MARK OF
ROYALTY

MARK OF
ROYALTY

A NOVEL

JENNIFER K. CLARK &
STEPHONIE K. WILLIAMS

Covenant Communications, Inc.

Cover image: *K4147164* © Fotosearch

Cover design copyright © 2010 by Covenant Communications, Inc.

Published by Covenant Communications, Inc.
American Fork, Utah

Printed in Canada
First Printing: February 2011

16 15 14 13 12 11   10 9 8 7 6 5 4 3 2 1

ISBN-13: 978-1-59811-775-2

To our parents who have always supported us in
our dreams and aspirations.

To our spouses and families who
have been patient and encouraging.

ACKNOWLEDGMENTS

Our deepest thanks and appreciation go out to those who read the first drafts of *Mark of Royalty* and provided valuable feedback throughout the various stages of its development. Our alpha readers: Jack Clark, Jared Kilgrow, Don and Linda Kilgrow, JoLynda Varner, Kelsey Wheadon, Anneli Byrd, and Catherine Byrd.

Thanks to Michael and Sarah for lending us your names, for your input, and for your enthusiasm.

And to Eliza Nevin, our editor, who stuck with us through the extra-long process that it took us to get *Mark of Royalty* to you in the form in which you see it now.

1. THE SECRET

Apollo felt knots twisting in his stomach and his mind reeled with the possible consequences of his treasonous decision. As icy mists encompassed the night air, he shivered involuntarily and tugged at his cloak, protectively pulling the small bundle he held closer to him. Was he saving the child's life? Or was he condemning her to death as well as himself?

He thought for a moment that trying to keep the baby a secret was hopeless. After all, in spite of his elaborate excuse regarding a sick friend, the servant must be suspicious at his request for a carriage in the middle of the night. And the bundle he held didn't exactly look like a bread basket, nor a collection of herbs and medicines. At least she wasn't crying anymore and had finally drifted to sleep. The driver pulled the horses to a halt in front of the castle's entrance and eyed Apollo with unfeigned curiosity as he climbed in, careful of the bundle he held snugly in his arms. It would be only a couple of hours before they would arrive in the small village, and he hoped that the warm blanket and the rocking motion of the carriage would keep the little girl asleep until then.

He thought of the infant's prospective new mother—the lovely twenty-four-year-old widow was as yet unaware of his plan, but he was certain she would agree. Miranda had married a fine man by the name of Antonio Benavente when she was nineteen, but he had died shortly after their marriage. She had no children and no family, which was fortuitous, he thought, because he would be asking her to take the baby and move far away. Not just far away, but to another country. Of course, he would pay her substantially to care for the child, but even he wouldn't be able to have any contact with them. No, that would be too risky. There were already too many people involved, and he wondered how long the secret would last. It would be best if he didn't know where Miranda would take the baby. He would have to be content knowing only that the child would have a good upbringing.

The sun was just starting to make its appearance, giving the horizon a faint glow when the carriage stopped at Miranda's house. Apollo knocked on the door and wished that it would instantly open. He shifted his weight from one foot to the other, firmly clutching the tiny bundle to his chest. Finally the door opened. "Is your mistress at home?" he asked the servant, trying to hide the urgency in his voice.

"Yes, sir," the woman replied as she ushered him into the sitting room. "I'll fetch her right away." She looked at the bundle in his arms suspiciously and then left the room.

"Apollo, what a surprise! It is always wonderful to see you, but what is so urgent that it brings you here this early hour of the day?" Miranda inquired as she entered the room. "I haven't had breakfast yet; would you like to join me?"

"No, thank you," Apollo said anxiously. "My business with you is urgent and of a royal nature."

Miranda raised an eyebrow. "At the very least you can have a drink with me while you explain. Please sit." She watched her old friend curiously as he stood, shifting from one foot to the other. She knew not to rush him. Their friendship of many years had taught her that he was not a man to be pushed. It was one of the qualities that secured him the position as one of the king's most trusted advisors.

"Are we alone?" Apollo asked in a whisper. "No one must hear what I need to say."

Miranda's curiosity piqued, but she calmly walked to the back of the house and gave instructions to her servants that would keep them in the kitchen.

Apollo nodded approvingly as Miranda reentered the room, then he nervously moved toward her and held out the bundle for her to take. She looked up at him with surprise, and then reluctantly took the bundle, clearly recognizing at once what was wrapped so carefully inside.

"The queen gave birth last night. Twins—a girl, then a boy." He began to pace back and forth across the floor, the significance of his task weighing heavily on his conscience. "It was an extremely difficult birth. The physician was fearful of losing the queen, and she became quite incoherent during labor. The queen survived, but she doesn't know of the girl."

Miranda removed the blanket from the infant's face, now just a few hours old. "Why bring me this child?" she asked, trying to mask the alarm in her voice.

"You know the great importance of the firstborn!" Apollo said as he kept up his relentless pacing. "The king's brother himself has sworn to kill the queen's firstborn if it be female. If this child had been the only one born, I could not have saved her from death, but as there was also a son. . . . It is better this way! You don't know the difficulties the king faces—with the country on the edge of revolution, the need to produce a male heir, the traditions, the expectations, the prophecies . . . " His voice trailed off.

Miranda looked at the sleeping child, unable to argue the point. It had been prophesied for years that if the country were to divide, it would be a prince, the firstborn, that would bring the people back together. And now that the country was on the verge of that separation, everyone had been awaiting the birth of that prince. She had also heard rumors about people who had sworn to kill any female child the queen might bear. These sinister plans had been justified and accepted by many as what was best for the country. But to take this child away from her mother. . . .

"Why not say that the boy was firstborn?" she asked.

Apollo glanced away nervously. "This child was wrapped when the physician handed her to me. I did not think to check. You know the prophecies—I assumed she was a boy. I . . ." he broke off, choking on his words.

Miranda looked up, alarm clouding her delicate face. "You marked her?"

Apollo didn't answer, but turned his back to her and dropped his head.

Miranda's voice rose forcefully, "Does she have the mark of the firstborn on her?"

"She was marked within minutes of the birth." Apollo turned and looked at the little baby and Miranda, his eyes reddening. "Only after it was done did we discover that there was another child. Upon seeing that she was a girl, we decided to give the boy child the mark of the firstborn as well . . . and now I bring this babe to you."

Miranda stood up and tried to place the baby back in Apollo's arms. "I beg you; don't ask this of me. This is a secret that cannot be kept! She will someday see the mark—someone else will see the mark. She'll know!"

Apollo, refusing to take the infant, moved to a chair and sat down. "Miranda, I ask this of you only because I know that you have a good heart, and you are worthy of this trust. There is no one else I can turn to."

Miranda sank into a nearby chair, her face ashen. "Who else knows of this?"

"The queen's physician and the king's other advisor, Master Samuel. They are both sworn to secrecy."

"This will not stay quiet. You know this!"

"I believe there is a way to keep this secret." He hesitated, then pressed on. "Miranda, I'm also asking you to leave—not just your home, but your country. You must go and never return. I'm prepared to give you a substantial amount of money, but you cannot stay here. If it is ever discovered that the queen had two children there will be a search. I will do all I can to prevent such a thing, but—"

"No, Apollo, I cannot do this! No matter where I go, the mark will still be there. What if a traveler—or a spy—were to see the mark and discover that she was truly firstborn? They would kill her, and what would happen to me? A life in prison? Execution? And what of you? This is akin to treason!"

Apollo reached out to touch her hand. "Leave those things to me. And to God. I believe this is the right thing to do, Miranda. Look into your heart and you'll feel the same. Please."

Miranda looked again at the sleeping baby and the tiny features pulled at her heart. How could she say no? If she returned the babe, the princess's fate would certainly be death. And Apollo's as well. He was right: in her heart she knew what she had to do. She sighed heavily as the child in her arms whimpered and turned her head toward Miranda. "Has she suckled?"

"No. We did not wish to risk discovery by hiring a wet nurse."

Miranda instinctively began rocking the infant as she gently patted the bundle and then whispered, "Has she a name?" But she knew full well that no one would have given a name to a baby that was not supposed to have been born.

Apollo stood. "That's best decided by you." He pulled from his belt a large leather sack that clinked as he put it on the table. "Here is enough gold to move you to another country and to sustain you in comfort for many years." He knew that Miranda was not extravagant and would not be quick to spend the gold.

"Please stay and eat," she said more out of politeness than sincerity, knowing that she herself felt too unsettled to eat, given the weight of her new responsibility.

Apollo moved to the door. "No. I must return. And I admit, I have no appetite."

Miranda gave him a half smile. "Nor do I."

She stood and walked him to the door. They paused before stepping outside to embrace one last time, reaching around the infant still tucked in the crook of Miranda's arm. Miranda choked back tears. Apollo was a remarkable man. If his first duty were not to his king and country, she thought he may have desired to court her. But a wife and family would be lost among his other duties. No, he would not ever marry. Not her, not anyone. He was destined to be alone in this world, and this secret would distance him even more. She felt numb as she watched her friend walk to the carriage and settle himself inside, hoping he had made the right choice.

* * *

Miranda knew that the infant would soon be awake and very loudly demanding food, so she reluctantly returned to the house, shutting the door behind her. She cooed to the newborn, who was beginning to squirm. The enormity of the situation caused a tightness in her throat and a sense of panic. She took a deep breath, trying to control the fear as she thought about how to explain the child to her servants. The baby began to fuss, and she began to rock her again as her mind raced to fabricate a believable story.

She can't be a peasant child, or the king's advisor wouldn't have bothered with her, Miranda thought. *A noble child? Perhaps, and how did she come by way of the king's advisor? Oh think, Miranda, there has to be something else. Someone from the castle? A lady in waiting?* Miranda stopped bouncing the infant and tipped her head to one side as she considered that thought. *A lady in waiting?* The queen did have several. Hadn't she heard rumors that one of the queen's attendants was with child? Instantly, she made up her mind.

"Rebeka, Adriana," Miranda called loudly to her two servants as she walked over and picked up the bag of gold. It was terribly heavy, but she tucked it between herself and the infant, rearranging the blanket to conceal it. She could only imagine placing it into the folds of her skirt and having her skirt fall off because of the added weight.

"Yes, my lady?" Adriana appeared in the doorway with Rebeka right behind her.

Miranda nodded toward the fussing child in her arms and then spoke with as much conviction as she could muster. "I have been given a very special charge by way of the king's advisor. This child's mother, a favored lady to the queen, died in childbirth, and her last wish was that the child be raised among her own people in Farellden. The queen wants very much to fulfill these wishes by placing the babe in the care of a trustworthy woman." She paused and took a deep breath. "The king's advisor has bestowed this honor upon me."

Miranda paused, wondering if her story was believable. She stared at Adriana's and Rebeka's faces and their wide questioning eyes. "I know it is unexpected, but I do want to do this. I need a change in my life. I need purpose, and this child brings that to me. You know how I have longed for a child of my own, and Master Apollo has given me an opportunity to satisfy that desire."

Miranda watched her servants carefully, and she thought now would be a good time to distract them by giving them a task as her own concerns quickly turned toward the whimpering child whose cries were growing steadily louder. "First we must find a way to feed this child. It has been too long for her to go without food. Any suggestions?"

Adriana quickly responded, "Would you like me to send for a wet nurse?"

"No," Miranda blurted out. She could just imagine another woman nursing the babe and discovering the mark on her shoulder. "No wet nurse. I wish to tend to this child myself."

Rebeka spoke up. "When my aunt died we fed her newborn on goat's milk. It was tedious, but he lived."

Miranda raised an eyebrow. "Has Nicholas milked the goats this morning?"

"Not yet, my lady," Adriana replied.

"Please have him do so immediately. And while you are at it, find something appropriate that we can wrap her in."

Proceeding to her bedchamber with the crying child, Miranda carefully laid the baby on the feather coverlet, then quickly buried the heavy bag of gold inside a nearby storage chest. Returning to the infant, she gently unwrapped the blanket and was somewhat surprised that Apollo and Samuel had not even taken the time to wipe off the child, let alone dress her. The blanket was crusted with dried blood and the white creamy substance that covers newborns. Gently she pulled the blanket away from the tiny naked body, and when fully exposed, the baby wetted. "Now, that was not very ladylike, Princess," Miranda whispered. She sighed softly as she tried to dry off the crying infant. "Now, what should your name be?"

Taking her softest shawl, she wrapped the baby and pushed aside the soiled blanket. She then picked up the girl, trying to hush her by gently bouncing her in her arms.

"Shhhh, Princess. Oh, we must have a name for you! A *suitable* name." Miranda tried to calm the crying babe. "Catherine? No. How about Angelique? Well, you are not exactly being angelic right now. No, you need a name befitting your true rank, but something that will also befit your new life. Mary? Miriam? Sarah? Hmmm. My little princess." She ran the names through her mind again. "Sarah. I like Sarah. Sarah Elizabeth. So you shall be named. Sarah Elizabeth Rankin Delacor. That will be your true and royal name. However, in this life with me, you will be Sarah Antonellis Benavente." Miranda followed the custom of using both her maiden name and her husband's surname. Somehow she would figure out how to get the child legally named and recorded by a clergyman, but she would worry about that later. Right now she had more pressing matters at hand. She bounced Sarah in her arms and wondered again what was taking so long; the child might lose her voice if she continued bawling like this.

There was a knock at the door. "Come!" The door opened slowly and in walked Rebeka with an armload of clean wraps, followed by Adriana and Nicholas. Nicholas approached timidly, his hat in hand. "I didn't believe her," he mused as he stared in awe at the infant, then presented a bull's horn that was half-filled with creamy, warm goat's milk.

Taking it, Miranda examined the highly polished horn, which featured a beautiful carving of a unicorn and was topped off with a piece of leather tied to the tip to simulate a nipple. "Thank you, Nicholas. This is beautiful."

"I was going to sell it at this year's festival, but I never got around to finishing it."

Miranda nodded appreciatively and maneuvered the makeshift bottle so she could rub the soft leather tip against the cheek of the wailing child. Sarah turned her head toward the object that had touched her, and Miranda pressed the nipple to her lips. She took it instantly and hungrily began to eat as the four adults stood in wonder and watched her take in her first meal.

"Thank you," Miranda said several minutes later as she handed the makeshift bottle back to Nicholas. "Please clean it for the next feeding, and would you please go to the village and tell a courier to come straightaway?"

Nicholas left and Miranda sent Rebeka and Adriana to prepare for the move. Her time was terribly short. Everything would have to be quickly packed, sold, or given away—a task that would normally take weeks, but needed to be done within the day.

While the infant slept, Miranda carefully rolled her onto her stomach and for the first time removed the piece of cloth covering the fresh burn mark on the baby's shoulder. She shuddered at the sight of the reddened wound. It was the mark of royalty, one that was supposed to distinguish her as the firstborn of the royal family, but the crest, featuring a unicorn, now only resembled a terrible disfigurement of red and weeping skin on the tiny innocent baby. She wanted to cry at the thought of Apollo pressing the red hot metal against the skin of this defenseless child.

The ointment originally spread on the burn had already been absorbed by the skin. Miranda cupped a hand over her mouth and shook her head as she studied the burned flesh, then hurried over to her dressing table and selected a small bottle, checking the label to make sure it was what she wanted: *comfrey cream*. She wasn't certain if this cream would prove as effective as what Apollo had used earlier, but it was good for scrapes, cuts, and sunburn. Miranda took a clean cloth, slathered the ointment over it, and then ever so gently applied it to the burn. Sarah whimpered, but Miranda continued and then gently bundled the tiny baby in clean wraps and laid her on the center of her large feather bed.

How would she be able to hide the mark? Would the princess be restored to her royal position sometime in the distant future? And what about herself? She was being forced to leave her life and everyone she loved behind. Miranda swallowed the mounting lump in her throat and began sorting through her personal belongings.

When the afternoon meal was served, Miranda sat down with Rebeka and Adriana in the dining hall. She preferred to dine with her servants. It made the meal less lonely since the death of her husband, but today it was unusually quiet. Miranda cleared her throat. "Thank you for your help today. We've accomplished a lot so far."

The two women just nodded without a reply. She tried to start up another conversation but it was no use. It was as if a heavy suffocating blanket had settled over the entire household and the meal ended as it had begun—in silence. Miranda helped to clear the table. She had never been too proud to do some of the small tasks most would leave for the servants.

Soon everyone was once again working at a furious pace, when Miranda sat down at her desk and quickly began writing a letter.

> *My dear cousin Andrew,*
>
> *I trust that this letter finds you and your family in good health and enjoying the happiness of this beautiful season. Cousin, I write this letter in urgency. I am to move to Farellden on urgent business. Since I must move to fulfill my responsibility, I look to you for help. I am reluctant to dismiss my faithful servants, for they have truly been devoted. And if you won't take them on, then I must do that which I most regret.*
>
> *I have many things with which I must part. I ask if you can find it in your heart, and if you have the means to do so, to assist me in finding a buyer for these items. I have very fine horses, as you know, and a carriage. I also have many fine household items that I cannot take with me. I beseech you, respond immediately, for I must go at once.*
>
> *Deepest regards,*
> *Miranda Secora Antonellis*

She finished the letter and immediately started another one to the local magistrate detailing the allocation of her property.

Miranda was just sealing the envelopes with red wax when she heard the sound of an approaching horse through her open window. She looked out, and seeing the courier, she hurried out of her room. "Nicholas," she called. It wasn't long before he emerged from the neighboring room where he had been packing. "Give these to the courier." She handed him the envelopes and a few coins for payment.

"Yes, mum." He turned to go, but then paused and looked back at her. "Would you like me to send for a carriage to take you around so you can make your goodbyes?"

Miranda swallowed hard and then shook her head. She would not risk saying goodbye to any of her friends. She was not a good liar, and knew that she would jeopardize everything if she tried to explain her departure.

It was best this way; besides, it was imperative that she leave as soon as possible. If the secret were found out, the castle would put out a search, and she needed to be far away.

She turned away from Nicholas and walked through the house. She was now beginning to realize how much she would have to leave behind. In the hallway she stopped and looked at the large painting of her beloved Antonio and put a hand over her mouth to muffle her crying. This all had been so unexpected. This morning had been just like any other, but from now on, nothing would be the same.

*　*　*

Apollo hung his head and listened to the carriage as it bumped along the road nearing the castle. His throat was tight as if he were being choked by an invisible force. He inhaled deeply, trying to relieve the ache, but to no avail. "What have I done? What in heaven's name have I done?" he said as he roughly ran his hands through his thick shaggy hair. He then buried his face in his hands and felt the hot sting of tears. "Please, oh please! Dear God up in heaven, please forgive me for what I have done," he pleaded. "And please! Please let the queen and Miranda forgive me too!" For a moment he had considered going back. How could he take this child from her mother and place this kind of burden on Miranda? His mind tried to wade through the deep emotions, the logic of his actions, and the reality of it all.

The sun had climbed much higher in the sky when the carriage entered the courtyard to the castle. He tried to ignore the noise created by the throngs of people and the music celebrating the birth of their prince and the fulfillment of the prophecy. The carriage slowly moved through the crowds and came to a halt. Apollo sat for a minute, reluctant to leave the confines of the carriage, but then the door opened, letting light pour inside. He laggardly raised his head and squinted to see who was intruding on him.

"My lord." It was the driver.

Apollo nodded but made no pretense of moving.

"My lord, are you a'right?"

Apollo nodded, then waved the servant away. At length he pulled himself to the door and stepped out onto the stone paving, having to instantly steady himself. He tugged at his tunic, collected himself, and then began the long climb up the castle stairs.

He was traversing the last few steps when Samuel appeared and reached his hand out toward him, but Apollo waved away the gesture of friendship. Slowly he raised his head to meet the gaze of the other advisor, his accomplice in this terrible secret, and then he simply nodded once. Samuel let out a heavy sigh, and both men walked reluctantly to the castle's entrance in silence, the subject on both their minds not to be discussed again.

2. A NEW LIFE

The warm spring sunlight filtered through the orchard leaves, causing radiant patterns below to shift and move with the breeze. Miranda inhaled deeply and let out a long sigh. She loved the morning hours in the orchard. The book she had been reading sat in her lap, and the peaceful morning vibrated with the sounds of her daughters playing nearby.

"Mother, Mother! Look what we made for you!"

"Young ladies! What have your father and I told you about running with your skirts up about your knees?" Miranda gently scolded the two girls.

Felicia, the smaller of the two, hung her head. "Sorry, Mother."

Both girls knelt in the grass near Miranda, and she pulled the dark-haired ten-year-old closer to her. "Now, what have my girls made for me?" The girls instantly forgot their scolding and began chattering like a pair of excited squirrels. With an affectionate smile, Miranda scooted over so that the older one could lean against her. "Sarah, take a deep breath and tell me what you and your little sister have been doing."

"We were picking flowers, Mother," twelve-year-old Sarah said, pulling her long, golden hair away from her face. The sun reflected off her natural curls, revealing the auburn undertones that seemed to magically appear whenever illuminated. "We decided to make you necklaces from the lion's tooth flowers."

"I was the one who thought of it, Mother," her younger sister added with a grin.

"Very well then, let me see these magnificent pieces of jewelry."

The girls produced the chained stems of the wildflower, but Felicia was obviously disappointed when she found that her chain wouldn't even fit around her mother's head.

Miranda hugged her. "I shall wear it as a crown!" She adjusted the small yellow flowers so they wouldn't fall off her head. "It is wonderful, my dear heart!" She gave Felicia a kiss on the cheek and watched the little girl glow with pride.

Sarah slid hers over her mother's wrist. "It's lovely, sweet princess." She gave Sarah a tight squeeze, and smiled at the thought of being able to call the girl by her proper title. She had been doing so for years now, and everyone simply regarded it as a pet name.

"But what about your own? Don't all the lovely ladies in the manor deserve such jewels?" They both nodded, and they went skipping off, giggling.

"And remember you are young ladies!" Miranda called after them. They were both so beautiful and growing up so quickly. It was hard for her to believe that it had been twelve years since she had made her hasty journey with the newborn princess. She watched the two young girls skipping between the trees. Sarah was practically a young woman now, and so happy, but Miranda still struggled with the unpleasant memories of that long journey, about which the young princess knew nothing.

As she sat watching the girls play, she recalled her struggle to cover their trail. She had said farewell to her servants and cousin at Quartermain and had hired some men to drive the carriage and wagon toward Farellden. At the tavern at the crossroads of LeShire and Cassington, she paid the drivers handsomely to change course and take her to Leshire instead. From there she hired someone to take her to the town of Botenfourt. Each time she told them a different story. She was going to help her ailing aunt, or her husband had moved on to find new residence. The men she hired had paid little attention to the infant and the goat that she had to stop and milk every couple of hours. Eager to earn the large pay she offered each team, they asked no questions. At last she crossed the border into Spain where she hired someone to take her all the way into France. Miranda sighed, remembering how slow and tedious it was traveling with a newborn.

At last she had stopped at an inn where she met a couple from Calibre, a small country on the other side of France. They were returning from a prolonged vacation, and quickly became friends with her. Miranda told them that she was recently widowed and was moving to get a fresh start. She did not give many details and the couple graciously pressed for none. They simply believed that Sarah was her daughter and had been born in another town on the other side of Spain. It didn't take much for the couple to convince her to accompany them to their home. It was a good move,

Miranda thought as she mindlessly pulled at the grass, for she had only spent a month with them when she met Clyde.

She looked over at Felicia who was gathering flowers. Her daughter was beautiful with long brown hair and dark eyes, both of which she had gotten from her father. At first Miranda had not wanted to marry, but finally complied when Agnes and Fitzjohn, her benefactors, encouraged the relationship, convincing her that no other man of means would want a widow. Though she had a comfortable supply of gold, she wished to provide the tiny princess Sarah with a lifestyle more in keeping with her birth and she knew that this was her chance to do that. It had been a small wedding and it held little joy for Miranda, but she felt Clyde was a good man and she could learn to love him.

As Miranda sat in the grass absentmindedly watching the two girls play, she fingered the gold heart-shaped pendant that she always wore. It was a wedding gift from her beloved Antonio. It was all she had left of him. Everything else of his had been given away and left behind.

She had moved her few belongings into Clyde's home, and had become the lady of the house. She had taken great joy in watching Sarah grow but she became pregnant only two months after the wedding, and when the realization set in, she was overjoyed.

Clyde had been disappointed that Felicia wasn't a boy, and even more disappointed when no other children followed. But he never took his disappointment out on Miranda or the girls, and he was a loving father. He doted more on Felicia than Sarah, but that was understandable.

"Mother." Sarah was calling her.

"Yes, Sarah?" Miranda left her world of reminiscence.

"Amanda says dinner is about ready. Felicia has already gone inside."

Miranda stood up and brushed herself off while Sarah ran over to her. "Would you be so offended, my princess, if we left my treasures here?"

"Better than if Lord Clyde were to see them."

Miranda wasn't surprised at the young girl's response. Sometimes Clyde scolded the girls when they didn't exemplify proper ladylike behavior in their manners and dress. She put her arm around Sarah and took her hand as they walked toward the manor. "You must scrub with soap before you sit at the table," she said as she looked at the green and yellow stains under Sarah's fingernails. "And remember, Clyde is expecting guests tomorrow."

"Who are they, Mother? Somebody terribly important?"

"I suppose they are. Your stepfather's sister, Lady Pendleton, and her attorney. They have legal matters to attend to concerning her late husband's estate."

"Is she a duchess?"

Miranda nodded. "She is, so you must call her 'madame,' or 'my lady.'"

"How long will they be here?"

"Perhaps just two nights or three, or they could even decide to stay a fortnight."

"Then I must be very, very good!"

Miranda gave the girl another squeeze. "You have never been anything but a good girl. Come, let's go inside, and remember—you and Felicia must work on your needlepoint after dinner, for I'm sure Lady Pendleton will want to see your work."

After the meal, preparations were made for their coming guests. Miranda made certain that the guest rooms were tidy, the blankets aired out, the rooms dusted, the fireplaces swept out, wood brought up in case the spring nights got chilly, and the beds remade.

Clyde spent the afternoon reviewing financial papers and giving orders to servants. During the evening meal he continued to give orders to the servants concerning the specific needs of his sister. "She prefers goose. Do we have a goose that can be prepared for her arrival?"

Joshua nodded. "Yes, sir."

"And ducks. Do we have ducks to spare?"

Joshua nodded. "Aye, sir, we do have plenty of them."

"Very well, dispatch a goose at first light."

The tall dark-haired servant bowed his head in response.

"Catherine," he said without looking up, "I want you to attend Miss Felicia while my sister is here. Make certain she's promptly dressed and always on her best behavior."

Catherine gave a small curtsy. "Yes, sir."

"Amanda, you are to attend Miss Sarah. See that she too is appropriately dressed and always available. No running off to the orchard." Clyde directed his last comment to Sarah, who sat at the end of the table.

Sarah sat straight in her chair and looked directly at Clyde. "Yes, sir." There was no hint of apology in her voice. Miranda suppressed a smile as she watched the little princess display her regal disposition.

"Amanda," Miranda said quietly after she had finished eating. She stood up and directed the servant down the hallway. "I shall help Sarah with her toilette and gowns as I always do. If you will, please attend to her hair and other needs."

"But my lady—" Amanda started to protest, when Miranda suddenly cut her off.

"I shall deal with my husband, if you will please attend to the child as I wish."

"Yes, my lady," Amanda said, as Miranda turned and walk down the hall. "How very strange," she whispered to no one in particular. "The Mistress does so dote on Miss Sarah."

"Miranda!" Clyde's voice boomed down the stone hallway, and Amanda quickly ducked into the kitchen, not wanting to witness the inevitable conflict about to happen.

"I will speak with you at once! In private."

He accompanied her up the stairs to their bedchamber. Once the door shut behind them he turned to look at her but said nothing. Miranda stood tall, silent, and patient. Clyde looked into her face, and it seemed as if he wanted to reach out and touch her but he restrained himself.

"Don't you love Felicia? Why must you insist on showing these extra affections to Sarah? Would it pain you so to have a servant attend her?"

Miranda lowered her head and groaned. She had a hard time keeping anything from Clyde. She could practically be anywhere in the manor, even behind closed doors, and he could overhear her. He had the ears of a fox.

He had turned away from her. "Perhaps it's me. I've always known that you didn't love me when we married. Do you resent Felicia out of spite for me?" He turned back to look at her, hurt clouding his dark eyes. He sighed and ran a hand through his graying dark hair.

Miranda reached out and took his hand, "Clyde, you're a good man, and I do love you. And you know I love Felicia as I do Sarah." She spoke softly. "Please understand. Sarah is all I have left of my former life, my only connection to the past."

Clyde looked at Miranda, his expression still one of pain. When he spoke, his voice was a hoarse whisper as he struggled to keep his emotions under control. "Do you love me even a fraction of what you loved him?"

The question stunned Miranda, and she felt an incredible urge to cry. Reaching out, she took his hand. "My dear husband! I do truly love you. The love for my previous is something different than the love I have for you, but my love for you is no less true and no less sincere than it was for him."

Clyde pulled Miranda tightly to him and kissed her softly. She returned the kiss, sensing his devotion to her, and after a long moment, she broke away.

"Let me settle the girls for the night and I will return soon," she told him, but Clyde buried his face in her shoulder. It was obvious that he did not want to share his wife with the two girls right now. She kissed his cheek. "I'll return soon, I promise."

He returned her kiss on the cheek and slid his hand across her shoulder and down her arm, reluctant to let her go.

"Wait for me here."

He let go of her hand and she hurried off to find the girls and put them to bed. She found Felicia sitting in the parlor working on her stitching and Sarah in the library reading a book. Each complained about going to bed early, but Miranda gently reminded them that guests were arriving the next day and everyone needed to be well rested.

She followed Felicia into her room and helped her daughter undress, then brushed her long dark hair. "Good night," Miranda said as she hugged her tightly and helped her climb under the blanket, then kissed her cheek. "Sleep well, my love." She leaned on the bed for a moment and looked at her daughter. "Do you understand I love you so very much?"

Felicia paused. "Yes, Mother. But sometimes I think you love Sarah more than me. You always want to help her with everything instead of letting the servants do it."

Miranda brushed a strand of hair away from her daughter's cheek. "I helped *you* dress tonight, and you are my dearest heart! You and Sarah are both unique, and that's why my actions may seem different toward each of you, but I love you both equally. I'll love you every day that the sun rises, and every night the stars shine, and then I'll love you even more."

Felicia smiled. "I love you too, Mother."

"Good night, darling." Miranda leaned over and blew out the candle and then found her way to the door by the glowing embers in the fireplace. She considered stoking the fire and adding another small log to take the chill out of the air, but she was in a hurry and so continued on to Sarah's room.

She knocked at the same time as she entered the room. With her dress laying neatly over the large chest at the foot of the bed, Sarah stood in the middle of the room in her shift, trying to see something over her left shoulder. She was pulling her shoulder forward with one hand while she strained her neck and head back as far as she could to get a better glimpse.

"Mother, what's this? I have never noticed it before." Miranda quickly shut the door and walked over to see what Sarah was trying so hard to look at, although she already knew.

"This?" Miranda brushed her fingers across the raised scar on her daughter's shoulder. She took a deep breath and slowly let it out, preparing herself to give the answer that she had been rehearsing in her mind for the last twelve years. "It's your birthmark, sweet princess," she said methodically.

"It looks different."

"Why do you say that?"

"It doesn't look anything like Felicia's. Her birthmark is dark, but not bumpy like this." Sarah touched the top of it with the tip of her fingers. "This feels strange. I can't really see it, but when I looked at it in the looking glass it almost looked like a unicorn."

Miranda pulled her toward the bed gently and sat on the edge so she could brush out her hair. She had waited for this day and although she had gone over it a thousand times in her head, she knew she needed to take care. "Yours is a very special birthmark. Very few people have a special mark like yours."

"Does that mean that Felicia is not special?"

"No, princess. Felicia is just as special as you are. She's just as lovely and just as important as you are . . . just in a different way. We are all God's children and need to be treated as such."

Sarah nodded.

"I know you might not understand now, but you will someday. I promise you."

After tucking in her little princess, Miranda hurried back to the room she shared with her husband. Someday soon she would write everything down for Sarah so that if for some reason she couldn't explain it all to her, she would at least have an explanation in writing, but in the meantime she needed to return to her dear husband.

3. THE VISITOR

The next morning the entire household was up early. Sarah grinned with excitement as she put down her needlepoint and looked out the window again. After she and Felicia had been dressed properly, they had been sent to the parlor to work on their needlepoint, but she had the feeling that it was more to make sure that their clothes would stay clean and to keep them out of the way than to make progress on their sewing. She looked at Felicia, who had also pushed her needlework aside. How could they work with all the excitement in the air and with the entire household alive with activity? She wiggled with excitement and looked out the window with anticipation at every sound in the courtyard.

It was midday when the large carriage pulled by four powerful brown horses noisily rolled into the courtyard, followed by a carriage loaded with trunks and bundles. The two girls had been taking turns peeking out the high, open window. The courtyard was filled with raised voices as the servants rushed out to greet the visitors, and Clyde ran out to greet his sister and assist her out of her carriage.

Felicia was now taking her turn at watching from the tall windowsill. "Oh!" She exhaled quietly.

Sarah nudged her younger sister. "What is it? What do you see?"

"She is so elegant!"

"What is she wearing?"

"The most beautiful black dress I have ever seen. The skirts are so very full!" Felicia said, the admiration evident in her voice. "She stepped out of the carriage like a queen!"

"Oh, what is she doing now? What color is her hair? Can you see her eyes? Does she wear gloves?" The questions tumbled from Sarah as she wiggled behind her sister. Felicia scooted over and let Sarah climb up, giving her full access to the window.

Sarah stuck her head out as far as she dared and stared at the scene. There were servants and attendants running around in what seemed to be controlled chaos. A short woman dressed in the most elegant black dress and veil was the center of all the commotion. She couldn't make out any specific features from where she was, but she could tell by the woman's manner that she was stern and forceful.

Sarah reluctantly slid from the window's edge. "Oh, Felicia, you were right! She's very elegant! Come see how she demands everyone's attentions." She dropped to the floor, allowing Felicia to occupy the spot next to the window again, then absently smoothed the front of her overdress, knowing that it wouldn't be long before they would be presented to their aunt.

"Oh, they are coming inside! Quickly, Sarah! Help me down!"

Sarah reached up to balance her sister as she hopped down from the window, then they scampered across the room to the chairs where they had abandoned their needlework.

It seemed like ages before their mother opened the door and entered the room. She smiled as she approached the two girls. "Are you ready to meet your aunt?" She straightened their overskirts and ran her fingers through their hair in an attempt to comb it. "Let me see your needlework." She looked at their work and smiled at them both. "Felicia, your work is marvelous. You are improving greatly.

"Sarah, you are also improving. I daresay that you still need some work, but your stitches are smaller and more uniform. Very good." She handed the material back to the girls. "You'll want to show Aunt Agnes your work." With that she turned and walked toward the door with both girls solemnly following her.

One would not consider the widow beautiful, but she was not by any means offensive. She had a short pointy nose, her lips were thin and pale, and her eyes were a cool blue. Her cheeks were slightly gaunt, with only the slightest touch of pink to them, yet she carried a certain air of sophistication that demanded the attention of those around her.

Sarah wasn't entirely sure what to think of her step-aunt, who was busy telling servants where to put all of the things she had brought with her. To Sarah it seemed as though she was moving in—at least she had brought enough luggage to appear that way.

Miranda stepped forward and urged the girls to her side. "Lady Agnes Pendleton, your nieces: Sarah Antonellis Benavente and Felicia Jennette."

The older woman turned to greet them and a soft smile crossed her thin lips. "Young ladies . . . a pleasure to finally meet you." She nodded to the girls as they each politely curtsied. "Benavente is a Spanish name. I daresay that you do not look to have any Spanish features, though you do take somewhat after your mother's red hair." She ran her fingers over Sarah's sun-kissed tresses, her faint smile having disappeared.

"Sarah's father was a blond with fair complexion." Lady Pendleton nodded at Miranda's reply and turned to Felicia, the smile returning as she looked at the lovely dark-haired child.

"And you, my dear, have been blessed with your mother's good looks and your father's dark hair." She was obviously pleased at the appearance of her only niece by blood. "Once I am settled I have gifts for you both. Now Felicia, be a darling and show me to my room."

Miranda stood with her hand on Sarah's shoulder, and they watched Felicia and Lady Pendleton walk toward the stairs. "Well, Sarah, my sweet princess, would you like to help me with the preparations for our afternoon meal?" She smiled down at her daughter. The older woman's preference for Felicia was not lost on Sarah, and it showed in her face as she looked up. This could prove to be difficult for Sarah. She touched a wisp of loose golden-red hair. "Come along. Shall we talk cook into letting us help make something special in honor of our guest?"

Sarah looked toward the stairs, then nodded slowly and turned with her mother to go to the kitchen.

* * *

Miranda jerked her head up, and then quickly asked God for a better day tomorrow and ended her prayer. She was too tired to concentrate, and after dozing off twice already she was sure that God had also had enough. She slid under the covers next to her already sleeping husband. She tried to force herself to think of something good to take her mind off of Lady Pendleton and how critical she had been of Sarah. It was obvious that she thought more highly of Felicia. On the other hand, she had brought some lovely material for both of the girls to embroider and that, in itself, was something good about the woman. Miranda set her mind to find another redeeming quality about her sister-in-law, but before she could think of anything else she found the sweet comfort of sleep.

* * *

The new day *had* been wonderful, Miranda thought. And it seemed that God had answered her prayer . . . until now. Clyde and Lady Pendleton had spent most of their time in the library with a lawyer, leaving Miranda to attend to her daily activities as usual. The girls had spent the majority of the day in the sitting room embroidering, but heaven only knew where they were now. Miranda sat silently at the table and stared at the meal that was now growing cold, trying to avoid eye contact with Lady Pendleton, who had already yelled at the servants to find the girls at once.

If God blessed me with a good day, even though I fell asleep in my prayers, perhaps He'll bless me more now, while I am wide awake, Miranda thought. No sooner had the thought entered her mind than she heard the girls coming. "Thank you, God, for your efficiency," she said out loud. Lady Pendleton shot her a harsh glance.

Giggling, Sarah and Felicia burst into the room at a dead run. Sarah was first and slid to a stop behind the large high-backed chair at her appointed place at the dining table. Felicia was not far behind her. As they caught their breath they realized that the room was unusually quiet.

"Sarah!" Lady Pendleton's voice was stern. "A lady is never late, and should never enter a room giggling. And she certainly should never run!"

Sarah pulled her chair out and sat quietly down. "Yes, Lady Pendleton. I apologize for my rudeness."

Felicia quietly slid into her own chair without uttering a sound. The chastisement that Sarah had received was more than enough for both of them.

The group gave thanks for the meal they were about to eat and then settled into a slightly tense conversation. Lady Pendleton and Clyde talked about family affairs, and the discussion was interrupted only by a soft thud every now and then. The sound was so soft that most everyone in the room seemed oblivious to its repeating occurrence. By about the seventh time Lady Pendleton stopped in mid-sentence and asked in a sharp tone, "What on earth is that noise?"

Miranda looked directly at Sarah, her eyes pleading with the girl to not make a scene. Sarah lowered her head, embarrassed and unable to look at anyone.

"Well?" No one was willing to speak. Lady Pendleton began to tap a finger on the table.

Sarah could no longer bear the silence. "Please forgive me, Lady Pendleton. I did it."

"You!" came the reply.

"Yes, my lady," Sarah muttered, still unable to look at anyone at the table. "I was kicking my chair."

"Hmmph. Do I need to tell you that ladies do not kick their chairs either?"

"No ma'am," came the soft answer. The meal was finished in relative quietness. Sarah asked to be excused as soon as courtesy would permit, and then retreated to her room.

It was a couple of hours before Miranda's duties permitted her to look in on Sarah. When she finally pushed open the door to Sarah's bedchamber she found her daughter lying on her bed with a large cat sitting on her chest. The cat purred contentedly as she petted his head.

Miranda laid down next to her and stroked the cat's long fur. She wasn't sure what to say to Sarah to ease her humiliation of being reprimanded in front of everyone.

"I think he likes me," Sarah said in a half whisper.

Miranda nodded, "I believe he does. He doesn't sit with anyone like he does with you."

"Is it unladylike to have a cat sit on me?" Sarah's question had a bitter tinge.

Miranda continued to stroke the purring cat. "Some people might think so. Some people think that riding horses is something a lady should not do either. Would you consider me to be unladylike?"

"No. I think you are very much a lady. But you are my mother."

Miranda nodded. "Not everyone thinks the way that Clyde and Lady Pendleton do. In our former country expectations of a lady were not the same as they are here. Antonio and I purchased two beautiful horses after we were wed, and I spent many hours riding across the countryside with him. And not sidesaddle, mind you. But some people are very stubborn and think that the old ways are the only ways. You, my sweet princess, will learn to use wise judgment, and will learn what is right and what is wrong regardless of what social custom dictates."

"How will I know if something is wrong?"

"Common sense, darling," Miranda said as she tucked Sarah in and kissed her on the cheek. "And if you ever are in doubt, pray about it. God answers prayers. He certainly did mine this night."

* * *

"Sarah! Where have you been all day? I looked and looked for you. You know it is not kind to hide from me." Felicia stood with her hands on her hips and her usually sweet voice was harsh with anger. "I had to spend most of the day with Lady Pendleton."

"How did Lady Pendleton like the needlework you did yesterday?" Sarah asked, looking up from the cloth she was working on, and then went on without waiting for a reply. "Because I spent the entire day up here, picking out every stitch I put in yesterday!"

"Oh, Sarah. All of it? I thought your work was very seemly, some of the best you have ever done. Lady Pendleton made you pick it all out?"

Sarah nodded grimly. "I think tomorrow I shall hide in the old privy until I am called for supper."

Felicia's face twisted into an agonizing frown. "Please, no. I can't bear to sit another day with Lady Pendleton if you're not with me."

"I thought you loved to spend time with her; she dotes on you so."

"I did enjoy it at first, but Sarah, she's always rubbing that smelly liniment on her hands, and then—" Before Felicia could finish she was interrupted by the thud of a dirt clod hitting the house next to the open window.

"Sarah," a voice called from below the window. Thud. Another dirt clod hit the house. "Sarah, are you up there?"

Sarah looked toward the window. "That sounds like Benjamin."

"Yes," Felicia said, folding her arms and rolling her eyes. "I wonder what the dirty little stink bug wants?"

Sarah shrugged, put her cloth down, and hurried to the window to look out. Benjamin, who was several years younger than she—and dressed in his usual layer of dirt, which was topped off with mud-caked hair—stood next to the tree that grew up past the window. She cringed at the sight of him, although it wasn't unlike him to look that way. She remembered one time when she and her mother went to collect rent from the tenants. They had just passed the large pond when the muddy bank on the other side of the hedgerow rose up and began moving toward them. Sarah had screamed at the sight of the earth heaving at them, convinced that it was the devil himself coming for her. Only after her mother had calmed her down had she realized that it was only mud-caked Benjamin.

"What is it, Benjamin?" Sarah called down to him.

"Jerry and I are trying to get a game of Hoodman's Blind on, and we need you to play."

"Now?"

"Yes," Benjamin called up to her. "Right away. Tyrell and Jordan are already out in the field. We're only waiting for you."

"Very well, I'll be right down." Sarah pulled her skirts up over her knees and stuck her foot out the window.

"Sarah, no!" Felicia said forcefully.

"I have to," Sarah told her as she balanced between the window and the branch. "You heard Benjamin. They need me. You know Hoodman's Blind is my favorite game. No one plays it as well as I do."

Felicia didn't look convinced. "It's wrong for you to go without permission."

Sarah paused, cocked her head to one side, and thought about what her mother had said about making wise judgments. "Perhaps. This might be a poor choice, but I'm not quite certain. If I go now I'll be back before supper, so no one should mind. I would pray about it as Mother suggested, but unfortunately there's no time. I think if God didn't want me to go, then He wouldn't allow me to be tempted so. He's quite aware that I am unable to resist the game, therefore I have no other choice." She scarcely finished her explanation when she pulled herself the rest of the way out the window and onto the large branch.

"Hooray!" Benjamin cried as he danced around the tree.

Sarah began working her way down from one branch to another, careful not to snag herself. She was only halfway down when Benjamin called to her again. "I see your family has a visitor."

"Yes," Sarah called back to him. "My aunt, Lady Pendleton from Madiea. How did you know?" she asked without breaking her concentration on her descent.

"Because she is coming this way," Benjamin said excitedly. "And she does not look very happy," he added.

Sarah's downward motion instantly reversed and she scampered quickly back up the tree. "Best not to be around when she gets here," she whispered loudly to Benjamin. But there was no need to warn him; he had already darted around the house, and in a matter of seconds would be halfway down the lane or taking refuge in the drainage ditch.

Felicia was gone when Sarah entered her room again, so she sat on her bed alone and waited. It took longer than she thought, but finally she heard footsteps coming down the hall, then suddenly her door was pushed open without even the courtesy of a knock. Sarah breathed out a sigh of relief. It was her mother and not Aunt Agnes who stood in the doorway.

Miranda closed the door behind her and then sat on the bed next to Sarah. "Sarah, what's gotten into you lately?"

Sarah let her eyes fall to the ground. "Mother, I'm sorry. I thought of what you said last night, about right and wrong, but I just couldn't help myself. Truly I tried. Was it so wrong?"

"To want to go play? No, but it was wrong to go without permission, and to climb out your window as if you were an escaping criminal."

"Am I to be punished?"

"You'll remain inside the rest of the day and go without supper tonight. And as soon as Lady Pendleton leaves, you will change rooms with Felicia at the front of the house, where there are no trees near the windows."

Sarah flopped back onto her bed. "Mother, I like this room," she protested. "And I shall starve tonight and be dead by morning."

"It's not so bad, my sweet princess."

"Princess! Why do you call me *princess*? I am the farthest thing there is from a princess. *Little black demon* would suit me better."

"That is not true," Miranda said in her most compelling voice. "There are times when I look at you and think that no one could be more regal." Miranda controlled herself, biting her bottom lip. "Besides, it's only a fond name I like to call you, just as I call Felicia *dear heart*."

"Better that her name be *dark heart*."

"Sarah, you bite your tongue! I never want to hear you speak ill of your sister again!"

"But if it weren't for her tattling, I would be fed tonight and not perishing from hunger."

"It wasn't her who got you in trouble, but yourself. Lady Pendleton was just out for her daily walk when she saw you in the tree. Felicia has said nothing."

"Sorry, Mother," Sarah apologized as tears welled up in her eyes. "I won't do it again."

"I know, my sweet princess." Miranda stood up and walked toward the door. "I'll be back to check on you after supper."

"I'll be here," Sarah said with a smirk.

Miranda marveled at how Sarah could move from tears to smiles in seconds.

"And Mother," Sarah said quickly, "thank you."

"For what?" Miranda asked.

"For you coming to talk to me and not Aunt Agnes."

Miranda turned and walked back to Sarah. "You are under my stewardship, not Lady Pendleton's. But Sarah, there is nothing wrong with Lady Pendleton's expectations of how you should conduct yourself. If you are to become a suitable lady, and with the right connections . . ." She paused, with a faraway look in her eyes, as if she were planning something. "Yes, it would do you good, and I will make arrangements." Without explaining herself Miranda stood and strode out the door.

4. A ROYAL SCHEME

Miranda sat quietly and looked around at the extensive garden that surrounded her, half wishing that someday she too might have such breathtaking grounds. She took a deep breath and drank in the sweet aroma. The hedge of roses that flanked the long pathways throughout the garden were starting to bloom and the fragrance permeated the air.

"Miranda, I was so happy when I heard you were coming. It has been such a long time since we have enjoyed each other's company." Adilia had her arms open as she came up the path and embraced Miranda before she sat down in the chair that bordered the small table between them. "Such a beautiful day. I hope you don't mind me receiving you in the garden."

"No, of course not." Miranda smiled politely. "The refreshing air does me good." Miranda had known Adilia for almost nine years now and had come to love and respect her as so many others did. The woman had a way about her that caused people to want to be around her. Her husband had passed away years ago, but that hadn't slowed her down any. She was still a favorite at court and among the nobles. She was a gentle woman, with a refined way that made her seem so elegant and graceful. Although she was almost twice Miranda's age, she was still beautiful, with dainty features and a delicate face softly etched with wrinkles.

"I'm glad you had time to meet with me," Miranda said with the slightest hint of nervousness in her voice.

Adilia threw her hands in the air. "Oh, this old woman has nothing but time, and you know how much I enjoy visiting. I tell you it's been too long. You really should come over more often, although I know you have been busy. I hear that Clyde's sister is visiting."

"Yes." Miranda nodded. Adilia seemed to know everything about everyone. "She is settling matters regarding her late husband."

"Yes, I thought that's what brought her here. I was expecting her to come with you."

"No," Miranda spoke hesitantly. "I do so enjoy visiting with you, Adilia, but I have neglected to inform you that this isn't a social call."

"Oh?" Adilia said raising an eyebrow. "Then to what do I attribute this visit? Come, tell me. Now I am intrigued."

Miranda sat up taller in her chair like her husband did when he was ready to do business with someone. "I'm in need of your services."

"My services?" Adilia questioned with a smile.

"Yes. It's my daughter Sarah. I wish her to get acquainted with a young man."

"Ahhh," Adilia nodded knowingly. "I understand now. Does Clyde know about this?"

Miranda dropped her eyes. "No."

"Well, no matter. You know that I would be more than willing to help you in any way that I can. How old is Sarah now?"

"Twelve years."

"So young. Miranda, are you sure about this?"

"Yes. You know these things take time, and when Sarah is of marrying age, I want her well acquainted with the gentleman. I know how hard it is on a marriage when you go into it blind. I want Sarah well prepared."

"Very well, Miranda. I can make some introductions. Now let me see . . ." Adilia paused and rested a finger on her cheek. "Lord Gilhart is quite influential and has a son around Sarah's age. Gregory is his name, I do believe."

"Yes," Miranda said. "I've met the lad, but I had something a little different in mind."

Adilia focused on her friend. "What did you have in mind, my dear?"

Miranda cleared her throat and then took a deep breath. "Royalty," she said firmly.

"Royalty?" Adilia exclaimed. "Well that does limit our choices. May I inquire why?"

Miranda fingered her heart-shaped pendant, thinking of her former life and what Sarah's would have been if she had never been taken from her country. She wanted to tell Adilia that Sarah deserved such a match. It was her birthright, a right that had been taken from her and one that Miranda felt was necessary to restore to her. Sarah could marry into nobility, but Miranda wanted more for her. A royal marriage was the only way to bring justice to the princess. Sarah was meant to lead such a life—to help rule, to have influence on important matters, and to bear children who would be blessed with the same privilege. But all this must go unsaid to her friend.

"I love Sarah," Miranda finally explained. "I want only what is best for her. I believe that life would suit her." Miranda let out a sigh. "Adilia, I know this doesn't make sense, but you must trust me. It is not for my or Clyde's benefit, but it is only Sarah I'm thinking of. I truly feel this deep in my heart. I beg that you believe me . . . she is deserving and capable of such an arrangement."

Adilia sat quietly studying Miranda's face.

"I'll pay you." Miranda set a small purse on the table and slid it toward her old friend.

"I'll not take your money, Miranda." Adilia pushed the coin purse back across the table. "But let me ask: Are you truly certain about this?"

"Yes," Miranda said with conviction. "Is it possible?"

"Well, yes, it is possible. His Majesty the Prince is sixteen years of age, and is not betrothed. But Miranda, you are aware that there are so many other courtiers that are trying to—"

"Yes, I am aware," Miranda broke in. "You say there are no future marriage contracts?"

"No, I have heard of none. He is free to choose whom he likes as of now, but of course that can change."

"And you can provide an introduction?"

"Yes, but—"

"Then, through your connections, you will arrange a private audience with His Majesty?"

"Perhaps." Adilia took in a long breath and sighed. "I have done so before, but that does not assure the presence of His young Majesty."

Miranda looked bewildered. "I am at a loss. What do you mean?"

"I have taken audience with His Highness on more than one occasion where he has failed to present himself. He has a mind of his own, is somewhat of a rebel, and regardless of his prior commitments or obligations, if he doesn't feel like being somewhere or doing something then he conveniently makes himself unavailable. Quite rude to my way of thinking. He is so volatile, impulsive, and changes with the wind. Too rash and inconsiderate of his position. So, the appointment I can make— however, I'm not inclined to promise an audience with His Majesty."

Miranda began to give up hope and sat back in her chair, deflated.

"Miranda, are you feeling quite well?" Adilia asked with honest concern. "Let me call for some refreshment."

"No." Miranda forced half a smile. "Perhaps I was being wishful to set my heart upon the prince."

"Yes, I must say that I'm quite astounded. You *are* being wishful. Now let us be realistic. Surely you must see it plainly; a match between Sarah and His Majesty the Prince is highly unlikely."

"I understand. But I believe it could happen."

"Come my dear, you have seen for yourself the many young ladies that are trying for his affections, and all from very notable families, I might add."

"Yes, so why not Sarah? Clyde is very—"

"Clyde is not Sarah's father," Adilia broke in. "Miranda, be sensible. Felicia is in a better position, but even then, the prince is more likely to choose a duke's daughter, or royalty from another country."

Miranda's heart was broken. "Oh, what am I to do? I will have failed her," she said softly as she sank back into her chair.

"I don't understand your reasoning. However, I've known you long enough to know better than to question your motives. Come, don't be so distraught. Perhaps your wishes for Sarah can still be realized. I have a thought. . . ."

Miranda looked up at Adilia and patiently waited while the woman sorted out the conspiring thoughts in her mind. Another minute went by, but Miranda kept silent, not wanting to hurry Adilia. She could see that her friend was plotting something great.

Adilia finally leaned forward and looked intensely at Miranda. "Is it your desire to put Sarah in position to become queen?"

Miranda made a quick glance around the garden to make sure there were no unwanted ears around. "It is," she said softly.

Adilia nodded. "To best fulfill your wishes, I think it would be advantageous to make a match between Sarah and the prince's cousin, Lord Chad."

Miranda gasped. "What you speak is treasonous."

Adilia waved a hand nonchalantly. "Oh, Miranda. You are just not accustomed to politics. Thrones are not always passed from father to son. Hear me out and then you may decide for yourself."

5. THE PRINCE'S REPLACEMENT

Five Years Later

"Are you still going over those political reports?" Miranda asked as she stuck her head into the study and looked at Clyde, who was obscurely hidden behind the piles of paper on his desk.

"Yes!" His reply was more forceful than he intended, and he quickly looked up with an apologetic look. "I'll be done soon. Make sure you call me when Lord Chad arrives, or when dinner is served, whichever comes first."

Miranda nodded and softly closed his door. In spite of her husband's growing ambitions, which seemed to her to be on the greedy side, she was glad that Clyde was interested in Lord Chad's visits. It hadn't always been that way. When Adilia had introduced Sarah to Lord Chad, Clyde had nothing positive to say about the budding relationship. But as years went by he took a growing interest in the young man that was now courting his stepdaughter. Miranda's plan for the young couple had gone just as she had intended, but sometimes she wondered if this was really what she wanted for her sweet princess. She pushed the doubts from her mind as she sat down at her small writing desk and set about answering the barrage of invitations to a series of parties and luncheons.

* * *

The summer day was warm and the added heat in the kitchen was almost unbearable. Sarah brushed a strand of hair from her sticky forehead and pulled the large round loaf from the heated brick oven with the long wooden paddle. Her mother had always insisted on keeping only a few servants, but despite the minimal staff to run such a large household, the manor had very fine amenities, including one of the few privately owned bread ovens in the province. Now the warm smell of freshly baked bread filled the air.

Sarah was a good cook, and now that she was seventeen she took the liberty of helping to make some of the meals for the family, despite her stepfather's complaints that it was below her position to be working in the kitchen. Today she had insisted on helping the cook and had even put some extra effort into the meal. Lord Chad had accepted an invitation to dinner, although he hadn't arrived yet and it was now getting late. Sarah scooted the hot loaf of bread onto a serving tray, followed Amanda into the dining room, and looked approvingly at the beautifully set table that was already laden with food.

"Well, you've certainly been busy," Felicia said as she strolled into the room and gave half a smile to her sister. "Where is Lord Chad? I expected that he'd be here by now."

Sarah looked out the window. "I daresay he forgot again," she said softly.

"Well then, are you finished cooking and doing the servant's job, or would you like me to help with anything?"

Sarah turned and met her sister's gaze. She knew that Felicia had no intention of helping. It aggravated their father for them to help the servants, and as Clyde's favorite, Felicia wouldn't do anything that her father disapproved of. Sarah finally shook her head. "No, but thank you; it's all done."

"Well I don't think we should have to wait for Chad," Felicia said. "Last time all of the food was cold."

"I remember," said Sarah. "You and the rest of the family can go ahead and eat. I think I know where Lord Chad is. I'll go get him."

* * *

"Good boy," Sarah said as she patted the horse on his thick neck and slowed him to a walk. Like her mother, Sarah was a good rider, but Clyde, who as a child had been repeatedly kicked by an ill-tempered mare, was distrustful of horses. Consequently, the family owned only two horses— horses that were more suitable for pulling the carriage than for riding.

Sarah found the marked path that led through the trees to the river, and there she slipped off the gelding and wrapped one rein around a tree. There was plenty of grass, and she knew he wouldn't go very far even if he pulled the rein free.

She was almost to the river when she saw the two attendants on horseback and knew Chad wouldn't be far away. He was always accompanied by one or two escorts that followed him like shadows. She thought it was frivolous to have them waiting on the young man hand and foot, but it wasn't her place to say. Chad's father had been killed in a fight resulting from a small argument while he was left unattended, so Sarah kept her thoughts on the subject to herself. After all, Chad was King Richard's oldest nephew. Besides, for the most part Chad's escorts minded their own business and she had become accustomed to ignoring them—as she did now.

She continued down the path nearing the river when she saw Chad. He was laying on the grass in the shade of a big oak tree. He was naked to the waist, his shirt lying on the ground beneath him, giving a soft buffer from the rough river grass. His breeches were dark and damp, indicating that he had gone for a swim. He was still, almost sleeping, and the only thing moving was his blond hair tousled by the breeze.

"Hello, Chad," she said as she drew close to him.

He sat up, startled, and looked around. His face quickly turned red as he looked down at his bare chest, then he grabbed for his shirt. "Ahh . . . good day, Sarah." He stood up and turned his back to her as he started to pull his shirt on.

He was quite handsome, just taller than she was, slim yet well built. This was the first time she had seen him without his shirt on, and she was about to giggle when something caught her eye. "Chad! Something's on you! A giant spider!" She pointed excitedly at the black leggy thing that lay across the back of his shoulder.

Chad jumped, almost dropped his shirt, and then quickly glanced over his shoulder to where Sarah was pointing. He relaxed. "My word, girl! That's no spider."

Sarah and Chad were close enough friends that they had dispensed with their more formal titles of address when they were alone and referred to each other by their given names, but being called *girl* was almost an insult and Sarah frowned at it. Seventeen, in her opinion, was not a girl. "Forgive me, my lord," she said reverting back to his formal title. She walked closer to get a better look at his shoulder. The stringy black spider evolved into five lines of fine lettering and she stepped even closer to read them. "What is it?" she questioned him.

"Those are my royal generations," he simply said, pulling his shirt on and covering the mysterious markings just as Sarah had gotten close enough to make out Chad's name and his father's.

"You mean the mark of royalty?" she asked. "I've heard about it, but I've never seen one."

"Many countries have the tradition, but each in their own way," Chad explained. "Some mark only their firstborn, but in our country, all the men connected with the royal crown are allowed the markings. I received mine when I turned fifteen," he said proudly.

Sarah nodded thoughtfully. Fifteen was the age that signified the passage into manhood. Chad was now nineteen, and she had not yet thought of him as a man, and certainly wouldn't have at the age of fifteen—but she just smiled and let him continue gloating.

"It's a way of identifying who I am. With this mark, no one can dispute my royal blood line and my link to the crown. You are aware that if my cousin died, the crown would pass to me."

Sarah had been told that many times before. Mostly by Chad himself. But she continued nodding as he spoke.

"My mark shows five generations of nobility."

"What if it washes off?" Sarah asked innocently.

"Wash off?" Chad scoffed. "It's permanent. It'll never come off even with the hardest scrubbing. The black ink was permanently put into my skin with a needle."

"Did it hurt?"

"It may for someone weak, but I don't remember that part. I certainly didn't cry."

She could tell that he was proud of it and didn't want to change the subject, but she was still mad at him for not showing up for the dinner she had worked so hard on. "Did you forget our appointment?" she asked, looking at him to see his response.

There was no change in his expression. "No. Is it that time already?"

"Yes." Sarah looked at the ground. "I told my family to go ahead and start without us."

"Good. I'm not really hungry at the moment. You know that I make those dinner appointments with your family just so I can come and call upon you."

Sarah could feel the blood rush into her cheeks. She realized that she, too, didn't mind that they were missing out on the meal.

* * *

Felicia pushed her food around on her plate. "Sarah has been gone a long time. I thought she would've been home by now."

"She'll be along soon enough," Miranda said. "She found Lord Chad, I suspect, and the two of them are just visiting."

"May I be excused?" Felicia asked as she pushed her plate away from her.

Miranda gave a concerned look at her daughter. "Is something on your mind, dear heart?"

"No, I must not be very hungry today."

"Very well, you may be excused. Would you step in the kitchen and tell Cook to save a plate out for Sarah and Lord Chad?"

Felicia nodded and slowly left the room, pausing to look longingly out the window for a moment.

Miranda's eyes followed her down the hallway and then she turned her attention to Clyde, who looked like his only concern was to devour the food on his plate with as few outside distractions as possible. But Miranda wasn't about to let that happen. "Clyde, I think Felicia needs to be seen after. I think she's feeling ill."

"Better not fret over her," he commented, without looking up from his food. "She's fine, just lonesome is all."

Miranda raised her eyebrows in surprise. This wasn't the first time Clyde had seemed disconnected to what was going on around him, yet still managed to have thoughtful insights. "Lonesome? How so?"

"Sarah isn't the only one who enjoys Lord Chad's visits." Clyde temporarily stopped his assault on his dinner and looked up at his wife. "You know, Miranda, you've done well with Sarah, but it's time you put as much effort into Felicia's future."

Miranda was astounded. "Whatever do you mean by that?"

Clyde had gone back to eating and took a big gulp of wine to clear his throat. "Only that Sarah is in a very beneficial situation in which her future will be secure. Don't think I'm not aware you're behind that. Now it's time to make arrangements for Felicia's future."

"I understand," Miranda said quietly. Now she was pushing her food around her plate just as her daughter had done minutes ago. "Do you really think Sarah's future is secure?"

"Yes," Clyde said, his voice muffled through a mouthful of bread. "It wouldn't surprise me if Lord Chad is making preparations for their marriage as we speak."

"Surely you jest, Clyde. I'm told that Sarah isn't the only recipient of Chad's affections."

"Nonsense, Miranda. He may enjoy flattering the other ladies, but it is Sarah who has his heart. Although I'm not quite certain she deserves it."

Miranda slapped her knife on the table. "I can tell *you*, Clyde Berack, that Sarah deserves more than that self-doting lord can offer."

Clyde's eyes once more wavered from his meal and focused on his wife. "Hold your tongue, Miranda. Lord Chad is a proper gentleman. Proper, I tell you. And Sarah, she is . . . unpolished," he said choosing his words carefully. "Too spirited."

"Character and self-assurance is what I call it."

"Any respectable lady knows her place and is attended to," he said gruffly.

"Don't worry about attendants—Lord Chad has enough for both of them."

Clyde glared at her. "Sarah is headstrong."

"You mean she is knowledgeable and assertive," Miranda retorted with an irritated smile.

"She cooks and tends to the animals like a servant."

"Implying that she is a well-rounded lady of many interests and talents."

"Nonconforming," Clyde grunted.

"Which makes her self-reliant."

Clyde's face was red now. "Miranda, there's no winning with you. If Sarah is lucky she will secure Lord Chad and she'll be well for it."

Miranda took a deep breath and relaxed, knowing the battle was over and Clyde was retreating. She knew she shouldn't take pleasure in this small triumph over Clyde but a slight smile touched her lips anyway. Trying to mask her wry look, she regarded her husband with a determined passiveness, but when she saw his eyes fixed on her neck she realized that she had been rubbing her heart-shaped pendant. Quickly she dropped her hand. "Well, in spite of my reservations about Lord Chad, I do believe he would be an advantageous match," she said in an attempt to engage Clyde in conversation again. "And I know you favor Lord Chad because he encouraged you to invest in Lord Bening's trading adventure."

Clyde glanced away, but the dejected look in his eyes was evident. He nodded and then cleared his throat. "Yes, it paid us well to do so, and therefore we are indebted to Lord Chad for that opportunity. All of

Lord Chad's endeavors have been prosperous, and many businessmen and officials see it the same way. Lord Chad will be a giant among men."

"You talk as if he is an accomplished and seasoned man of experience," Miranda scoffed. "You forget that he has scarcely emerged from his own childhood."

"He may be young, but he has a cunning mind for business and government."

Miranda rolled her eyes.

"Well then," Clyde said firmly, "let me tell you what I heard today while I was in town with Mr. Connor."

"Very well, do tell," she said, trying not to sound too eager to hear the gossip.

Clyde leaned back in his seat, taking great pleasure in sharing the story. "The dignitaries that are visiting from Spain were treated to a royal banquet yesterday after which they offered gifts to Their Majesties the King, Queen, and Prince in an elaborate ceremony." He paused for effect. "However, the prince had slipped out right after the feast and was nowhere to be found. Supposedly, just as the situation was becoming uncomfortable, guess who took the place of the prince in the ceremony? None other than our Lord Chad. The dignitaries were satisfied with the substitution, because it'd been Lord Chad who had accompanied them on their travels around the kingdom, and endeared himself to them. It's said that the king himself was so upset by his son's disappearance that he let Lord Chad keep the gifts from the Spaniards. I'm told these included a prized hunting falcon and a relic from Saint Babylas—I haven't the detail of what that is, but I'm told it has the power to grant wealth."

"So he adds more to his many treasures," Miranda said flatly.

"No," Clyde groaned at his wife. "The point is that Lord Chad took the place of the prince in an important ceremony, and it was acceptable. Not only to the Spanish dignitaries, but to the king's court as well." He leaned forward on the table, not noticing his sleeve drooping in the gravy on his plate. "The rumors have already started that Chad assumes the position of the prince better than the prince himself. I tell you, Miranda, if you could refine Sarah she will be able to secure Chad now, and with a few political maneuvers, Lord Chad is going to be in a position you would've never thought possible."

6. THE LOST SECRET

Sarah poured hot water over the horehound and mullein leaves that she had gathered and let them steep. She had gathered many herbs during the summer, but now that the weather was getting colder, she looked at her dwindling supply of dried plants and decided that she had better go out once more before winter set in. She moved everything on the large shelf, grouping and organizing while she made a mental note of what she needed more of. *More lobelia, yarrow, and mullein, and it's the perfect time to collect the rose hips.* Every herb was good for something, her mother had taught her. Horseradish clears the sinuses and aids breathing, yarrow sweats out fever, horehound quiets a cough. And now that her mother had been coughing and feverish lately, she didn't want to find herself in the winter months without her remedies.

After a minute, Sarah pulled the leaves out of her concoction, added a bit of honey, and carefully took the cup into the sitting room were her mother was. Miranda smiled at her daughter, but her face looked pale and hollow, and Sarah noticed that with each cough, her mother's body shook as if the sickness had penetrated to her very core.

Sarah held the cup in her mother's hand to steady it while Miranda sipped from it. "Mother, do you want me to send for the doctor?"

"No, as I told you before, I just need some time. I'll be fine in a few weeks; just let it run its course." She coughed again. Even speaking seemed to take all of her energy.

"I think I should gather some more herbs today."

"Very well; don't be gone too long." Miranda thought it was too late in the season to find much of anything, but decided it would take too much out of her to convince Sarah to stay home. She was getting weaker and needed Sarah to help her get around, but Felicia was home and would assist her if needed, so she settled into her chair to rest while Sarah was gone.

Wrapping her cloak around her and grabbing a basket, Sarah stepped out the kitchen door at the back of the house and headed toward the fields. The air was crisp and the colorful leaves had faded and now covered the ground, crunching and crackling with each step.

"My lady," Amanda called from the back door. "Lord Chad has come to call."

Sarah thanked her and ran around the manor. In the small courtyard, two escorts were still mounted on their horses, and Chad stood in the open doorway of the manor. It was unusual for him not to come inside, but then she heard her mother coughing from the sitting room. She realized that he must have felt uncomfortable with it and had decided to wait at the door.

"Good morning," she called.

Chad turned and smiled. "My lady, you look splendid this morning," he said with a bow.

"Thank you, and you as well, my lord."

"You shouldn't be out in this brisk weather," he said, eyeing the basket hanging from her arm. "Perhaps you should take your walk later when the sun is warmer."

"I find it refreshing," Sarah said.

Chad stepped over to her, taking her arm. He took a deep breath and led her to where the faint sun filtered through the clouds and was warming the horses. "I see your mother is still ill. Would you like me to send for a doctor?"

"I've already asked her, and she will not see one at present, so I'm going to the field to gather some herbs for her. Would you like to join me?"

Chad shook his head. "I was rather hoping to spend the morning indoors. I brought a game to play, but it needs at least three people. Your servant mentioned that Felicia was home, so I thought we could all enjoy it together."

"I would dearly love to, but my mother is so very sick."

"Yes, I heard her coughing; she sounds very bad off indeed. It can't be good for you to be around it. If you'd like, I'll send my rider for a carriage, and the three of us can go to Mendierlan. It's been so long since you have come to visit—my mother would love to see you, and I'll have you and Felicia home by nightfall."

She loved to visit the grounds at Chad's estate, but she knew she couldn't leave her mother alone for that long. "It's kind of you to offer, but I really mustn't."

Chad frowned. "I must have your company today. I'm lonely and need you to cheer me."

"Then stay. Come with me to the field and I'll show you some different plants and what you can do with them. It will be a wonderful outing, and you can stay for dinner."

"The thought of plants doesn't thrill me in the least," he said, ignoring the pleading look in her eyes. "Am I to understand that you are determined not to entertain me?"

Sarah dropped his arm. "I'm afraid not. I must stay and help my mother." She paused. "I am sorry, sir. Perhaps when she is well again, I'll play your game." She stated it, hoping he would see the double meaning.

"Very well, I won't keep you from your chores. Good day, my lady."

Sarah watched as Chad mounted his horse and nudged it down the lane and then called out to him, "My lord, please come again soon, and I promise to be at your disposal."

Chad turned, flashed her a smile, and nodded politely.

* * *

Clyde sat at his desk and diverted his focus from the snow piling up on the window ledge to the ledger in front of him. In the last few months it seemed like his concentration had deteriorated right along with Miranda's health. Sarah had taken over much of the household management and now he was trying to make sense of the figures she had written in his finance book. He rubbed his face and sat back in his chair, looking out the window again. It was no use; he couldn't concentrate on anything for more than a few minutes. He closed the ledger and hoped Sarah's figures were right. Instinctively he reached out for the flagon of brandy sitting on his desk, but he stopped himself, thinking better of it. Tipping his head back, he closed his eyes. He was always so tired lately. Perhaps he needed to get out. He cursed himself for the thought. What if Miranda were to pass away while he was gone?

The squeaking of a heavy door upstairs drew his attention and he strained to listen. This had been the doctor's third time to come and see Miranda, but today Clyde had refused to go up to her room with him. He couldn't bear it, and besides, he already knew what the doctor would say. There was nothing he could do for her, and he was surprised she had held on this long. He didn't need confirmation from the doctor to feel any worse about his wife's condition. Two of his tenants and close friends had already died of the same sickness, and several others throughout the village, but why did it have to take hold of Miranda?

He listened to Sarah and the doctor whispering something about a balm to rub on her chest and back to ease her breathing, then he watched through the window as the doctor climbed into his cart and left. He shook his head and grunted about the cold draft coming into his study, then noticed that a large carriage was approaching the house. He watched as Lord Chad stepped from the carriage and hurried over to the house where Sarah still stood in the open doorway. He strained his ears to listen again.

A moment later he was up, pacing the floor with his hands tightly clasped behind his back. "The wretched girl," he mumbled as he walked over to the window and watched as Lord Chad stepped back in his carriage and shouted to his servant to drive on.

Clyde grabbed the flagon and took a long draw of brandy from it, then quickly walked to the hall and caught Sarah by the elbow just as she started up the stairs. "What on earth are you doing?" he growled, allowing his pain and heartache to turn into anger.

"Pardon me?" Sarah asked with surprise.

"Lord Chad. What are you doing turning him away like that?"

"I simply can't keep company now. I must attend to Mother."

"Surely you fail to understand the consequences of your actions. You've been tending to your mother for almost three months now. You need to tend to yourself." He paused, not wanting to admit what he was about to, and then he took a deep breath and continued through tight lips. "With your mother, it's only a matter of time, but you have a whole life yet, and Miranda wouldn't want you to close those doors that she has opened for you."

Sarah gently pulled her arm out of Clyde's grasp. "I'm not closing doors. I'm doing what I need to, and that is caring for Mother."

Clyde scowled. "Miranda is delirious and out of her mind much of the time. I'm quite certain she wouldn't know if you took a day and spent it with Lord Chad."

"Perhaps she wouldn't, but I would," Sarah said flatly.

"For more than a month, you have not even given an hour of company to Lord Chad, and I dare say it won't be long before he turns his affections to someone who will reciprocate them."

"Be that as it may, at least I'll have a clear conscience, knowing that I had compassion for my mother while she was ill." Sarah took in a quick breath and held it, surprised at her outspoken manner. She wished she could somehow take back her hurtful words.

Clyde's ears turned red and he looked as if he were about to explode. "I'm not asking you to abandon your mother, but only to take some time for yourself and continue to build those prosperous relationships. There will be a time when you will want to turn to Lord Chad, but he will be secured in another's affections and leave you to become the poor wife of some feeble merchant, and Miranda would be disappointed in that." Clyde snapped his mouth shut and marched away.

* * *

Hours later, Sarah carried a bowl of broth into Miranda's room. "I'm sorry I woke you," she said, turning her red, blotchy face away from her mother. "I just brought you something to drink and some broth."

"Sarah?" Miranda said weakly between coughs. "Come here a minute and sit by me."

Sarah walked over and sat on the edge of the bed next to her mother. "Let me feed you some broth, Mother. It's been so long since you have eaten anything."

Miranda tried to lean forward and with Sarah's help, managed to prop herself up enough so she could get a good look at her daughter. "My, you're getting so beautiful," she said as she reached a pale, thin arm over and pulled Sarah's hair to the side and over her shoulder. Using all her strength, she slid her daughter's sleeve down just enough to see the scarred royal seal on her shoulder—the seal that she had protected and hidden for more than seventeen years. She traced the emblem with a frail finger and then slid the sleeve back up and let her arm fall to her side. It took a minute for her to recover what little strength she had. "Sarah, I want to tell you something," Miranda said as forcefully as she could, but her voice escaped her mouth as no more than a hoarse whisper.

Sarah looked at her mother. Miranda's pale face was etched with seriousness.

"I've been living with a secret," she started, then drew in a deep breath and began to cough. It was several minutes before she could go on. "I want you to know . . ." She paused, gathering her thoughts. "I want you to know, sweet princess, that you really and truly are a princess." Miranda stopped and looked at her daughter. Sarah smiled and leaned over and kissed her on the cheek. Just then Clyde appeared in the doorway, and Sarah jumped to her feet. She'd been avoiding him since their earlier confrontation and didn't want to talk to him now.

Clyde stood in the door looking awkward. "How are you feeling today?" he finally asked, ignoring Sarah and staring at his feeble wife. "I see you're sitting up."

"I was just going to give Mother some broth," Sarah said quietly.

"I have no appetite for broth," Miranda whispered.

"I'll do it," Clyde said, ignoring Miranda's comment. He quickly walked over and picked up the bowl.

Sarah gave her mother another kiss on the cheek and then walked out, quietly closing the door behind her. She breathed a sigh of relief, glad she didn't need to stay in the room with Clyde.

That turned out to be the last conversation Sarah had with her mother. For the next three days, Miranda stirred and mumbled but never became fully coherent. She quietly passed away in the middle of the night, with Clyde asleep in a chair next to her. Two days later, the small family and their close friends, with tears stinging their cheeks, huddled around the frozen grave, trying to brace themselves against the harsh weather and the bitterness of facing life without Miranda.

Not only had her gentleness and love been buried with her but also the secret she had kept for so long.

7. SABOTAGED LOVE

It was June now and Sarah had cried herself to sleep again, as she had so many times since Miranda's death. She rolled over restlessly, her face still wet with tears. Suddenly she sat up with a jerk, her eyes wide and chest heaving. Fresh tears slipped down her cheeks until the nightmare slowly abated into the darkness. Quietly she climbed out of bed and tiptoed down the dark hall to Felicia's room. As children they used to slip into each other's beds anytime they were scared, but it had been years since they had done that. She paused for a minute, and then feeling foolish, she turned and snuck back to her own room.

She couldn't bear it. She knew she had started secluding herself from everyone, but she couldn't help it. Miranda had been the one holding them all together, and now that she was gone, things were changing. Clyde tried to soothe away his grief with his brandy bottle and consequently grew increasingly angry and volatile, and Felicia denied that anything had happened. She would talk about Miranda as if she had just gone on vacation and would return at any moment. Even Lord Chad had distanced himself, as Clyde had predicted. Unable to console Sarah, he found it more comfortable to just leave her alone. And now that's what she felt—dreadfully alone.

Falling onto her bed, Sarah buried her face in her pillow and cried.

* * *

Clyde looked out the window at the unexpected visitor approaching the manor. Lord Chad met with him and other businessmen almost weekly in the village to discuss politics, but Chad's visits to the house happened only on rare occasions now. He shook his head in dismay as he imagined how this impromptu visit would go, considering Sarah's cool demeanor lately. Miranda had worked carefully to establish their union, and now Sarah was letting the relationship slip through her hands. Clyde let out a long breath, then stood up with determination. He wasn't going to let this visit end as the others had. Lord Chad was an opportunity. Miranda must have known that, and now with some assistance, perhaps Felicia could take advantage of that opportunity. With renewed hope, Clyde hurried out to where Chad stood in the entryway, looking rather unsure about coming to visit.

"Ah, good day, sir," Chad said with obvious hesitation. "I hope you don't mind me calling at such an early hour this morning."

"Of course not," Clyde said and motioned toward the sitting room. "Come in, come in. I heard about the speech you gave at court this week. Sorry I missed it. Had business down south, you know."

Chad nodded. "Yes, I talked to Lord Bening yesterday. I understand things are going quite well for you now."

"Yes, quite well, but somehow I think that you are here for matters other than business."

"You are perceptive, my friend. I came to call on Sarah. Is she home?"

"I believe so. Please sit down." Clyde held a hand out toward a seat near the window. "It's good of you to take the time to come for a visit; I know you are busy with the Austrian matter."

Chad nodded. "Yes, I received another letter regarding the issue just this morning. Things are even more dire on our northern borders than I previously thought. We have farmlands and homesteads that are being attacked almost daily now."

"Should we be concerned about their advancement, do you think?"

"No, I believe we'll be able to manage the situation. The Austrians are coming across the border by Midway, and it's so favorably situated that we'll have no trouble defending the area. I have faith that the king will trust me with command of his soldiers, and we will indeed have success."

"I heard that the prince has been given command of the soldiers," Clyde commented.

Chad frowned. "That is only a rumor. His only role will be to form an alliance with one of our neighboring countries through marriage. After all, this matter is not to be toyed with for the amusement of my cousin."

"These are the sentiments of myself and my colleagues as well, I assure you. We hope for your personal management of the situation."

"Thank you," Chad said with a nod. "I'm sure I'll secure the support of the king's council regarding my defense plans and will be able to put them into effect as soon as possible."

"Good. I see we are in capable hands." Clyde waved a hand graciously. "Please make yourself at ease, and I'll send for Sarah right away."

Clyde walked out of the room, but instead of going upstairs to wake Sarah, he made his way to the sewing room where Felicia sat quietly putting small, uniform stitches in a lacy cloth. "Lord Chad is here," he told her. "Would you please keep him company until Sarah is ready to come down?"

"Of course," she said, and then eagerly hurried into the sitting room.

"I hope you don't mind me sitting with you until Sarah comes," she told Chad moments later.

Chad smiled graciously. "Not at all."

Clyde stood by the doorway just out of sight, listening to them for a few minutes before he went outside, leaving the two to visit—and Sarah to sleep.

More than an hour later, Clyde smiled as he saw Felicia walk Chad out to his horse, deeply satisfied that both seemed to have had a pleasant time with each other.

After Felicia had waved to Chad, she walked over to her father. "Where is Sarah?" she asked.

"Still up in her room. You know how she's been lately." Felicia nodded and turned away, but he caught her by the arm. "I think it best that you don't mention anything to Sarah about Chad. I believe that will just worsen her moods." She nodded again.

Felicia had just walked in the house when Sarah came down the stairs. "Why didn't anyone wake me for breakfast?"

"We haven't had breakfast yet," Felicia explained.

"At this late an hour! What has everyone been doing?"

"Uhh, nothing of importance," her sister said with uncertainty, "but I am getting hungry now. I'll go see if Cook is ready." She turned and hurried off toward the kitchen.

Outside, Chad glanced back over his shoulder at the manor before it disappeared from view. This was the first time in months that he had actually enjoyed a visit at the Berack manor. He wondered why Sarah hadn't come in to see him, but even so he enjoyed being there. Sarah was obviously still out of sorts about her mother's passing, but he didn't understand why she just couldn't get back to her own life. Why was she so withdrawn? He shook his head and decided that he would go back to visit in a few days and see how she was doing.

* * *

"I think she went out for a ride," Felicia explained. "But she should be back by now."

Chad raised an eyebrow curiously. It had been three days since his last visit to the manor, but the situation seemed oddly the same. Clyde had answered the door, led him to the sitting room, briefly discussed politics, and then went to get Sarah, and again it was Felicia who appeared in the doorway to keep him company.

An hour later, Sarah walked in the back door. Clyde heard the door shut and met her in the hall. "Sarah, Chad is here," he said matter-of-factly.

"And no one came to get me?" she asked as she hurried toward the sitting room.

"I was on my way out to get you just now. He hasn't been here long," Clyde muttered.

Felicia stood up blushing when Sarah walked in the room. "Sarah, I . . . I've just been keeping Chad company until you came. I'll leave you two alone now."

"Thank you," Sarah said gratefully as she watched her sister flash a smile at Chad before leaving the room.

"I hope you haven't been waiting long," Sarah said as she sat down opposite him.

"Oh, I didn't mind," he said truthfully, still watching the doorway Felicia had disappeared through. "I find your sister quite entertaining." He turned his attention to Sarah. "But I am happy to see you. Sarah, how have you been doing? It's been such a long time since I've seen you, and in truth, I've been quite worried about you."

"That is thoughtful of you; however, I'm fine."

"I'm glad to hear it. I just wanted to check on you, but unfortunately I can't stay much longer. I failed to tell my mother where I was going and she's expecting me, but I wanted to tell you that it's our country's centennial anniversary this year, and a magnificent celebration is being planned. An open feast, a grand ball, fireworks, and a day fair! Mother's been able to talk of nothing else. Announcements are even being sent out to all of the neighboring villages."

Sarah's face lit up. "Oh! That sounds like so much fun! When is it scheduled for?"

"Not for a couple of months, mid-August I believe, but preparations are well under way. His Majesty is posting the announcement tomorrow so that everyone in the kingdom can make ready. I myself have been appointed to oversee much of the preparation, and Mother is getting involved too. She made me accompany her to town yesterday so she could pick out material for the new gown she is planning on wearing."

"I suppose I'll have to buy a new gown too."

Chad nodded, then stood up and walked over to the window. Sarah watched him closely. The sun filtered through the thick glass and made his hair look a bit more blond than it really was. She had forgotten how handsome he was, and she didn't realize how much she had really missed him. She wished that they could just go for a walk together and talk like they used to. Her grief had sufficiently healed enough that she felt ready to confide in him again and rebuild their friendship.

He turned around and caught her looking at him and smiled. "Well, I must go," he said somberly. "If it is all right I'll come back in a day or two."

Sarah's heart sank. "Must you go now? I haven't even had time to visit with you. Please stay," she pleaded and then crossed the room to where he stood. "We really must catch up. Just a little longer, please."

"I'll come again soon." He took her arm as he walked to the door.

"Please do. I so miss our conversations we used to have." She waved farewell to him and slowly closed the door. It hadn't been a long visit, but still it was something, and she really needed that—to know that he still cared for her. Sarah was sure that when it was time for the big celebration, things between her and Chad would be back to normal. After all, he was making an effort and coming to see her, and she was ready to move forward. Perhaps by this time next year she would find herself married and the mistress of her own household at Mendierlan.

* * *

Sarah walked in through the back door, and peered into the kitchen where Catherine was standing at the large table making dinner. "Where is everyone?" she asked.

"Out front I believe, miss. Your young man came a-calling today, and is just leaving."

"Today? Clyde told me that he was coming tomorrow!" Sarah ran to the front door, threw it open, and saw three men riding away. She instantly recognized the traditional red tunics worn by servants of Mendierlan, and she could just make out Chad on his dapple gray horse in the lead nearing the bend in the road.

She stomped her foot on the ground. This was the third week in a row that she had missed him. Last week Clyde had given her permission to go riding, and although she hadn't gone far, no one had bothered to go find her when Chad arrived. She had returned an hour later only to find out that she had just missed him. And the week before, he had stopped by unannounced while she was out collecting rent from the tenants.

Today, with summer in full swing and the hot July sun making the house unbearable, she had taken one of her favorite books and gone for a walk to the orchard to read. The apple orchard was one of her favorite places to get away from daily pressures. It was peaceful and secluded. A road ran between the orchard and a small forest, but it was seldom traveled, and with the thickness of the trees, Sarah felt like she had her own secret little hideaway. It was a special place that she had hoped to share with Chad. She grumbled as she watched the riders disappear around the corner, scolding herself for staying out too long.

"Lord Chad is sorry he missed you," Felicia said as she joined her older sister in the doorway. "He talked about the celebration coming up. I can hardly wait! He mentioned such wonderful things! Although I'm surprised that such a celebration is being planned while the Austrians threaten war on our border."

Sarah was not in the mood to talk. "You fail to see that there's no better time for a celebration. It will raise morale." She turned and ran up the stairs, taking them two at a time.

Felicia was just stepping up the first stair when she heard the door to Sarah's room slam, and decided to leave her alone.

Sarah threw herself down on her bed and buried her face in her pillow. She had really wanted to talk to Chad. The celebration was only four weeks away and she was sure that Chad would be asking her to accompany him. The thoughts of it ran through her mind again. They would be together for hours. Dancing, talking, and laughing. She wanted to be in his arms, to have him hold her close to him, to feel him near her. But she wanted that now. She didn't want to wait four weeks.

Oh well, she told herself. *Tomorrow I will go to the tailor and get fitted for a new dress, and since it is also market day, there's a good chance that I'll see him.* Chad could often be found wandering through the market, looking at the different vendors' goods. He was a competent swordsman and spent a lot of time at the sword maker's guild. He could not pass up a good-quality sword, and he often searched the shops on market day for unique items.

The next morning Sarah woke early, did her own hair, and slipped into one of her nicest dresses. She counted out the twenty-two coins that Clyde had allotted her and placed them in her sachet.

Catherine was standing by the door with a basket, ready to accompany her. "You ready, miss?" she asked.

"Yes. I want to hurry so I have plenty of time at the market. Did you remember to bring the horseshoes for the blacksmith?" Sarah asked.

"Yes, miss. Got them right here in the basket."

Sarah enjoyed Catherine's company, but they never had deep conversations like she and her mother used to have. Nevertheless, it still made short time of the walk with Catherine along.

The blacksmith's shop was the first place they stopped so that Catherine's basket would be lightened, and as they neared the old shop, Sarah noticed a little bay pony in the corral. She walked over to it and reached across the fence to scratch his neck. The blacksmith stepped out, rubbing his hands on his leather apron. "Ah, hello, Miss Sarah, what can I do for you today?"

"Just a few shoes that need reshaping." She motioned for Catherine to give him the horseshoes.

The blacksmith looked in the basket and nodded. "For the large gelding? It won't take long. Have Joshua bring him by tomorrow and I'll make sure I've got the fit right."

Sarah nodded, then turned her attention back to the little pony. He was quite small, but fat, and had a shaggy, thick, brown coat. His black tail was exceptionally long and touched the ground behind him; his mane was equally as long, hanging past his neck, and his forelock hid his eyes. Sarah reached out and pulled the long hair back so he could see. "This little one is cute. Where did you get him?" she asked the blacksmith, who was taking a look at the horseshoes he had taken from Catherine.

The man frowned. "I took him in trade for some work that I did," he said bitterly. "The blasted thing is lame." The blacksmith gave a disgusted wave toward the pony. "Back leg is crippled. Not good for anything but meat for my dogs."

"That's terrible to say." Sarah rubbed the pony's forehead. "Why not just sell him?"

"Believe me, I've tried. No one wants to buy a lame animal, and I can't afford to keep feeding him. I have half a mind to take him and put him out of his misery."

Sarah turned and looked at the man. "No! You can't do that. It's not right."

"If I could find someone who would take him off my hands, I would gladly give him away."

"Well then, that settles it," Sarah said as she turned and faced him with a grin. "I'll be back to pick him up when we are done with our shopping."

"But, miss," Catherine jumped in, "What will Master Clyde say? He might be against it."

"Nonsense! We have plenty of pasture, more than our two horses will ever need." Catherine just shook her head, pressed her lips tightly together, and grimaced.

"Are you sure, miss?" the blacksmith asked. "I'm more than willing to send him with you, but not if it will cause problems with Mr. Berack."

"I am quite certain; there will be no problems. I'll be back soon," she said, more to the little pony than to the blacksmith, and then she turned and walked toward the tailor's shop to see if they had any gowns for sale. Halfway down the street, she excused Catherine to go get the few items that they needed. Catherine objected to leaving her unattended, but Sarah wouldn't hear it. She needed her space.

Sarah stepped through the small door of the tailor's shop and found her attention drawn to a striking gown hanging against the far wall. It was pale, icy blue silk with beadwork across the bodice. The top of the sleeves were puffed and billowed out and then tightened at the elbow. It was stunning, and Sarah wondered if the tailor was making alterations on it for the owner, or if he had displayed it to sell. She walked closer to examine the wonderful craftsmanship when she noticed the tailor working on an article of clothing in the back of the room.

"Excuse me," she said, "about this blue gown, do you mind telling me who it's for?"

"It was for the Baroness Raildega," he answered without looking up. "I was making it for her to wear to the centennial celebration."

"It's beautiful. You do wonderful work."

"I wish the baroness were as gracious as you. She was just here a few minutes ago and it wasn't to her liking, and now I'm making another for her."

Sarah's hopes soared. "Then am I right in presuming that you will sell this one?"

The tailor laid down the cloth he was working with and looked at her. "I will ask the baroness what she wants done with it the next time she comes in. I'm sure she won't take it, and then I will be forced to sell it."

"Will you tell me how much money you would ask for it?" Sarah held her breath, hoping that she would have enough.

The man stood up and walked over to the dress, then took the fabric and rubbed it between his thumb and forefinger. "This is very expensive fabric." He paused. "I could take no less than twenty-five silver florins."

Sarah's heart sank. She was lacking just three coins, but she was not about to ask her stepfather for extra money. The tailor had read the look on her face and went back to his work, leaving Sarah to admire the dress that she would never wear.

"It's beautiful, is it not?" The voice caught her off guard. There was an accent to it that seemed familiar, almost reminiscent of the way her mother had talked. Quickly she turned to see who was standing behind her. Sarah didn't recognize the woman. She was elderly; her face was etched with wrinkles, and she was small and bent over with rounded shoulders.

"Yes! It's a lovely gown," Sarah said, but her expression was crestfallen.

"My dear, what's wrong?" the woman asked, putting a hand on Sarah's arm.

"Oh, nothing. I was just . . . nothing," she broke off.

"Ah . . . I think I understand." The old woman looked at Sarah thoughtfully. "A special occasion of some kind? You are shopping for a new gown?"

Again Sarah noted the woman's accent and wondered where she was from. "Yes," she finally sighed. "The celebration in four weeks."

"Oh yes! That is a special occasion. Is someone taking you?"

"Yes. Well, I think so. Lord Chad, but it's not certain yet."

"Ahhh, the king's nephew. I know him well."

"You do?" Sarah looked closer at the woman to make sure that she had not met her somewhere before.

"Yes. He seems to be a charming young gentleman. My name is Carlina Sarter Fales. I'm a seamstress, and his family has used my services on many occasions," she explained.

Sarah nodded in understanding and looked back at the dress.

"I make wonderful gowns. Would you like me to make one for you before the ball?"

"I can't afford more than twenty-two silver florins," Sarah responded.

"Well, I am sure I can come up with something wonderful for that price, something much like this but more flattering to your young figure."

Sarah looked into the woman's eyes. "Would you? I would really appreciate it."

"Of course, my dear. Come with me. I have a place just down the street and I can get your measurements." The old woman completed her business with the tailor, then left the shop.

Sarah walked with her down to the end of the street, discussing style and color as they went. "I never knew there was a seamstress shop down here," she said as they walked inside the little building.

"I worked privately out of my home up until a month ago," the old woman explained as she rummaged through a box. "I have been in this part of the world for only a year now," the woman went on. "I'm from Kyrnidan. My son travels a lot and he moved here to Calibre, married, and then settled down here. I moved here so I could be close to my grandchildren," the seamstress said. She had just found her tape measure and stretched it out as she looked Sarah up and down. "Now then, let me see." She stepped forward and pulled the tape along Sarah's arm, marked down the number on a piece of paper, and then measured her again from her waist to the floor. The little woman proceeded to measure and mark down numbers—her bust, then her waist, then shoulder to waist, always moving slowly and double-checking the numbers.

"One more," she finally said as she took Sarah's hair and pulled it around so that it fell in front of her. Scooting a little stool next to her she stood on it, making them the same height, then she pulled the measuring tape across Sarah's shoulders. She leaned forward to make sure the tape was in the right spot before she took a mental note of the measurement, and then stopped. "What happened here?" she asked innocently, tapping a small dark area barely showing above the neckline.

"Oh, that's just a birthmark," Sarah explained, still holding very still.

The seamstress folded back the edge of Sarah's dress to reveal the entire emblem. She looked hard at it for a minute, and then stepped down.

"Are you done?" Sarah asked.

"Yes." The old woman turned her around so they were facing each other and then took both of Sarah's hands in hers. "My dear, you haven't even told me your name."

"I'm sorry, please excuse my impoliteness. My name is Sarah. Sarah Antonellis Benavente."

"Now tell me who your parents are."

"My mother died last winter. Her name was Miranda." Sarah looked down at the floor as if she were studying the cracks in it, trying to hide her pain.

"I'm so sorry, my dear," Carlina said with sympathy.

"My stepfather is Clyde Berack," Sarah went on, trying to move away from the subject of her mother.

"I'm afraid I don't know who he is." The old woman just stood there silently for a long minute studying the young girl's face. "And how old are you?"

"Eighteen now," Sarah replied with a curious look.

"I see." Finally the old women let go of her hands.

Sarah took out her sachet and counted the coins out to the woman.

"Thank you so much for your business. I will have the gown ready in three weeks—"

"Three weeks?"

"Three weeks, maybe longer." The seamstress shrugged. "I'm an old woman and things have been so busy lately . . . but I will have a gown ready in time for the celebration."

"But that leaves no time if the dress needs altering."

"Not to worry. I have all your measurements and I never misjudge on sizes."

Sarah reluctantly agreed, then stepped back out onto the street and looked around. She still had a little time before Catherine was supposed to meet her at the blacksmith's shop, so she took her time looking around the market. Not that she was really looking for something in particular, but some*one*. By the time she made it back to the blacksmith's shop, Catherine was already waiting. Sarah was disappointed. It was time to go home, and she hadn't seen Chad at all. She pushed the disappointment aside and looked forward to the next time that they were sure to meet. Clyde was taking Felicia and her to the castle next week to celebrate the promotion of their friend Sir Tyson to the position of chancellor. Chad was sure to be there.

8. THE STRANGER

Sarah was outside by the stables brushing the two workhorses. She was spending more and more time outside with them, especially since she had brought home the little bay pony. The horses were her friends, and when she was lonely, they kept her company. Since her mother's death, her sense of isolation lingered despite her attempts to return to her old routine, and her best escape from the loneliness was to ride the horses.

Even with the days growing shorter she had plenty of time to go for a ride before supper, but she decided to spend the time with the small pony she had named Pooka. She put the two work horses away, grabbed the smallest halter, and walked toward the little woolly horse. Pooka was an odd name, but it suited the mischievous little horse. He reminded her of a wood sprite or the mysterious impish spirits called pookas. Clyde wasn't happy when he found out that she had brought the pony home, but reluctantly he gave in and let her keep the animal. Sarah suspected that he had given in to make her feel better after she had discovered that she had missed Chad yet again. She had come home from the market with the little pony when Felicia told her that Chad had spent more than two hours at the manor that day. Since then, Pooka had become her confidant. She took him for walks and talked to him as if he were a person, sharing those thoughts and feelings that would have been entrusted to Chad—or to Felicia, had they not grown apart this last year.

"Come on, little one." She pulled the halter over his head. "Look at your long shags. I see you're due for a good brushing." She loved his long mane and tail and felt like a little girl brushing the hair on a doll. When she was done, she led him over to the stone trough and he plunged his muzzle into the water to drink. The hair from his forelock and mane drooped in the water and swirled around his head. "I really should take some shears and trim that mane." Pooka lifted his head out of the water as if he had understood her. She grabbed the long wet hair between his ears and twirled, twisted, and pulled it up until it stood like a black spike on top of his head. She let it go, and it stood on its own for a brief moment before toppling over.

Sarah threw a hand over her mouth and started to laugh. She twisted the pony's hair once more, giggling at how funny he looked. She scanned the yard and her eyes rested on a bucket of old thick molasses. Amanda had set the molasses out two days ago but hadn't yet gotten rid of it. "Perfect," she said with a mischievous grin.

She took the bucket and dipped her hand into the dark, thick, glue-like syrup and pulled out a glob. "You're going to look so cute!" she laughed, and went to work coating Pooka's forelock with the thick goo. She pulled, twirled, and twisted it, coating it with more sludge until it formed a tight cone on top of his head. The dark molasses blended perfectly with his black hair and she slicked it up so it looked like a perfect spike. Once she had it standing up on its own she stepped back to admire her work. She couldn't help but laugh out loud, and Pooka simply looked at her, unaware that he was the cause of her amusement.

As she wiped her hands on her apron she saw her stepfather coming around the corner to meet her. "Sarah, I want you to go to the orchard right now and gather a basket of fresh apples."

Sarah just looked at him. Why would he ask her to pick apples? It was something she was sure he would never ask Felicia to do, and hadn't he rebuked her in the past for doing that same task?

Clyde sensed her hesitation. "I asked Cook to make an apple pie. She would go pick them herself, but she's already busy making dinner and I thought you would . . ." he broke off, thinking carefully through his words. "I thought you would enjoy the walk. Or if you wouldn't, then perhaps you could help Felicia finish embroidering the altar cloth."

Given the choice, she would much rather go to the orchard to fetch apples.

"Now, do you intend to pick apples, or shall I call for Amanda to bring the sewing?"

Sarah nodded. "I'll go to the orchard right away."

"Thank you." Clyde was just about to turn when he noticed the little pony.

Sarah looked back at him too, coloring as she saw the spike still standing on top of Pooka's head.

Clyde raised an eyebrow and shook his head. "Take that beast with you, too," he mumbled, then turned and walked back around the house.

* * *

Chad didn't mind when Clyde told him that he had just missed Sarah. After all, he was starting to get used to it.

"She left a few minutes ago," Clyde explained when he returned from the yard.

"I'm sorry. My timing seems to be off," Chad said, shaking his head. "Will she be back soon?"

"I can't say. She is so unpredictable. She went to the orchard to pick apples. She's a wonderful young lady, but unlike Felicia, she is so . . . well, unrefined, if you take my meaning."

Chad nodded. "I'm beginning to see that. Is Felicia at home? Perhaps I could visit with her awhile."

"Certainly." Clyde's lips curled slowly up into a shrewd smile. "I'll send for her straightaway."

* * *

Sarah was almost to the orchard when she reached out and touched the pony's forelock, which was still formed into a tight cone. It was slightly sticky, but the sun had baked it into a hard mass.

"Oh no! You poor little animal. I should have washed this out before we left. You look so funny!" she giggled. "It's a good thing you can't see yourself." She looked at the pony and rubbed his back. "Well even if you did, you wouldn't hate me . . . would you? No, you like me, don't you Pooka?" Sarah rubbed his back and then slid her arm around him. "Come on, little one. We're almost there."

The orchard was a cool sanctuary from the hot sun. Many apples had already fallen into the tall grass, but the trees were still loaded with the ripe fruit, and birds were chirping happily among the branches. Sarah led Pooka between the trees and dropped his lead rope. She knew he wouldn't wander very far with his crippled leg.

"Go on," she encouraged him. "Go eat some apples." The pony was eyeing the apples in the grass but apparently the movement to get them was too much for him after their long walk. He stood motionless with a pathetic longing look that was accentuated by his peculiar hairdo.

"Come on, Pooka, eat some apples," she directed him with a gentle nudge. When he still didn't move, she finally took pity on him and quickly gathered up several of the yellowing, bird-pecked apples from the orchard floor, placed them in her basket, and put them in front of the little horse.

Pooka nuzzled the apples curiously before taking one in his lips, and Sarah sat down next to him and watched him for a moment as she let her mind wander.

Calibre's anniversary celebration was only three days away, and she wondered why Chad was delaying in asking her to accompany him. Of course she had missed several of his visits the past month, and they hadn't had any private time together. Even at Sir Tyson's appointment celebration last week, Sarah recalled getting sidetracked by Lady Adilia Menford while Felicia and Clyde disappeared with Chad for the whole afternoon. That's how things had gone all month, but Sarah was sure that if Chad had really wanted to, he would have found a way to talk to her. He could have left a note, or sent a letter. But he hadn't. Lately she wasn't so sure how she felt about Chad. She had hoped that their relationship would be strong again by now, but it seemed more unstable than ever.

Sarah picked up another apple and examined the worm hole. Her life was like that, she thought. Almost perfect, but then spoiled and devoured by something from inside. She tossed the apple away in frustration as she contemplated her failing relationship with Lord Chad—the relationship that her mother had encouraged, and that Clyde had foreseen as doomed. She wished that she could take back the last several months and make time for the man she had grown so fond of, but it was too late for that now; the damage was done.

Angrily she pulled at the grass in front of her and tossed it away, then stood and brushed her skirt off. "I better get these apples picked," she said. She examined the nearest tree and decided that the better apples were probably higher up. She really didn't need to climb the tree, but she remembered doing it as a little girl and wondered if she still could, so she hiked up her skirts and started her ascent. "Why worry about acting like a lady anymore? It hasn't helped me so far," she grumbled to herself. She was halfway up when she heard a horse coming down the path adjacent to the orchard. Bending down and leaning forward, she tried to see between the branches.

Whoever was coming down the path was riding a large, dark horse. She looked more closely. The horse was the most beautiful she had ever seen, with artistically carved features. It was pitch black and the sun reflected on its coat, giving off a beautiful sheen. It was tall, with powerful quarters and a thick, crested neck held in a graceful arch. Its mane and tail were wavy and remarkably long and flowing. It picked its front feet up high in the air with every step as if it were dancing, and she marveled at the feathering of long hair that almost covered its hooves. She had never seen such a majestic horse.

As it came closer she started to look more closely at the rider. He was no one she recognized. He must have been about twenty-two or twenty-three, and was strikingly handsome. His hair was thick and dark, almost black. His white shirt hung loosely, open at the neck. His face was tan from the sun, and he had a strong jawline, thick eyebrows, and a straight nose. She couldn't help noticing that he was an experienced rider by the way he moved easily in rhythm with his mount, and she leaned forward to get a better look. Suddenly her foot slipped, causing her to gasp, and she tightened her grip on the branch, which creaked ominously.

* * *

The young man astride the horse had been out riding for several hours when he passed the orchard and saw the girl perched in the tree. She clung to a branch precariously and was watching him intently. At first he thought her to be a peasant, but a closer look revealed that she wore the gown of a lady of upper class, and he could make out the beads woven in her hair. It was the apron and the fact that she was up a tree that had caused him to misjudge her as a servant. She had long, shimmering, golden hair with streams of light auburn scattered throughout, and if it weren't for her homespun apron and dumbfounded stare, he would have thought she was beautiful. He was fully aware that all of her attention was on him, but he had received many such looks from other girls before, and normally he would have just smiled and nodded his head in greeting and then continued on his way; and that is what he was just about to do when something else caught his eye.

With his curiosity mounting, he turned his horse toward her. The horse tossed his head as they approached, and he eased back on the reins, stopping only a few feet from her tree. He leaned on the front of his saddle and just looked at her for a moment without saying anything, just studying her up and down as she had done to him moments ago.

He was wondering a few things. One of which was why a lady of the upper class was wearing a commoner's apron and standing in a tree. This, however, was not what piqued his curiosity most. After eying her for a minute he finally asked, "Please forgive my intrusion, but I must know. What is that supposed to be?" He raised his arm and pointed at something behind the tree.

Sarah turned and looked through the branches. There, standing only a few feet away, was Pooka, his forelock still standing straight up on top of his head. Withholding a laugh, she turned and began to make her way out of the tree. In a serious tone she said, "Have you never seen a unicorn before?" She dropped to the ground and watched him as he leaned forward in his saddle with interest. He smiled playfully at her, causing her stomach to knot with excitement.

"I have seen unicorns, but only in books. Aren't they supposed to be white?"

Sarah looked over at Pooka again. "Usually, but this one is uniquely special."

He sat there for another minute, looking her up and down before he decided to ask her his second question. "What were you doing in the tree?"

"Picking apples."

Slowly his eyes fell upon the basket near the base of the tree and he scrutinized the yellow, decaying, bird-pecked apples piled inside. He narrowed his eyes suspiciously. "What are you going to do with them?" he asked warily as he looked closer at the mushy rotten fruit.

Sarah smiled sweetly. "They're for an apple pie," she said. The stranger made a noise that sounded like he was gagging, and when he wrinkled his nose in disgust, she followed his line of sight until she saw the basket of rotting apples. Sarah closed her eyes in brief humiliation. The man must have thought that she was going to make a rotten apple pie. "Oh no! Not *those* apples!" she started to explain. "Those apples are for the . . . unicorn. I was just about to start picking the ones for the pie."

"I'm glad to hear that," he said with honest relief.

He swung his leg over the back of his horse and dropped to the ground. He was taller than she had expected. She herself was tall for a lady, but he was almost half a head taller than she. He appeared to be from a wealthy family, although she couldn't tell from his clothing—but only someone with wealth could own such a fine horse.

He took a couple of steps toward her, then reached up into the tree and picked a nice big apple, looked it over, and took a bite. He chewed it for a minute as he watched her contentedly, then swallowed and continued. "I suppose you climb the tree to get the best apples?"

"Of course," she said defensively.

"I have always favored the apples that come on in summer," he said casually. "They have a sweeter taste."

Sarah nodded her head in agreement, then plucked her own apple from the tree. "If I were as clever as Jerry Scotts, I would build me a fire, right here on the ground, and roast me an apple. I love roasted apples."

"Who is Jerry Scotts?" he asked, surprised at how easily they had fallen into a conversation. She was not tight-lipped like most women and he liked that.

"He's one of our tenants' sons. He is quite young, but very clever and talented. He can do anything, like start a fire using flint and dried grass, or build the most amazing things using just wood and twine."

"He sounds interesting."

Sarah nodded, then bent down and dumped the rotten apples out of her basket and placed the one she had just picked in it.

The man watched her closely with a contemplative expression, and when she reached back up in the tree he quickly stepped over to her. "Let me help you," he insisted.

Sarah's heartbeat quickened at his nearness, but she consented and held the basket while he picked the apples for her.

When the basket was full he turned to her. "Will you give me your name?" he asked.

Sarah quickly thought of what Clyde would think and decided to tread cautiously. "Sarah," she said simply.

The stranger's horse started pawing uneasily at the ground. She walked over to him and stroked the velvety black hair along his neck as she wondered who the man was, and where he had gotten such a magnificent horse. She had never been ashamed to speak what was on her mind, and the fact that they had just met wasn't about to stop her now. "This is the most beautiful horse I have ever seen. What breed is he?" She stopped, instantly feeling foolish for the unladylike question.

The young man was unabashed and reached out and rubbed the horse along the bridge of his face. "He is a Friesian stallion. He arrived yesterday. Not as magical as a unicorn, but I like him."

"Friesian—I have never heard of that breed."

"They're new to this area," he explained. "This one came from the Netherlands. My family is going to start breeding them."

Sarah stopped petting the horse, and looked inquisitively at the stranger. She thought she knew all of the families in the province that bred horses, but she didn't recognize this man. Despite the risk of sounding too bold, she decided to press the matter. "Will you tell me your name, sir?"

He stood there for a minute without answering. He had a puzzled look on his face, like she should've known him. She looked closely, and the faces of all of the people she had ever known ran through her mind. She was absolutely positive that she had never met him before. She would have remembered him if she had.

"Alex," he finally said, giving his name with some apprehension just as she had done.

Sarah wanted a last name to follow, and then remembered that she had not offered hers, but she wanted more information, and so she went on. "Do you live nearby?"

He gave her another puzzled look. She thought for a moment that she was being too bold for a lady, but then she noticed a smile playing on his lips.

"Yes, I live nearby," he answered vaguely, "and you?"

"I live on the other side of those fields." She pointed in the general direction.

She waited to see if he would say where he lived, but he only nodded at her and pushed a piece of dark hair away from his eyes. She was amazed at how blue his eyes were and she couldn't help but want to stare at them. Suddenly she realized why he was being so vague. No one that handsome could go around without having admiring women constantly flirting and pressing for personal information. But he wouldn't have to worry about her; she wasn't trying to lure him into her affections. She already had someone. She and Chad had some work to do on their relationship, but things were certain to improve soon. However, she didn't know how to explain the butterflies she felt when this new stranger smiled at her.

"Well my lady, it's getting late and I'm afraid I must leave you," Alex said, interrupting her thoughts. "Besides, your unicorn is eating your apples . . . and not the rotten ones either."

She looked back to see Pooka with his nose in her basket wrapping his lips around one of the apples. She ran over and picked the basket up. "I need to return home as well, sir."

Alex gathered the stallion's reins and smoothly stepped up into the saddle. He looked at Sarah again, smiled, and nodded to her. "It was a pleasure to meet you, Sarah."

She waved to him as he nudged his horse into a graceful high-stepping trot and headed back out onto the road. She watched him for a minute and then grabbed Pooka's rope and started back to the house with her little unicorn.

9. A FATHER'S WRATH

Sarah walked slowly home, trying to focus her thoughts, which was a lot harder than she would've liked to admit. She tried to force herself to think about Chad, but her mind kept wandering back to Alex. Why had she enjoyed that brief interlude so much? She knew she was lacking in friends her age, and meeting someone new felt like taking in a breath of fresh air.

When Sarah got home, she retired to her room and only came out when called for the evening meal. It was an unusually quiet meal. Sarah wasn't very hungry, and found herself wanting to return to the orchard. Finally she broke the silence. "Do you know of any families around the province that are breeding a new kind of horse?"

Clyde put his goblet down and called for Amanda to refill it. "What kind of new horse?" he asked as he looked with eager eyes at the wine bottle that Amanda brought in.

"It is called a Friesian."

Clyde pursed his lips. "If I had any questions about horses, it would be I who would be asking *you*—disregarding the fact that it is an improper interest of yours." He raised his eyebrow pointedly at Sarah for a moment longer, making sure she understood, before he lifted his goblet and drank deeply, draining its contents.

Sarah cringed when he called for Amanda again and this time took the wine bottle from her and set it protectively by his plate. She ate the rest of her meal in silence. Not that she ate much after what her stepfather had said, but rather just pushed it around her plate before excusing herself to go to her bedroom.

"Proper!" she said once she was alone. "Does he think I'm not proper because I have my own interests?" Of course her stepfather's idea of a proper woman was one who did not speak unless she was spoken to, and one who blindly followed tradition without thinking for herself. Sarah often spoke her mind and she was full of fire, spirit, and a love for life that few women showed and fewer men appreciated.

Sarah lay in her bed staring at the moonlight that fell across her floor through the open window. It had been more than three hours since she had heard anyone in the house, but still she couldn't sleep. Tonight, her customary thoughts of Chad were intermingled with those of Alex, the mysterious gentleman she had met that afternoon. Or was he a gentleman? He hadn't really explained who he was but only looked amused that she didn't know him, and still she couldn't place him. Somewhere between those lingering thoughts, she finally drifted off to sleep.

Sarah awoke early the next morning and, despite what had transpired the night before, she was in a good mood. With a smile on her face she went down to the kitchen where Amanda was just starting on breakfast. "Good morning, Amanda."

"Morning, mistress, can I get you something?"

"As a matter of fact, I would like to bake something this morning."

"But my lady, you know what the master thinks about you working in the kitchen!"

"I know." Sarah made a face as she remembered her stepfather's words last night. "'Tis not proper," she mocked. "But am I to have no pleasure in this house? I have been craving something," Sarah said as she pulled out a mixing bowl. "I am going to make honey cakes."

"Are you quite certain, my lady? The master has been on pins and needles, with the bad news and all. He will be cross if he finds you in here."

"Bad news?" Sarah asked.

"Were you not in the parlor with the master, Felicia, and Lord Chad yesterday?

"Lord Chad was here yesterday?"

"Yes, my lady. I thought you knew. I thought you were with them."

Sarah set the mixing bowl on the large wooden table and stared blankly at Amanda. "No, I was unaware of this."

"I am terribly sorry, miss," Amanda flushed as she turned to go about her work.

"Amanda, what bad news?"

Amanda turned back around. "Oh, mistress!" She went on quickly, "The Austrians have taken over Midway."

Sarah looked stunned. "It cannot be. What of the soldiers?"

"The prince ordered them to retreat last week."

"Retreat? But why would the prince do such a thing? Isn't Midway impenetrable?"

"Midway is a great stronghold, my lady, but I don't think anyplace is impenetrable. But oh, you should have heard Lord Chad and the master talking of it. Lord Chad said he advised against the retreat and could have held the ground if it were he in command. He said we just gave the Austrians our northern border, and we shall never get it back again! Says that it will give them the position to invade farther in and take over more of our lands!"

Sarah's expression showed her alarm. "Amanda, doesn't your brother live at Midway?"

"Near Midway, yes. He works a field on Sir Robin's land; but not to worry. He and his family are safe. They left Midway several weeks ago and are with his wife's relation at Millfork."

"I can't believe our soldiers would just leave Midway and let the Austrians take it." Sarah mindlessly gathered the few ingredients she needed for the honey cakes and went to mixing them in a disturbed silence, deep in thought.

* * *

Clyde came into the dining hall where Felicia was already seated at the table. "Where is Sarah?"

Felicia frowned at the mention of her sister's name. While they were growing up they had gone through bouts of sibling rivalry, but they had always managed to forgive each other. It seemed different now. Since their mother died, feelings between her and Sarah had become more tense than she could ever remember, and it didn't help now that she was starting to care for Chad. She suspected that Sarah still loved him, but she couldn't help secretly longing for Chad to choose her over Sarah. She would've been able to keep her feelings in check, but she knew that her father was encouraging it, and she had always done her best to please him. "I don't know where Sarah is, Father," she finally answered. "I haven't seen her all morning."

"Well, we mustn't wait." Clyde sat down at the table and hollered for Amanda.

The servant appeared a moment later with the meal. "Good morning to you, my lord."

Clyde glared at her. "The morning would be good if I had two daughters at the breakfast table." He glanced through the doorway to see if he could see Sarah. "Always running off, that girl," he mumbled under his breath. "Amanda! Have you seen Sarah?"

"Yes, my lord."

"Well, where is she?"

"In the kitchen, my lord. Would you like me to go and fetch her?"

Clyde's face went red. "No. I will have a talk with her later."

* * *

Sarah was sitting in front of her dressing table in her room that afternoon when she heard Clyde stumbling up the stairs. Amanda had warned her that he wanted to talk with her, but from the sound of him falling against the wall and his uneven step, she knew this wasn't going to be a pleasant visit. She waited and hoped that he would pass by her room, but then there was an unrhythmic pounding at her door just as he pushed it open and staggered in.

Slowly she stood up, the stench of hard alcohol wafting toward her. "Do you need something?"

Clyde motioned her to sit down again. "I need to talk to you." His words were slightly slurred and he took another step forward, but swayed and had to reach out and grab the bed post to steady himself.

"It wasn't that long ago that four people surrounded our table at mealtimes, sometimes even five when Chad visited, but now . . . now . . ." He broke off, his red eyes resting upon her. "Your behavior has been unacceptable. You are supposed to be ladylike, not like some heathen child without manners and without any concept of what your place is! Do you think you are a common servant?"

Sarah stared at the floor in silence. She knew her stepfather wasn't done and it would only make things worse if she tried to defend herself.

Clyde continued, "There must be a stop to this! You are at the age where you should be thinking about getting married and taking a husband! You are a lady and 'tis time you start acting like one! You are an embarrassment to your sister and me!" He was getting more furious by the moment and his voice quivered with anger. "No more acting like a servant! No more working in the kitchen or tending after the horses! You are to conduct yourself like a proper lady, engaging in activities that are more fitting for your gender and station in life! No more barbaric talk of horse breeding or matters of the like, and no more running off without an escort! You are to be prompt when called for, and you are to be present at every meal, and I expect you to be on time!"

He stopped and looked at her, but she sat stone-faced, withholding any emotion. She could see the frustration clouding his expression, but she tried to remain stalwart.

"Of all men, you had the king's own nephew taking interest in you, but honestly Sarah, he shouldn't take a wife like you. He needs someone who is more conformed to the role of a lady. Someone more self-controlled, more refined."

Sarah turned away, unable to mask the sting of his abusive words anymore. Dropping her head, she tried to blink away the tears that were starting to form in the corners of her eyes.

When she looked back, Clyde glowered at her and then pushed on. "I wish your mother was here, God rest her soul. She could handle you, something I have failed to do." He stopped and made his way over to the window and looked out for a long moment. "I sent word to my sister today, requesting that she take you for a time. She will be able to mold you into the proper woman you should be. As soon as I receive her response, you will leave."

Sarah jumped to her feet, tears now streaming down her face. "I can't believe you would do this! I won't go!"

Clyde turned, his face coloring with anger. Without warning, he raised his hand and slapped her across her cheek, leaving a burning red mark below her eye. "You will go! And do not think you can defy me!" With that he turned his back to her and stalked out of the room.

Sarah fell on her bed sobbing. A moment later, she heard a horse neigh outside her open window, and she got up and quickly pulled back the curtain, afraid to see who may have just heard the insulting words of her stepfather. To her relief, it was the servant Joshua who was standing there, holding the reins of her stepfather's horse. This wasn't the first time that he had heard her stepfather raging. Just then, Clyde burst out from the front door, quickly mounted, and then sunk his heels into the horse's ribs. Sarah shook her head and wiped at her tears. It was just like him to have planned an escape before he carried out an attack.

There was no way that she was going to stay here. She needed to get out, to get away. She ran down the stairs, through the back of the house, and out the back door. She paused just long enough to reach down, grab her skirt with both hands, and hike it up around her knees. Then she took off at a sprint. She ran out into the field, hot tears still streaking down her face and stinging her cheek where Clyde's hand had left its mark. She pushed herself to run harder and faster. A sharp stabbing sensation crept into her side and her legs began to ache, but she welcomed the physical pain. She could deal with it much better than the emotional pain she felt. Finally she reached the orchard, but she kept on running despite being out of breath. She ran from one end of the orchard to the other until she leaped over the hedge that separated the orchard from the road. Then she finally stopped and bent down, with her hands on her knees, and took in big gasps of air.

Still breathing hard, she straightened up and looked around. She walked up the secluded road a little way, then jumped over the ditch and walked into the small forest on the other side. Usually she preferred the orchard over this wooded area, but right now she wanted to hide. She made her way through the brush, pushing aside branches and twigs and stepping over the bracken until she made her way into the heart of the small forest and slid down the trunk of a large oak tree, nestling herself between its roots. Pulling her knees up to her chest, she wrapped her arms around them and then buried her face in her skirt and started to cry again.

Sarah's heart ached. She had never been scolded so sternly before nor had anyone ever struck her, but most of all she hated the idea of going to live with someone else. She had met her aunt Agnes only a few times and had never liked her. She was a stern woman, and Sarah had never seen much of a smile come from her tight, thin lips. Nor had she ever heard her aunt give her any praise, although she seemed to have plenty of criticism for her.

Pulling her knees in tighter, she curled up into a ball. She was tired, perhaps from the lack of sleep last night, or it could be that she was so hurt that sleep was the only way to escape the pain. Whichever it was, it didn't matter now. She laid her head on her knees and, softly crying, said a silent prayer before allowing her senses to deaden and her mind to drift away.

10. THE RIDER

Slowly Sarah became aware of her surroundings, and she noticed a change in the light and shadows. She brought her head up and looked around. The sun was getting low in the sky. Had she fallen asleep? How long had she been there? One hour? Two hours? She didn't know. But one thing she did know; she wasn't going to be late for the evening meal. She wasn't going to risk Clyde's wrath again. She jumped up and started bolting through the woods, determined to run all the way to ensure that she would be at the supper table before Clyde was.

She pushed through the bracken and the thick foliage, trying to protect her sore face from the branches as she bounded through the thicket. Finally she could see the road, and with one giant leap she broke through the brush and bounded over the ditch, only to find herself leaping right in front of a horse and rider. The horse spooked, rearing back and almost dumping its rider. Sarah was startled herself and stumbled, nearly falling into the ditch. She recognized the large black stallion immediately and then looked up at the startled Alex, who was trying to gain control of his steed and stay in the saddle at the same time.

"Excuse me, sir! I'm sorry, I didn't see you coming."

"You?" Alex said, a little flustered.

Sarah glanced at him as he steadied his horse. "I am sorry." She turned and started running again.

"Aren't you full of surprises," he said as he nudged his horse into a fast trot to catch up to her. "Unicorns and apple trees one day and then leaping out at me the next. Now please tell me, what is so urgent, my lady, that makes you take flight down this road?"

Sarah, not slowing, just glanced over her shoulder at her handsome pursuer, his clear blue eyes steady upon her. "I need to get home, sir."

"Will you not even stop for a moment to converse with me?"

She looked at him again but kept her pace up. She did want to stop. She wanted to tell him everything, but she couldn't just share her personal problems with someone she barely knew. "No," she said, running even faster now. "I mustn't be late getting home."

Alex nuddged his horse forward until he was even with her. He rode for a minute in silence before he spoke. "I beg your pardon, but I don't quite know what to make of you. You jump out at me from nowhere, I almost get dumped on the ground, and you run off as if the devil were after you. Will you not even stop to see if I'm all right?"

Sarah slowed and looked up at him. His eyes washed over her then lingered on her bruised cheek, his expression clouding with concern.

"Perhaps it is I who should be asking if you are all right," he said.

Embarrassed, she averted her eyes.

"Would it help if I were to give you a ride home?" he asked softly.

Sarah had intended on ignoring the offer, but there was something in his voice—an honest kindness that almost seemed to plead to her. She stopped, out of breath, and turned to face him. "You would do that?"

"Of course, my lady."

Again, her stomach twisted excitedly as she saw the corner of his lips pull into a soft smile. She wondered why he had that effect on her, but then she noted his dark hair and steady blue eyes, and decided it was no surprise. She wanted to kick herself for even considering letting him give her a ride home. A proper young lady would never do such a thing.

She was about to refuse and take the risk of being late, but then Alex reached his hand out to her, and slipped his foot out of his stirrup. Instinctively, Sarah reached out and took his hand. His grip was warm and strong, instantly giving her a sense of security, and with his help, she easily swung up behind him. Then suddenly, the horse began to prance.

"Easy boy." Alex reached down and stroked his neck. "He has never had two people astride him before, and I'm not certain how he's going to take to it. I think you had better hold on tight."

Sarah could tell by how the horse moved under her that Alex was not being forward with her, and she didn't want to end up on the ground, so she slid closer to him and slipped her hands around his waist, feeling the subtle strength of his muscles tighten beneath her hands as she locked her fingers together in front of his stomach.

Alex coaxed the stallion into an easy lope, and Sarah tightened her grip and softly pressed her cheek against his back. She found herself relaxing, feeling comforted and safe next to him. She was sure that he wasn't aware of the emotions that were swirling inside her. To him he was just helping her as any gentleman should, but to Sarah it was so much more. He was someone who cared, at least enough to show her some kindness. He was someone who was there for her when she needed it. Someone who was there with her so she didn't have to be alone.

Sarah basked in the feelings she was experiencing. She wanted the ride to last, not wanting to go home and face her stepfather and his promise to have her sent away to live with his sister.

Alex brought the horse into a slow walk. Feeling the change in movement, she opened her eyes and saw him looking over his shoulder at her, and then there was that kind playful smile that she liked.

"I thought you had fallen asleep," he said. "Which way now?"

She sat up, looking around. They were back where she had met him yesterday. Lifting her arm, she pointed past the trees. "Follow that trail over there through the field." She felt him nudge the stallion back into a lope, and she quickly wrapped her arms around the security of his waist again. It felt like a hug, although she knew it wasn't. Of course Alex was not embracing her, but it was close enough. She hadn't realized how desperately she had ached for someone, anyone, to put an arm around her. Nobody had done that since her mother died—not her stepfather, not Felicia, not even Chad. Actually, Alex hadn't done that either, but he was allowing her to hold on to him, even if it was only so she didn't get dumped off the horse, and it gave her the comfort that she needed.

Several minutes later, she felt a change in the horse's gait again and knew that they were close to her home. She kept her eyes closed for a moment longer, not wanting the ride to end, but then she slowly sat up. Alex turned his head and she saw him frown as she removed her hands from around his waist. She couldn't help but smile shyly at him, then she looked around.

They were near the bottom of the field and the manor was in sight. "Those are the stables over there." She pointed at a small outbuilding. "If you don't mind, please let me off there. I don't want anyone to see me coming home." Alex gave her a curious look so she explained further. "I wasn't supposed to leave this afternoon, and I am afraid I left without the permission of my stepfather."

"I'm glad you did," he said.

Not knowing what to make of his comment, she didn't say anything until they reached the stables. "This is close enough," she said as they neared the building. Alex pulled back until the stallion stood still, then twisted around in the saddle and offered his arm to her. She slid off, letting him lower her carefully down to the ground before he let go.

"Thank you." She smiled appreciatively, and then walked over to the stable door and peeked in.

"Is he in there?" Alex questioned.

"Pardon? Is who in there?" She looked back at him and noticed the playful look on his face.

"The unicorn." His attempts to hide his smirk failed.

Sarah smiled. "Yes, but he's disguised himself as an ordinary pony today."

Turning back to the stables, Sarah peered inside. She hadn't seen Alex step down off his horse and quietly walk over to her, and when he nudged her arm, she jumped, a slight scream escaping her lips. Alex had to duck as she flung her arms at the same time.

He laughed quietly, but Sarah wasn't amused. "What are you doing?" she demanded.

"I'm sorry. I only wanted to take a look at your unicorn."

"His name is Pooka, and I was trying to see if my stepfather's horse is in the stable."

"Is it?"

"No, but it's getting late, and I am sure he'll be coming any moment now."

"Then will you allow me to escort you to the house?"

She hesitated, but Alex already had his horse by the reins and was walking in that direction. "Pooka," he said quietly under his breath. "What a funny name."

She barely heard the words but was instantly annoyed. Quickly, she spun around and caught up with him. "Pooka is not a silly name."

Alex's expression was slightly amused. "Ah. I did not say silly. I said funny. There is a difference."

"Silly or funny, it doesn't matter. Neither describes his name."

Alex tried to give her an understanding smile. "Sorry, I must have been mistaken."

The irritation left Sarah's face as she accepted his apology. "Names are important, and should reflect the qualities of the bearer."

"And what qualities does the name *Pooka* reflect?" he asked, now curious.

"Pooka is another name for a wood sprite, a mischievous little creature that can sometimes change its form." She paused, looking at Alex, trying to read his face to see if he was genuinely interested. "Don't you think that describes the pony?" she continued without waiting for his answer. "He is small. He has a woody quality about him with his thick shaggy hair, and he is cute and curious just like a little elvin creature."

Alex paused for a moment and regarded Sarah thoughtfully. He appreciated someone who put so much thought into simple things, making them more meaningful, and he liked that Sarah was quick to defend her ideas. "Yes, the name is fitting for the little thing," he said, catching up with her. "And I do see that he has changed his form from yesterday."

"Thank you, I am glad that you agree. What is the name of your stallion?"

Alex reached up and patted the horse's broad neck, "I haven't named him yet. I've been thinking of calling him Brutus or Clyde."

Sarah made a face and marched around him to the horse, taking his massive head in her hands as if he were offended by the names and she was consoling him. "Those are horrible names for such a magnificent animal. Besides, Clyde is my stepfather's name."

Alex felt the color rising in his cheeks. "Oh! I beg your pardon. I didn't know. Tell me what you would suggest."

He wasn't surprised when Sarah didn't answer right away. He could see that she was thinking; she stood for a moment while she rubbed the horse's head, and he was content to watch her.

"He needs a strong name. Something like Midnight, or Prince, or maybe Phantom. You know him better than I do."

"Midnight and Phantom are well enough, but Prince?"

"I would name a horse Prince if I had one that was so gallant and noble."

"I don't suppose you have a horse, at least one that is pompous and proud enough to be called Prince?"

Sarah frowned and started walking toward the manor again. "My stepfather doesn't care for horses. The pony is lame, but still, he is my own." She turned and looked at him. "Someday I will have my own horse and he'll be as majestic as a real unicorn."

Alex could see the desire in her eyes—something that she ached for but was never allowed to have. Instead she had to make do and find joy in a small lame pony, something that she could not even take pleasure in riding.

He was still trying to find something to say that would bring a smile back to her lips when she interrupted the silence. "I'd better get inside before my stepfather gets home."

He didn't want to leave, but it was improper to press his company on her when they were so little aquainted. "Then I shall take my leave," he said, not trying to hide the disappointment in his voice, and then gracefully bowed.

Sarah curtsied. "Thank you for the ride. It was kind of you and it truly saved me."

"You are worth saving." He enjoyed being able to speak his mind and seeing the smile it brought to her face. He nodded to her once again and then gathered his reins and swung up onto his horse. "I hope I will have the pleasure of seeing you again."

Sarah's cheeks flushed red and her smile broadened. She gave another curtsy, turned, and walked into the house.

Alex trotted the stallion around the house, eyeing the manor. It was a large and fine house, although not overly extravagant. Everything looked well tended, but he wondered why he had seen no one else. Usually a manor of this size would have a full staff of servants, but all seemed to be quiet and almost vacant. He looked at the front of the house, hoping to see Sarah looking out at him from one of the windows. *I wonder which bedroom belongs to her?* he thought, and then smiled as he realized how foolish he must look, staring at her house. He turned his horse and headed down the road.

Up ahead a rider came around the corner. The man was big and almost looked out of balance perched on his mount. He was dressed fine enough, as a gentleman, but his face was stern. He guessed that he was Sarah's stepfather. As they passed, Alex politely tipped his head to the man. "Sir."

Clyde nodded his head also in acknowledgment, but said nothing. Then after a moment, he looked thoughtfully back over his shoulder at the young man.

When Clyde walked into the dining hall, both Felicia and Sarah were seated at the table. Sarah kept her eyes lowered as Amanda brought the meal in and Clyde seated himself across from her. He seemed to be more sober, but he clearly was not interested in eating right away.

"I passed a young gentleman on the road coming from our house. He looked familiar, but I couldn't place him. I want to know who he is and why he was here."

Sarah had just taken a bite of her meat and tried to swallow, but choked on it instead. She started coughing, then grabbed her goblet and began gulping water.

Felicia stared at her sister. "I'm sure I know nothing about it, Father. I was unaware that anyone was here."

Clyde looked at Sarah, who was still drinking from her goblet and making the most unladylike noises as she tried to clear her throat between swallows. "Sarah?"

She put the goblet down and started to fidget with her spoon. "Umm . . . His name is Alex." She paused and saw that he wasn't satisfied with her answer. "I don't know his surname. I met him yesterday when you sent me to pick apples."

Clyde's face hardened. "Why didn't you tell me this before?"

"I started to last night but . . ." She knew this wasn't helping the matter any and she quickly composed herself. "I am sorry. I should have, but really the meeting was brief. Nothing really, I assure you. He was just riding by and stopped. I asked him about his horse and—"

"If it was nothing, then why was he here at the house today?" Clyde raised his voice.

"He was just riding by again and I happened to be outside," she said truthfully. "He recognized me and stopped to visit for a moment. He wasn't here long."

"But you were with him alone?"

"He was only here briefly, and no one was around. Is it my fault I have no maids to attend me?"

Clyde's face went red. "Well you certainly will when you go to my sister's!"

Sarah clenched her hands into fists under the table and bit the inside of her lip, waiting until she knew she had her emotions under control before saying anything. "I am sorry." She forced her voice to be calm and gentle. "I'll try to do better."

Clyde seemed to be satisfied and started to eat. "He did look familiar," he commented. "And I guess it's good that you're making friends," he mumbled as he concentrated on eating. "I'm expecting both of you girls to make your appearances at the celebration. And I hope both of you have someone respectable to accompany."

Felicia's eyes brightened. This was a subject to her liking. "Oh! I can't wait another day! It's so exciting."

"Has anyone asked you to go yet?" Sarah asked curiously. Clyde had been taking Felicia to all the royal functions just as Miranda had done with her, and it was frustrating that Clyde hadn't invited Sarah to go with them since Miranda's passing. Felicia was apparently becoming quite well known in noble circles, and Sarah had no idea if someone had caught Felicia's eye.

Felicia was obviously enjoying the attention from Sarah and stalled a minute before she answered. "Not yet, but when father took me to town earlier this week all the ladies were talking about how many of the gentlemen and noblemen were waiting until the last minute to ask for companions. I do know that Lord Chad hasn't asked anyone yet."

Sarah's heart raced, and she didn't hear anything Felicia said after that. There was still a chance that Chad would ask her. He would be coming to visit tomorrow, she was sure of it.

* * *

Sarah had just slipped into her nightgown and had sat down to brush her hair when the sound of a carriage rolling into the courtyard below echoed up through her open window. She quickly moved to the window and looked out. It was dark, but by the lantern's light she recognized Chad as he climbed out from the carriage along with another man, one whom she didn't know.

Sarah quickly dressed again and then waited to be called down to the parlor, but when no one came to get her, she quietly opened her door and crept down the hall to where she could hear the voices as they drifted up the stairway to where she was standing.

"I can't believe the crown prince would do such a foolish thing," Clyde's voice boomed.

"Yes, I quite agree," another gruff voice said. "Our only stronghold and we shall never get it back."

"No, not now," Chad's voice sounded clearly. "I just received the statistics of the Austrian army and they outnumber our soldiers three to one."

Sarah frowned. He hadn't come for a social call, but to discuss business and politics, and at the moment, it almost sounded like Chad was campaigning against his cousin. She wanted to go down and join in the discussion, but she knew she wouldn't be welcome. She couldn't help it if she liked to debate politics, but knowing that Clyde wouldn't allow it, she sat down on the top stair, content to just listen to the muffled voices below her in the parlor.

"Outnumbered three to one?" the stranger exclaimed. "How will we ever take Midway back? There's no way—our soldiers will be massacred, and then once our army is destroyed, the Austrians will come in and take over the rest of the country!"

"I have visited with the grand duke," Chad said reassuringly. "He has a good strategy of how we can hold our ground. I've set an appointment for the prince to meet with him tomorrow, and with any luck, my cousin will be persuaded to not make any more stupid mistakes, and we won't lose any more land to the Austrians."

"Here, here," Clyde's voice boomed. "These mistakes could've been avoided in the first place if the army had been placed in your charge."

Clyde's voice had a little too much flattery for Sarah's taste, and she cringed.

"Yes," the stranger said quietly. "We all agree. In fact, several of us have decided to push for a change of command."

"I do thank you for your support," Chad said. "It is most welcome, and if things go as planned, I assure you, your support will not go unrewarded."

Sarah shook her head, not liking the direction this conversation was going. She wanted to hear more details about the takeover at Midway, not just complaints about the leadership and how these men could use the situation to promote themselves. She stood up and walked back to her room, tired and depressed. It was bad enough that she wasn't able to see Chad, but maybe when he had gotten his fill of politics, he would come back tomorrow for a more enjoyable visit.

11. PREVAILING FEELINGS

Sarah stirred in her bed. She heard the faint sound of footsteps and then opened her eyes. "Oh, pardon me, mistress." It was Catherine. "I was trying to be quiet. The master told me not to wake you." Her arms were full of fresh linens.

Sarah sat up in bed. "Lord Clyde told you not to wake me?"

"Yes, mistress. He said you needed your rest. Are you feeling all right?"

"Yes. I'm quite well. Have you already set breakfast?"

"Yes, my lady, almost half an hour ago. That is why I can't understand the master. One minute he's asking that you be to every meal and the next he's insisting not to wake you for breakfast." Catherine set the linens down on the bench by the window. "Don't fret; I saved your meal for you in the kitchen. Would you like me to help you dress, my lady?"

"No, I can do that quite well." Just then Sarah heard a knock at the front door. She flew out of bed and rushed over to peer out her window. Chad's dapple gray horse was standing out front being held by one of his family's stewards. "Catherine, I changed my mind. Please hand me my blue gown and stay to help me with my hair," she said as she darted behind the dressing screen.

She could hear muffled voices downstairs. She dressed quickly, then hurried over to her dressing table where Catherine waited, holding a brush. "Please hurry, Catherine!" For the most part Sarah usually did her own hair, but it looked so much nicer when she had someone help. While the servant was pulling her hair back and interweaving it with a strand of pearls, Sarah lightly powdered her face. She didn't need to do much; she had good skin and natural color in her lips and cheeks, so she never applied the coloring that other ladies had to use.

Sarah looked in the mirror, pleased with the result. It would have taken her much longer if she had done it all herself. She sprinkled some rose water on herself and hurried downstairs.

She could hear two people talking in the parlor. At first she had recognized Felicia's voice, but it was Chad's voice that she was hearing now.

"It's going to be a great evening, my lady," he paused, "and I am hopeful that you will . . . Sarah!"

Chad jumped to his feet when Sarah entered the room. "Umm . . . it's good to see you." He ushered her to a chair before returning to his own seat across from her and Felicia.

If Sarah noticed the stunned look on Felicia's face that quickly turned into irritation, she made no indication of it. But she was aware that Chad was suddenly uncomfortable. He sat silent for a moment, wringing his hands.

"Uhh . . . I was just speaking to Felicia about the ball tomorrow eve. You'll be there, won't you Sarah?"

She smiled at him. "If it will please my lord."

"Oh, ah," he stammered and glanced at Felicia. "Of course, I had hoped to see both you and Felicia there." Chad was growing more flustered by the minute, and after a long moment of silence that seemed to last forever, he stood up, fiddling and brushing at the front of his doublet. "Ladies, I regret that I cannot stay any longer."

Sarah was on her feet now. "But you just arrived!"

"I do apologize. I have matters to attend to that are of a pressing nature."

Sarah walked up to him, begging him with her eyes not to leave. "What is so pressing that it would take you from us?"

"If it were my choice, heaven knows I would stay, but it is a royal errand I am on. My cousin failed to show at a meeting with the grand duke, and I must go smooth things over." He looked back and forth between Sarah and Felicia as if he didn't know which one to address. "I was just passing by and couldn't resist stopping even for a brief moment, but now I must go." He turned to Felicia and gracefully bowed. "My lady." Then he turned. "Sarah." He bowed again. Without waiting for a response, he turned and walked out the front door.

Sarah was stunned into silence. She had not expected it to happen in that way. But how could he ask her to the celebration with Felicia sitting there? Perhaps he was nervous about it, because things had been a little awkward between them lately. He did say that he wanted her to come, and in a roundabout way, maybe that was his way of asking her. And besides, who else would he go with? They had been intended for years now, and they had always gone to his mother's balls together, and to all the social events. True, they hadn't been out together recently, but he still made visits to the Berack manor. There had been times when he hadn't asked her to accompany him, but it was just known between them that they would go together, and this surely was one of those times.

With renewed excitement for the ball, Sarah almost skipped her way into the kitchen to see what was left over from breakfast. She had completely forgotten about Felicia and didn't hear her when she stomped up the stairs and slammed the door to her room.

Sarah was excited. Tomorrow she would go to the seamstress's shop and pick up her gown. That is if she had a gown. She had gone to the little shop twice before to see how it was coming along. Both times the old woman had given excuses as to why Sarah couldn't see the dress. The first time the seamstress said she was too busy to show it to Sarah, although she didn't look very busy. She said that she was working on another garment for a member of the royal family and that took priority. Sarah didn't press the issue and left disappointed. The second time was just a week ago when she and Catherine had stopped in on market day. The seamstress walked into the back but then came out moments later without the gown. She explained that she had been working on it, but she must have left it at home, and told her that she would need some extra time to finish it. With the celebration and the high demand for new gowns and alterations, she simply found herself swamped, and asked Sarah if she could wait until the morning of the celebration to pick it up. Sarah was beginning to wonder if there really was a gown or if the old woman had just swindled her out of her money.

"Oh well!" she said, trying to force the negative thoughts from her mind. "She did tell me to come the morning of the ball and she would have it ready, and that's what I'll do. I will go tomorrow and hold her to her word. I won't leave her shop until I have what I paid for, even if she has to pull some scraps of material together to make me something."

That afternoon Sarah was walking past the kitchen when she saw Catherine step out the back door with a basket. Sarah hurried out after her. "Catherine, where are you going?"

"To the orchard. We're running low on apples again. I think Joshua's been sneaking them to feed to the horses. Do you need something before I go?"

"No . . ." Sarah thought for a moment. "But I think I'll go along with you." She saw the worried look on Catherine's face, so she persisted. "I won't be stuffed up in this house all day. A walk would be so enjoyable."

"Of course, my lady."

Sarah waited on the trail while Catherine ran into the stables to question Joshua about the missing apples and to tell him about an unwanted snake that had taken up residence in the bean patch. It was a full ten minutes before she reappeared, and Sarah was getting tired of waiting.

"My lady," Catherine called as she ran out from the stables. "Joshua just brought Mr. Berack home from the village!"

"I am happy to hear it," Sarah replied sarcastically, impatient from the wait. "May we go now?"

"Of course, miss, but it might interest you to know what Joshua overheard."

The servants were always up on the latest rumors going around, so Sarah let her irritation dwindle and gave Catherine her full attention.

"Joshua said that His Majesty the Prince has just officially announced that when the time is right, we will retake Midway!"

"When the time is right? What does that mean?"

"Joshua didn't understand that part either. He said that Master Clyde and Mr. Bening were talking to Lord Chad and the grand duke, and they said that there was never going to be a right time. They said that it was a mistake to give up Midway in the first place and that it will be a bigger mistake to try to retake it! Oh, you should have heard everything that Joshua said! I'm so scared! What is to become of us?"

"I am sure that everything will be all right . . ."

"But what about Amanda's family? They live near there, you know. And my sweet Wayne, he's one of the king's soldiers. They just got home and then when they go back, he'll never come home again!"

"Wayne is a good soldier. I'm sure he'll be fine."

"I wish he were here right now. He does comfort me so."

Sarah nodded. "He is a good man. And we must not think the worst. Let's be positive and hope that God will assist our armies."

"Yes," Catherine said, wiping a tear from her cheek and turning to walk down the trail. "But I do wish Wayne were here."

It was disturbing news, and Sarah, too, wanted someone to tell her that everything would be fine. She thought back to yesterday and how Alex just happened to show up when she needed someone to comfort her. She remembered the solace she felt, and longed for it to return. Perhaps that is why she found herself on the way to the orchard now. She wanted to see Alex and to feel his comfort again.

She walked behind Catherine, silently watching the tall grass wave in the breeze as she scrutinized her motives for going to the orchard. She tried to deny it, tried to convince herself it was the peace she felt there, but it was no use. She wanted to see Alex again. She couldn't stop thinking of him. Every time she closed her eyes, she could see his face, his tantalizing blue eyes, and his smile that had a way of making her tingle.

Why couldn't she get him out of her head? She tried to make sense of it all. Maybe it was the way he made her feel at ease when he was around, like she didn't have to worry anymore because he was there to protect her. She had to admit that there was something between them, if only the beginning of a friendship, and friendship was something she hadn't enjoyed since before her mother had passed away. She kicked at a tiny pebble in front of her and watched it bounce into the tall grass that bordered the dusty path, hoping that he would happen to show up again today.

"Would you like me to stay with you, my lady?"

The voice yanked Sarah from her thoughts and she looked up. They were already at the orchard. "No, go ahead. I'll just walk around a bit, but come and get me when you are finished picking the apples." Catherine nodded, turned, and walked away.

Sarah walked over to the road and looked up and down both ways. Nothing. She paced back and forth and with every little noise, her heart jumped and she turned to look, anticipating a rider on a dark horse. And each time her heart sank. She tried to think about Chad, but it was no use. It was Alex who filled her thoughts. Finally, after some time, she sat down in the grass and just watched the road, listening and hoping.

"Are you ready, mistress?" Catherine came walking up to her, her basket heavy and overfilled with apples. "I'm sorry if I took too long. This time of year, it's hard to find good apples that the birds have passed up."

Sarah stood and took one more long look down the empty road. *Please come now,* she prayed in her heart. She waited a moment longer. Nothing.

"Very well, Catherine, we'll go," she said, the corners of her lips pulled down with disappointment. "I shouldn't even be thinking of him!" The words escaped her mouth out loud and Catherine looked at her strangely. Sarah pushed the thought of Alex out of her mind. *I must forget him,* she told herself. *It's Lord Chad I should be thinking of.*

She was going to the ball with Chad, and by all means she should. She had been friends with Chad for years now. She didn't get the same feeling around Chad as she did around Alex, but maybe that was because she was comfortable around Chad now. She knew him better than she did any other man, including Alex. They had spent a lot of time together and that must account for something. She wasn't happy about his brief visit this morning, but tomorrow she would have him all to herself and maybe that would give her time to sort out her feelings for him. She was very well aware of her mother's wish for her to marry Chad, and with a little bit of luck, it could still happen.

12. LOST LOVE

Sarah knocked on the door to her stepfather's chamber and waited. There was no answer. *Where could he be?* she wondered. She had already looked for him downstairs, and it was still quite early in the morning; she couldn't imagine him having anywhere pressing to go on the day of the celebration. She knocked again . . . still no answer.

Giving a long sigh, she turned and walked down the hall. The door to Felicia's room was slightly open. She tapped on it and pushed it aside, peering in. "Felicia?" No one was there, but she stepped in and looked around anyway. Several of Felicia's gowns were lying across her bed. She picked up the sleeve to one of the gowns and examined the cuff. Felicia was able to keep her garments in much better condition than she could. Of course her sister was more refined, and would never be found climbing trees or running through the woods. Sarah dropped the sleeve as she glanced at the other gowns. Felicia had obviously been going through her dresses to find one to wear tonight. "I wonder which one she picked?" she said out loud. "I hope it's this one." She ran her eyes over the deep green dress and thought of her own gown, ready to be picked up from the seamstress. She wanted to leave right away, before the morning wore on too long, but she needed to tell her stepfather where she was going. That is, if she could find him. She stepped over to the window that overlooked the grounds and scanned the area for any signs of Clyde. She looked out toward the stables. Both of the doors that led into the stables were wide open. Sarah turned and hurried downstairs.

"Amanda! Catherine!"

"Yes, mistress?" Amanda came out from the kitchen wiping her hands on her apron.

"Do you know where my stepfather is?"

"Yes, my lady. Joshua took the master and your sister into the village to market. Left a few minutes ago. Just missed them, you did."

Sarah huffed a sigh of frustration. "Why did no one tell me?"

"Did you want to go along?"

"Yes, I have a gown for the celebration that I need to pick up from a seamstress."

"Joshua forgot to take a bushel of vegetables to sell, so I planned on taking them into the market myself. We can walk in together, if you like."

"Very well. We must hurry. Get what you need and I'll fetch Pooka."

Sarah hurried out toward the stables. It was times like these that she wished her stepfather would allow more horses. Now it would take them twice as long to get to the village. She looked at the sun. It was still early and she figured that, even walking, she would still get back with plenty of time to spare, but she didn't want to waste a single moment. She was anxious to see the new gown. She tied a rope to the pony's halter and led him, limping, toward the house. The blacksmith had said that there was no use for the poor animal, but Sarah had found one. She swung sacks over his back with one hanging on each side. Amanda walked out the back door carrying a basket full of vegetables, and Sarah helped her load them into the sacks. Despite his lame leg, he still did very well at packing, which made things a lot easier for the servants.

"That's everything," Amanda said, putting the basket back inside the kitchen door.

Sarah handed Amanda the pony's rope and started walking down the road. She walked quickly, and when she had reached the bend in the road she stopped and looked back. Amanda, still several yards behind her, was struggling with the pony, pulling and tugging at him to move faster. She knew she should slow down for them, but she was too excited and eager to get to the village. She always enjoyed holidays, but this promised to be particularly delightful. The thought of the celebrating that they would do tonight—and that she would finally have some time to spend with Chad—filled her with an energy that made her want to run and skip all the way to the village. She couldn't wait any longer, and she turned and hurried down the road. Chad would be going around getting things ready for tonight too, and there was a good chance that she would see him in the village. She smiled at the thought of it and almost felt like a little girl awaiting the gifts at the feast of Saint Nicholas.

She had it all planned out. Her jewelry was already laying on her dressing table, and she pictured how she would look in her new dress, her hair perfectly done up with ribbons and curls. She imagined how Chad would react when he saw her tonight. If he had any doubt about their relationship, it would be remedied that very evening. She was going to prove to him that she really was a lady—one that was worthy of being his wife. She was determined to put everything she had into convincing Chad that she was a good choice for him, and therefore fulfill her mother's wish.

Sarah was well aware of the benefits of being wed to a nobleman, especially one of Chad's status. Many maidens had tried for that very privilege, but she had an advantage over them; she had a longstanding intimate friendship with him. Yes, she convinced herself, it would be wise for her to secure him as her husband. Even Clyde would approve and realize that he did not need to send her away. She would be elegant and charming, and would carry herself with the bearing of a noblewoman. This was the night she would prove herself to be all that Chad and Clyde expected.

As Sarah reached the center of the village, she looked around with surprise. The street was bustling with people. She knew that it would be busy today, but she had no idea it would be like this. It seemed like everyone in the province had gathered at the marketplace. This was truly a day of festivities, and people from all over the kingdom had come into the village to socialize, shop, sell, and celebrate.

She walked down the cobbled street and drank in the sights and smells of the market. Children were running around, laughing and chasing each other. Hearing the clacking of sticks, she turned to see a couple of boys involved in play fighting with wooden swords. A vendor stood by with a small cart selling the wooden weapons among hobby horses and other toys, and a group of children hovered around him, calling to their parents for a few coins.

Sarah smiled and looked back down the street. People were laughing and talking. She saw mothers chasing after their little ones, elderly folks visiting on the sides, and women gossiping by the public fountain. A juggler with his brightly colored clothes was tossing small round balls above the gathering crowd. A musician stood nearby, plucking a merry tune on his harp while a band of dancers swung long colorful silks through the air as they wove their way through the audience. It was amazing to see so many people gathered together from all different classes—from the poor beggars in rags to the noblemen in their extravagant clothing.

She continued down the street, thrilled just to be part of the busy scene. Merchants and apprentices were out in the street showing off their wares. "What do you lack? What do you lack?" was being called from every corner. She passed the baker's shop and the sweet smells reminded her that she hadn't had breakfast yet. A mother and her daughter walked out of the small shop carrying fresh pastry tarts, and Sarah glanced in at the baked goods. She was tempted to go in and try a sample, but she hurried on her way, crossing the street toward the sword maker's guild. Rows of shiny metal blades were displayed outside, but it wasn't the swords she was interested in. A finely dressed man was admiring one of the weapons, and she thought it might be Chad. But then he turned . . . no, this was nobody she knew, so she continued on.

Just then she saw the Baroness Don Marcos walk out from the tailor's shop with her two young daughters. The baroness had been a good friend to her mother and she crossed the street to greet her.

"Oh! Good morning, Sarah!" the baroness called to her when she saw her.

Sarah curtsied. "It is a good morning."

"We haven't had the pleasure of visiting for some time; I hope all is well with you?"

"Yes," Sarah replied. "Everything is quite well." Sarah noticed the little faces peering at her from behind their mother's skirt. "Hello Olivia, hello Kerry Ann."

Both girls grinned and popped out from behind their mother and began jabbering on about the new dresses that their mother had just bought for them.

The baroness smiled approvingly at her daughters, "Yes. It wasn't long ago that they both received new gowns, but they grow out of them so quickly," she explained. "But I guess this is the perfect time to get them new ones."

"Of course," Sarah said as she looked at the packages the baroness carried. "And if the truth be told, that's what brings me here today as well."

"Then you'll be at the castle tonight, too?"

"Yes." Sarah bent down to the two girls who had been listening to the conversation. "And I'm sure you two will be the prettiest ladies of the court tonight in your new gowns."

The two girls smiled and giggled, then waved as their mother ushered them down the street.

Sarah started walking again but as she passed the open door of the tailor's shop she glanced inside. The pale blue gown that she had admired four weeks earlier was still hanging in the front of the shop. She stopped and looked through the door at it just as the tailor carefully took it down and carried it into the back.

Sarah frowned. *I wonder who the lucky maiden is?* she wondered. Out of curiosity, she stepped through the door and took a few steps toward the back of the room.

Her heart raced. Chad was there. He was standing in the back of the shop next to a pile of neatly folded fabric talking to someone, but as the tailor made his way to the back of the room he blocked Sarah's view from seeing who it was. Sarah smiled at Chad, but when he didn't see her, she started walking toward him.

"Oh, thank you. It's a beautiful gown." Sarah froze in her tracks, her stomach lurching as she recognized the voice. The tailor handed the gown to the lady and then walked around her, giving Sarah a full view of the maiden. Her stomach turned as she watched Felicia run her fingers over the silky fabric and then thank the tailor as she dumped a handful of coins into his hand. For a moment Sarah felt paralyzed. She couldn't move. It seemed like a dream, like she was watching it happen to someone else, but not her. No, this couldn't be happening to her! Chad stepped closer to Felicia, smiling at her—a smile that Sarah hadn't seen for a long time. One that he used to offer her.

"My lady." He took Felicia's hand and slowly raised it to his lips, then gently kissed it. "I daresay that you will take my breath away in that gown tonight. I won't be able to lay eyes on another lady the whole evening."

Sarah gasped. Chad and Felicia turned toward the sound and looked at her. Chad still had hold of Felicia's hand and stared blankly at Sarah. She shook her head, turned, and ran out the door, her vision blurring from the tears welling up in her eyes. She stepped onto the street and turned to run, but after only two steps she slammed right into someone.

Her stepfather stumbled backward, rubbing his chest where she had hit him. Sarah glanced back at Chad and Felicia, who were now standing in the doorway of the shop, still holding hands.

Clyde had furrowed his eyebrows angrily when Sarah collided with him, but his anger quickly cooled as he realized what had just taken place.

"I'm sorry, Sarah. Didn't you know that Chad asked Felicia to accompany him to tonight's festivities?" His expression showed awareness of his involvement in the matter, but his voice was more matter-of-fact than apologetic. "You know, it really is for the best."

Sarah tried to stifle her crying and ducked her head, then lunged around Clyde and ran up the road, soon unable to control her sobs.

* * *

Sarah opened the front door to the manor and began to wander mindlessly. Realization finally started to dawn on her that every time she had missed Chad, Felicia had been spending that time with him. She felt numb, and her eyes were dry and stinging. Finding herself in the parlor, she looked at the chair where Chad had sat yesterday morning. *I was just speaking to Felicia about the ball tomorrow eve,* he had said. He was likely about to ask her younger sister to accompany him, and Sarah had just interrupted him.

She rubbed her face with her sleeve. She had to get away—to focus her mind on something else. She wished her mother were there to comfort her. But thinking of her mother now intensified her heartbreak. Sarah longed to feel her mother's arms around her. She walked up to Clyde's room, and without even pausing, she pushed the door open and went in. It looked like a man's room now with all of Clyde's personals lying around. The man who had raised her, cared for her needs, and who she thought had loved her, had not cared one whit about how much she was hurt.

She scanned the room again looking for things that were left behind by her mother, but everything had been put away, except one small chest that her mother had kept for as long as she could remember. She ran her hand over the old hardwood and looked through the books that had been stacked on it, pulling a familiar one from the pile. She remembered seeing her mother read the book when she had first gotten sick. Clutching it to her chest, she left the room.

Outside, Sarah walked slowly through the back gardens and into the pasture, unconsciously heading toward the apple orchard. The sun was directly overhead, and she imagined the others would be getting back soon. She didn't care. She didn't care if she missed the midday meal, and though she had previously hated the idea, she didn't even care if she was sent away to live with her aunt. All she could think of was Chad and Felicia and the image of him kissing her hand. Tears welled up in her eyes again at the thought. *I will not be able to lay eyes on another lady,* he had told Felicia. Sarah wrapped her arms around herself and let the tears come again as she gritted her teeth. "Why?" she cried, pressing a hand firmly against her chest in an attempt to stop the pain that had knotted there. "Oh Lord, help me. I hurt so much." Feeling she'd explode with the pain, Sarah began to stumble forward, running as fast as her legs would take her.

Once in the orchard, she stopped and looked up, watching the sun filter through the leaves that were shimmering in the breeze. How could the sun be so cheerful, the leaves be so festive, when she was so miserable? She dropped her head. Seeing the book she had taken from Clyde's room still in her hand, she walked over to a spot where the grass was thick, kicked the rotting apples away, and lay down. Hoping to distract herself, she opened the book and attempted to read.

13. A NEW FRIENDSHIP

Alex pulled back on the reins to slow the stallion down. "Good boy," he said as he reached down and patted its broad neck, which was now wet and frothy. The horse bobbed its head and snorted, eagerly taking the chance to slow down.

Alex was pleased that he was acquiring a good working relationship with his newest mount. He had made an effort to ride the horse every day since it had arrived, and the stallion was responding well now.

The horse had almost cooled off when they reached the orchard. Alex stepped down and walked into the trees, picked an apple, and held it in front of the stallion's nose. It didn't take long before the stallion wrapped his lips around the treat and then took the whole thing in his teeth. Alex turned and started to lead the horse back toward the road when he saw the girl.

He stood still for a moment, staring, and then realized she was asleep. Quickly he tied his horse's reins around a sturdy tree limb and then quietly made his way toward the sleeping form.

He had suspected—hoped—that it was Sarah, and when he was close enough to see that it was, he smiled to himself. A book lay upside down on her stomach with one hand still holding onto it. He walked closer, trying to be quiet, but the grass rustled around his feet and with every step he was sure that she would wake up. When he was standing over her, he grinned, pleased with himself. She hadn't even stirred.

He squatted down and looked at her face. Her skin was smooth and glowed in the afternoon light. Her hair fell softly on the grass and around her shoulders, and the sun filtering through the trees caused the light to dance on her face and her shimmery golden auburn locks. He reached out and touched a piece of her silky hair, but she still didn't move. Her chest rose and fell in a slow, deep rhythm and he felt it would be a shame to wake her from such a peaceful sleep, but he couldn't seem to leave her alone.

Plucking a piece of grass, he twirled it between his fingers and then stuck the end into his mouth to chew on as he watched her for a minute longer. There was a slight smudge on her cheek and he could see that she had been crying. His heart lurched at the thought; he wanted to put his hand on her cheek and gently wipe the smudge from it, but that would certainly wake her, so he restrained himself. Alex sighed. He longed to comfort her, but he knew she didn't know him enough yet to trust him, so he just waited. He tried to make out the title of her book, but her hand lay over it. He reached out and gently put his hand on top of hers and then slid the book out from under her fingers.

He started to turn the book upright to read the name on its cover, but pulling the book from her hand had made her stir. She breathed in deeply through her nose and brought both arms up by her shoulders. He watched her face, fascinated by the light dancing across it. She yawned and stretched, opened her eyes, then her breath caught in her throat and she froze.

"Alex?" she exclaimed. His dark hair looked black from where she lay, but his eyes were still an incredibly piercing blue that seemed to look right through her, yet without being threatening—they were kind and reassuring. She relaxed and smiled at him. "What are you doing here?"

Alex turned his head slightly to the side but kept his eyes steadily on her. "Forgive me, my lady. I was just enjoying the beauty of this orchard."

Sarah's cheeks turned pink. She looked up at him, unsure of what to say or do and wondered why he always seemed to show up when she was hurt and felt alone. She was glad he was there and smiled appreciatively.

He watched her for a moment without saying anything else as he chewed on the piece of grass he held in his mouth. Finally he raised the book and looked at the cover. "I wanted to see what kind of book would put my lady into such a sound sleep."

Sarah sat up. "I'm sorry you found me here. I don't normally sleep in the orchard. . . ."

"Don't be sorry," Alex interrupted. "I, for certain, am not."

She blushed again, not knowing how to respond. There weren't many men who could leave her speechless. Mindlessly, she began making a little grass nest at the edge of her skirt.

"It's a nice day to be out reading a good book," Alex commented, handing it back to her.

Sarah took the book and set it on her lap. "I must've been tired. I read only a few pages."

Alex turned around and sat next to her in the grass. He caught the smell of her perfume on the breeze and breathed it in deeply. They sat in silence for a moment, and Sarah, oddly enough, didn't feel pressured to talk. It felt like they were long-time friends that didn't need to force conversation.

Alex took the grass from his mouth, tossed it on the ground, and looked at her. After several minutes he said, "I am surprised to see you here today."

Sarah looked at him with a raised eyebrow. "Why? I'm out here almost every day." She thought of being there yesterday, watching the road and hoping to see him.

"I'm still surprised. I thought that most ladies would be home getting ready for tonight."

Sarah's face instantly fell, and the pain of seeing Chad and Felicia together returned. "Perhaps I'm not like most ladies." She plucked at the grass more intently.

Alex reached down, placing his hand over hers. She stopped pulling at the grass and looked up, meeting his gaze.

"I know. You, my lady, are not like any other, and I mean that as a compliment."

Her heart beat faster and her body turned warm at his touch.

"I was hoping that I would see you at the ball tonight," he said softly.

Sarah pulled her hand out from his. "I'm sorry, but I won't be attending tonight."

"But why? What keeps you from going?"

She paused for a moment, thinking of how to answer him. She had been hurt enough, and the last thing she wanted was to go to the ball and see Chad and Felicia together or even Alex and whichever lady he was taking, but she didn't want to explain all of that to him. "I haven't had the pleasure of being asked," she said truthfully, "and I don't wish to go alone."

"This isn't a function that requires people to come in pairs," he said. "At least that's what I keep trying to tell my parents . . . but still they are expecting me . . ."

Sarah's head came up in surprise. Hadn't Alex asked anyone to the ball?

"I had hoped to see you at the castle tonight," he went on, "so perhaps it would benefit us both if . . . Perhaps . . . you would like to accompany me tonight?"

Sarah's eyes widened with astonishment and then her mind began to race. Could she go after all? Perhaps the night wouldn't be a total loss and she could still go to the celebration with someone she genuinely liked. Then she remembered. She didn't have enough time to go back to the village to get her new gown. She frowned. "I have nothing to wear."

Alex's eyes lit up mischievously and a grin flashed across his face. Sarah instantly turned red and regretted her words. She hoped that he wouldn't tease her.

"That's all right, my lady." Alex paused, choosing his words carefully. "Wear what you have on. It's the lady I wish to take to the ball, not the gown."

Alex watched her closely as he waited for her to answer. Slowly Sarah started to nod her head. "Yes, Alex, I would very much like to go with you tonight."

Alex smiled and sprang to his feet, brushing off his breeches. "My lady, that would give me great pleasure." He reached out to her and took her by the hand, then pulled her to her feet. "Then I'll return home to make ready, and this evening I will bring a carriage to your house."

Sarah nodded her approval and walked him to his horse. She stroked the long black mane. "Have you given him a name yet?"

"No, but I have been trying different ones out on him. The stablemen think I'm crazy changing his name every five minutes—Storm, Phantom, Blacky . . ."

"Well, I'm sure you'll find something to suit him."

"My lady," Alex said, "may I offer you a ride home?"

Sarah didn't even have to think before answering. "It's kind of you to offer, and yes, I would appreciate it greatly." From the time he had given her a ride home a couple of nights ago she had longed for it again. And that's why she had found herself in the orchard yesterday . . . hoping to see him, so she could be near him. And perhaps that is why she went to the orchard today.

Alex mounted the steed, then reached down and pulled Sarah up behind him. The horse took to it much better today and didn't prance or show any signs of uneasiness. She almost wished it had. It would have given her a reason to reach her arms around Alex to hold on, and although she felt somewhat better now, she still desperately wanted to feel comfort in his strength. But to her disappointment, the horse was fine, and Alex nudged him into an easy walk toward the field.

The first few minutes of the ride were spent in silence, each of them deep in their own thoughts, but then Alex broke the silence. "You mentioned your stepfather's name is Clyde?"

"Yes. Clyde Berack."

"His name seems familiar. Perhaps I have met him, or at least heard of him. And the rest of your family? Tell me about them."

Sarah groaned inwardly. "I have a younger sister," she said simply, hoping to leave it at that. But Alex didn't respond. Clearly he was waiting for more. "My mother's name was Miranda. She passed away last winter."

Alex leaned to the side and turned in the saddle to see her face. "Forgive me . . . I truly am sorry. You were very close to her?"

"Yes," she whispered, then shifted the attention to him. "Now tell me of your family."

"There's only me, my mother, and my father. They'll be at the castle tonight, so I am quite certain you'll meet them."

Sarah waited for him to expound, but to no avail. Perhaps he was just as uncomfortable talking about his family as she was talking about hers. But it made her wonder. She had entertained the notion that he could simply be a stable hand to one of the wealthier families, but he dressed and spoke too well for that. And thank goodness! If Clyde ever suspected that a mere stable boy held the attention of his stepdaughter, he would most certainly put an end to it. No, she would rest her hopes on the possibility that he and his family were well connected but simply new to the area, and that Clyde would approve of this young gentleman.

After a minute of silence, Alex glanced back over his shoulder. "Will you tell me more about yourself?"

Sarah groaned again. "I'm not trying to hide anything, but there's not much to tell." She was glad that he was interested in her, but she didn't want to ramble on about herself.

"Then am I to guess?"

Sarah laughed at the notion. "Oh yes! Please do."

"Very well." Alex shifted back and forth in the saddle as if he were getting ready to pounce on top of something. "I guess that you're around the age of nineteen?"

She laughed. "Very close. I am but eighteen."

He nodded. "You . . . You enjoy having the freedom to do what you please, and you love life." It was not a question this time, but a statement. "And take pleasure in simple things."

Sarah nodded, content to let him explain his perception of her.

"Let me see," he continued. "You like to read, and . . . oh! You have a passion for horses unlike any I have ever seen in a lady and in only a few men."

"A fault that I'm frequently reminded of by my stepfather," she said.

"A fault or a rare quality—it's a matter of opinion, and I tend to think the latter." He glanced over at her and noted her appreciative smile. "Am I to go on then?" he asked.

"No, that's enough," she said, nudging him. "You're just trying to flatter me."

"No, it's not flattery. I'm completely sincere, I assure you."

"Thank you, but now, no more about me. I want to know more of you, but I'm not going to guess. I'm afraid you'll just have to tell me."

"Oh, but there's no fun in that."

"Alex! Please!" She nudged his back again.

"Very well, I'll concede." He was silent for several minutes as he contemplated what to tell her. "I'm afraid that I'm misjudged by many who think they know me," he finally began. He had a serious tone, and Sarah listened intently. "I'm more serious than many people think . . . And I wish to lead my own life without regard to my station." He paused for a moment to think before going on. "I have a great interest in issues of this country."

"Ah . . . then you are politically minded?"

"Yes, very much, contrary to what many might say."

Sarah nodded knowingly. "Do you seek for a position at the king's court?"

"Y-e-e-es," he drew out slowly. "You might say that. Would that please you?" he asked, glancing back at her.

"Yes, if you can obtain a position that suits you." She knew of many young men who came from all over the kingdom to seek their fortunes at the king's court, and it wasn't easy to obtain a salaried position. There were few jobs and many who sought them. There were very few who were as lucky as Chad, who were guaranteed a paid position.

"And what of you? A lady of the court? Or perchance have you had the opportunity to meet the royal family?"

Surely he didn't expect her to provide an introduction to the royal family. She wasn't that important. Chad was one of the few of great status that she personally knew, and as much as she would like to help Alex, she wouldn't introduce him to Chad either. "No, I have never had audience with the royal family. However, we have a long-time friend of the family, Lady Adilia Menford, who is well acquainted with the queen, and who introduced my mother and me to Her Majesty at the celebration of her fortieth birthday. It was only a brief introduction, but I was impressed."

"Unbelievable!" Alex exclaimed as he turned in the saddle to look at her again. "I too was so fortunate as to be at Her Majesty's birthday celebration. How is it we haven't met before?"

Sarah too was surprised and her mind raced to try to place him.

"Do you attend some of the royal functions?" Alex asked.

"Yes, some of them, most recently when Sir Tyson was appointed the new chancellor. Were you also there?"

"No, I was away," he said cautiously.

Sarah's curiosity piqued. "And where did your travels take you?"

"North."

"North? Isn't that a dangerous direction? How far north did you go?"

Alex shifted in the saddle. "Midway," he said, letting it catch in his throat.

"Midway?" Sarah said with utter amazement. "By the saints, is it true? You were at Midway? Whatever took you to Midway?"

Alex suppressed a chuckle at her reaction, and paused for a long time before he answered. "I went to handle some business matters for my father," he finally said.

"Did you see any Austrians?"

"Yes, but only at a distance. At night you could see the light from their campfires."

Alex waved an arm out as if motioning to several imaginary campfires, and Sarah could imagine hundreds of men around them all clad in heavy leather and armor. "It would've been a terrifying sight for me. I've never been to Midway. Tell me, is it as they say, a great fortress?"

"Yes, the best our country has."

"How so?"

"The terrain is very different from here. They have sprawling fields as far as you can see, but there is a great ravine that winds through the land, and Midway is built in such an area that one side is bordered by a river, and the other three sides of the city are bordered by the ravine. The cliffs into the ravine are steep and covered in shale. Have you ever walked on shale?"

"No," Sarah admitted.

"The rocks are flat, and slick, and support no weight, but slide off of each other when any pressure is put on them. It's difficult, at best, to walk on, and impossible to climb, therefore making entrance into the city from those three sides impossible."

"I see," Sarah said, nodding her head.

"The city itself is entirely encircled by a great stone wall," Alex went on. "There is but one entrance, and to get to the gate, you must cross the river on a long, very narrow bridge."

"I see," Sarah said again. "No wonder it is such a great fortress. What army would dare to come against it, if they could only attack from one side and would have to take such great risks as to cross a bridge where they must funnel their ranks to one or two wide?" Sarah stared out into the field as they rode through it as if she were looking at the great walled fortress. "I can't see how it could have been overtaken unless . . ." Sarah broke off her sentence.

"Unless our army were to desert it upon the news of approaching troops, leaving it vulnerable," Alex finished. "You are observant, my lady."

Sarah blushed.

"The great Midway, such a profound loss," Alex said.

"Admittedly, but just yesterday I heard that our army will try to retake it."

"That is rumored," Alex commented casually. "Do you believe it can be retaken?"

"I don't know about war strategies, but according to my stepfather and his associates, it's a lost cause. My stepfather says our soldiers should've never abandoned Midway in the first place. The Austrians outnumber our men three to one, and too many lives will be lost in the attempt to retake it."

"Is that what he says?"

"Yes, he and others. Many people are calling the army's retreat an act of cowardice."

"The decision of a weak, cowardly fool. I've heard it all too. But what do you think? Do you share your stepfather's opinions?"

Sarah thought for a moment. "I believe we can retake Midway," she said tentatively. "I might be foolish to think so, but it is our people's land and homes. Surely a man fighting for his own property will fight more fiercely to protect what rightfully belongs to him. With a clever stratagem and strong leaders. . . . But what do I know of such matters . . ." Sarah let her voice trail off, afraid that she had overstepped her bounds. "I'm sorry. I have no right to speak on such subjects."

"Ahh, but I believe that you do, and I respect your opinion," Alex said as he looked at her over his shoulder. "I prefer a lady to speak her mind and to know of the world around her than to be mindlessly self-absorbed. There is much wisdom in what you speak. There is no greater cause than a man's home and family."

Sarah sighed, relieved that she hadn't offended him by her forwardness. She had listened to many such conversations between Chad and her stepfather, but was constantly ignored when she tried to join in, and then later scolded for trying to voice her opinion.

Sarah looked around in surprise as she realized they were already passing the stables behind the manor. She looked around the yard for the carriage. It was still gone, but the afternoon was waning and Felicia and Clyde should be getting home any minute now.

Alex pulled the stallion to a halt at the back of the manor, then swung his leg forward over the horse's neck and jumped easily to the ground. Sarah followed suit, swinging her leg over the front of the saddle, but before she had a chance to slide down, Alex reached up and placed both hands on her waist to ease her descent. She blushed at his touch, but giving in to it, she placed her hands on his arms and let him lift her gently to the ground.

They walked over to the manor and Alex plucked a rose from the flowering bush that grew next to the back door. "For you, my lady," he said as he handed it to her.

"Thank you. You are so thoughtful."

"Yes, and my thoughts are full of you, my lady."

Sarah began to twirl the stem in her fingers. "That is a bold statement."

Alex glanced at Sarah's mouth and then back to her eyes. "But it is a true one. The last few days, my thoughts have been pleasantly spent dwelling on you. You are the first thing I think of every morning when I wake up and the last thing I think of as I go to sleep."

Sarah suddenly found the tips of her shoes quite interesting. After a moment gathering her courage, however, she took a deep breath and boldly looked back at him. "I too have spent an inordinate amount of time thinking about you."

He grinned admiringly at her. "It's only natural to think about someone you like."

"Yes, but we are barely acquainted."

"But don't you believe that you can know a person within a few moments of meeting him? I mean really know him, who he truly is."

Sarah considered the statement. "To know a person intimately and the many details of his life, I believe, would take years. But I also believe that a person's character can be revealed within moments of the acquaintance, unless he purposefully tries to hide it."

Alex flashed a smile, and stepped closer to her. "Yes, that's exactly what I mean."

"I haven't tried to conceal my character," Sarah said, "so what you know of me must be in line with my true nature."

"Yes, and I feel as if I really know you." Alex reached out and softly took her hand in his. "And I would love to take those required years to get to know the many intimate details of your personal life."

Sarah's face flushed at what his words implied, but she managed to speak, albeit breathily. "Then I look forward to this evening, when we'll have the opportunity to get to know each other more."

"And I too," Alex said, giving her hand a tender squeeze. He gently pulled her closer to him, raised her hand, and affectionately pressed a kiss to it. "'Til this evening . . ."

Sarah nodded, looking up into his eyes and trying her best to suppress the desire for another kiss. "'Til this evening."

Alex stepped back, letting his hand linger with hers for a moment longer before letting go. He bowed, then slowly turned and walked away, leading the big black stallion behind him.

14. A TEMPORARY TRUCE

Sarah stepped inside the back door and saw Amanda in the kitchen sorting out what had been brought home from the market. "Are Felicia and Lord Clyde not home yet?" she asked as she walked through the kitchen without stopping.

"No, miss. Saw them as I was leaving the market to come home. They were with Lord Chad. Must have gotten something to eat at the village, or perhaps they went to Mendierlan with Master Chad, but I would expect them home any minute now."

"Thank you." Sarah was already through the kitchen and hurrying up the stairs, taking them two at a time. In her bedroom she skipped over to the window. Alex was still in view riding down the road. She watched him for a second. Then her smile faded. A small carriage had just come around the corner, and she recognized the lanky man that sat atop driving. It was Joshua. She had hoped that Alex would get to the main road before having to pass them. She watched as they drew closer together. At least Clyde was in the carriage, and perhaps with the noise from the horses and wheels, he wouldn't notice Alex passing by.

Alex tipped his head to Joshua and she saw Joshua do the same. Neither slowed down and Sarah relaxed when they had passed, but then a head quickly poked out the carriage window and looked back down the road at the rider. Nothing must have been said, for they both kept going in opposite directions.

"Thank heaven," Sarah said softly as she watched the carriage slowly make its way toward the manor. She thought of her encounter with Chad and Felicia earlier that day. The hurt returned as she pictured Chad kissing her sister's hand and then turning to look at her. But she could see now that her hurt wasn't for a lost romance. The hurt stemmed from that look he had given to her—a look that said, *I don't care if you see me this way. You should have known.* But she hadn't known, and didn't he have any regard for their friendship? A friendship that had spanned six years. And Sarah didn't even wish to consider the deception her sister and stepfather must have been practicing.

She shook her head. She had been so confused earlier, but now she could think, and she saw it all clearly. All those times that Chad had come to call and Felicia had been keeping him company—when she would walk in, Chad would suddenly have to leave. This romance wasn't a sudden development—Chad had been coming to see Felicia, not her. But when did this all start? Sarah shook her head. It didn't matter now. She realized that she didn't love Chad. She hadn't for quite some time. She had been angry and disappointed in him since her mother's health started failing. He hadn't helped her nor shown any care for her after she lost her mother, and now she saw that it wasn't Chad that had distanced himself from her, but it was *she* who had pulled away from him.

How had she been blind to all of this before? It seemed quite simple now. And Alex—what of him? He was intriguing and charming, and it was he, not Chad, who had occupied her thoughts the past few days. She felt comfortable around Alex, but at the same time he was new and refreshing. She was willing to turn her full attention to this new suitor, but what if Clyde wouldn't allow her to see him?

She heard the door shut. "I guess I'll find out soon enough," she said, then sat down at her dressing table and waited.

She heard Clyde mount the stairs, even heard him grumbling as he came straight for her room, and she braced herself for what was about to happen.

He pushed her door open. "Sarah, I presume that man I saw the other day is the same man I just saw leaving here—" He broke off, scratching his head. "Remind me of his name."

"Alex."

"Yes, Alex. Then that was him? What was he doing here?"

Sarah stood up from her dressing table and Clyde instinctively stepped forward, showing his dominance, but Sarah didn't cower. She never did, and it frustrated him that she would not submit to his authority. Instead, she took a step forward, pulling her shoulders back and standing taller. It was a gesture that made him feel uncomfortable, as if he were the one who should make way for her.

"Alex came across me as I was reading out in the orchard this afternoon," Sarah said unabashedly. "He asked me to go to the festivities with him tonight, and I accepted. He then gave me a ride home on his horse. When he left, he promised he'd bring his carriage for me later."

Clyde's anger flashed at her boldness, but he kept silent as he sorted things out. Sarah was too headstrong to conform, but he wasn't about to let that interfere with his plans. In fact, maybe he could use her situation to his advantage. He thought of what Chad had mentioned that afternoon. He hadn't been able to think of anything else since.

Stroking his chin, he took a moment to think. A judge's position was coming open, and Chad had mentioned that Clyde might be a likely candidate to fill the office. It had helped him socially over the past years to have his stepdaughter, and now his daughter, associated with Lord Chad. And it was Lord Chad who could give him a recommendation for the judgeship. However, the position would be guaranteed if he could get several other influential men to recommend him. He needed to impress more people. He needed to make more contacts.

He narrowed his eyes. The man who appeared to be taken with Sarah—for whatever reason—was clearly a gentleman and most likely had influence. Perhaps it would do him good to have both his daughter and stepdaughter at the castle escorted by fine gentlemen. At court, looks and appearances carried just as much weight as other qualities. Perhaps this Alex, or his father, was also in a position to recommend him to the office. And if not, then perhaps he had connections to someone who could. After all, despite her strong will, Sarah was a pretty young woman who could be charming if she would only make the effort. He eyed Sarah, who stood patiently in a regal stance, waiting for his response.

"Very well. You have my blessing to go with him." Clyde gave no notice to Sarah's expression as her mouth fell open; he just turned and left the room.

Sarah stood there for a moment, shocked, staring at the empty doorway. Had she heard right? She had his blessing to go with Alex, a man he hadn't even been introduced to? But with such a pleasant result, she really didn't care what motivated him to give in to her, so she went back to her dressing table to get ready.

Sarah daydreamed about the ball for nearly half an hour before she sat down and tried to weave some ribbons through her hair. Finally she called Amanda up to her room to help her until it was perfect. After excusing the servant, Sarah sat for a while fingering the necklace that lay on the small table before her. She was amazed. She felt such misery this morning yet now felt such happiness. Finally she put the jewelry on and looked at herself in the mirror. She was pretty enough . . . but Alex—he could have his pick of any girl in the kingdom. She frowned at herself and then laughed at her sour expression. *What are you thinking, Sarah? Remember what your mother taught you! You're just as becoming and worthy as any other lady.* She eyed herself in the mirror again and made a little curtsy to herself. Truthfully, she was pleased with everything but the gown. Yet there was no use changing into anything else—she was already wearing her best one. She hadn't been to a formal event since her mother had taken ill, and her last suitable gown had been given to the poor when an unfortunate stain had made it unpresentable.

"Amanda!"

Sarah jumped at the sound, startled. It was Felicia, screaming at the top of her lungs. Sarah walked over and looked down the hall to where Felicia had stuck her head out of her doorway and was yelling.

"Amanda! Catherine! Anybody!" She turned and looked at Sarah. "Where did everybody go?"

"I don't know," Sarah said with a shrug.

"It's getting late now and I need help dressing. Will you help me, Sarah?"

Sarah raised her eyebrows.

"Sarah, please! I can't do it alone, and I don't have time to chase down the servants."

Sarah let out a long sigh, and without saying anything, walked down the corridor and into her sister's room. Felicia was standing in her underskirt and was holding the pale blue gown from the tailor's shop. She pushed it into Sarah's arms and turned around. Sarah hated holding the gown and wanted to throw it on the floor and leave, but knowing what her mother would want her to do, she went about helping Felicia into it without a word. What torture. The gown that she had wanted so much, she was now putting on her sister so she could go to the ball with the man who was supposed to be going with her instead. She moaned inwardly. *I don't even want to go with Chad now,* she acknowledged to herself, but still, she didn't rejoice in the fact that her sister was going with him either. She was tempted to pull the bodice of the gown tight, perhaps tearing it a little, but she pushed the temptation from her mind as quickly as it came.

No, Sarah had resolved to act the part of a lady this night, and wouldn't drag herself down by being cruel and childishly taking revenge. She knew that the satisfaction from such actions would be short-lived, so she forced herself to lace the gown up with great care.

"You look beautiful, Felicia," she said, forcing a smile.

"Thank you, Sarah. I was afraid you'd be very angry."

She thought about it for a moment before answering. "No, I'm not mad at you."

"I'm glad of that. I had hoped that you wouldn't be cross with me." She smoothed the gown as she looked at herself in the mirror. "It was quite an accident—me running into Chad today. I saw this gown in the tailor's shop and went in to ask if he would sell it, when Chad came in. We visited for a while and then he asked me. I accepted because Chad and I have become quite close lately." She turned, looking at Sarah again. "But I hear you'll be going with someone too. Who is it?"

"Someone I met earlier this week. His name is Alex—" There was a loud pounding at the front door. "That must be Chad coming for you," Sarah said.

Felicia just laughed. "Oh, Sarah. You know that Lord Chad is practically royalty. He had other obligations tonight and won't be able to pick me up. I'm to meet him at the castle," she said smugly. "I imagine Chad has some business with the king or something."

"I'm sure," Sarah replied curtly.

Amanda tapped on Felicia's door and Sarah opened it. "Here you are, Miss Sarah. I was just looking for you, and your room was empty. There's a young man awaiting you in the parlor, my lady. And if I may say so, he's quite striking."

"Thank you, I'll be right down."

"Amanda," Felicia broke in. "Will you please come in and help me with my hair?"

Sarah started down the stairs when Clyde came around the corner, obviously headed to his room to change his clothes. He was already pulling and untucking his shirt as he turned up the stairs. He stomped along and cursed bitterly under his breath, mumbling something about Joshua, when he looked up and saw Sarah. He hurried up the rest of the stairs to meet her.

"Sarah, the knock at the door, was it for you?"

Sarah looked at him curiously. "Yes, Alex awaits in the parlor."

"He's brought a carriage, hasn't he?"

Sarah raised her eyebrow and looked at him, trying to figure out what he was getting at.

Clyde quickly grew impatient. "Well, I assume he's not going to let you ride behind him astride that beast of his."

"Yes. I'm sure he brought a carriage."

"Good then. Would it trouble you to ask him if Felicia and I could ride along with you to the castle?"

Sarah didn't answer, but stood looking grimly at him.

Clyde continued, "That dunce of a servant has unhooked our carriage and turned the horses out to pasture after I had told him not to, and now he's nowhere to be found! The dimwit!" He cursed under his breath again. "I don't have the time or the desire to round up those animals and hook them back up. I'm late as it is, and still need to dress!"

"All right," Sarah conceded, then walked around him and down the stairs.

"Now that's a good girl," Clyde muttered and then hurried down the hall to his room.

15. THE HIDDEN MARK

Sarah stepped into the parlor. Alex was standing by the window looking out with his hands clasped behind his back. He turned and faced her, letting his gaze wash over her until their eyes met. Sarah was immediately self-conscious and quickly looked at the floor. They would be a mismatched pair. Alex was wearing a striking green and blue doublet over his white shirt, setting off the color of his eyes. It was fitted to the waist with decorative buttons and had ornate sleeves with openings where his white shirt was pulled through and puffed below a padded roll of blue velvet that ornately concealed the seams. To complement the ensemble, he wore black breeches and proper long boots that came just above the knee.

"Sarah." Alex walked toward her. "You look beautiful."

She quickly looked back to the floor. "You are too kind, but thank you." His comment seemed sincere. Could it be that he hadn't noticed that her dress was no more than supper attire, and the hem had turned a light shade of green from walking though the tall grass? His eyes gleamed and were full of life as always, and he smiled honestly at her, either unaware of or indifferent about her dress.

"I know I'm here sooner than you expected," he said. "I hope it's not an inconvenience."

"Don't think that you have imposed. It is quite the contrary, and I am ready to go, however, I need to ask a favor of you." Her lips tightened as she thought about her stepfather's request, and how awkward it made her feel right now.

"Anything, my lady. Tonight I am at your disposal."

"Thank you." She hesitated and then let it all come out in a rush. "My stepfather and sister are also going to the castle tonight, but as of now, they lack the means of getting there."

"Say no more. They're welcome to ride with us."

Sarah smiled and nodded gratefully.

"Shall we wait for them outside?" Alex motioned to the door. "It's a bit warm in here."

"Yes, I agree." Sarah led the way.

She stepped out the door and looked at the carriage. It was large, and hooked to it were a matching team of four white horses. She looked around. There were no drivers, no escorts. She was still trying to figure out who Alex was, but he made it hard. His dress tonight was extravagant, like that of a noble, but he came without even so much as a servant, as if he were a commoner.

"You came alone?" she asked nonchalantly, trying to disguise her prying words.

"I insisted on it. You might not believe it from our recent encounters, but it's not often that I get out without the accompaniment of a steward or escort. You don't mind, I hope, my informality?"

"No, I don't mind at all." She truly didn't, but she wasn't sure if he was telling the whole truth. He was so different from Chad, who never went anywhere without someone to wait on him, flaunting those who served him as a display of his exalted station. In Chad's mind, the more servants, the more important the person was. But Alex was different to the extreme. He didn't even bring a driver for the carriage. Did he truly insist on it, or did he not have any servants? Perhaps his family had fallen on hard times. She gave him a questioning look, but if he noticed, he paid no attention to it and offered no further explanation.

She walked up to the team of horses. Although the reins were loosely gathered to the head of the carriage, the horses stood absolutely still, and Sarah knew that they were well trained. "They are perfectly beautiful!" She rubbed the muzzle of the horse in front of her.

"I tried to find four unicorns to pull the carriage, but this is the best I could do."

"They're perfect! Do you ride them also?" She stepped over to the next horse, spreading her attention between them.

"No, not these four. They haven't been broke for the saddle. We only use them to pull carriages." He watched her move between the animals, amused at her simple pleasure with them.

"They are a perfect match—each one completely white. Where did you get such a perfectly matched team?"

Alex ignored the last question. "They are brown at birth, but gradually turn white as they mature."

Sarah was impressed with the team of horses. They were all the same height and beautifully conformed. Strong and compact, they stood squarely, each with its head tucked, giving the crest of each neck a beautiful arch. And they were meticulously groomed, with each mane trimmed and knotted.

"I should like to see your stables someday." Sarah stopped, silently scolding herself for her unusual request, and decided to make a more ladylike attempt at it. "You said your family breeds horses. I would like to meet your family, and see your establishment . . ." She let her words trail off, realizing that there was nothing ladylike about her request no matter how she worded it.

Alex just smiled, "Certainly, and you shall—" His words were cut short as they both turned to look down the road toward the sound of someone approaching.

A small grey horse pulling an equally small cart lumbered toward them with a woman bent over the reins. Sarah tried to make out who it was, but it was hard to see her above the bobbing head of the horse. "Surely she must be lost, for we certainly aren't expecting anyone."

It wasn't until the woman had stopped the cart and Sarah had walked over to her that she recognized the old seamstress. "Good afternoon," Sarah said, greeting her with a puzzled look.

"Oh, my lady. I'm glad I caught you," she said in her thick accent as Sarah helped her down from the cart. "When you didn't come today, I got worried. As soon as I closed my shop this afternoon, I asked around to find out directions to your manor. I am glad I found it."

Sarah was still baffled, and stared dumbfounded at the old woman.

"I've brought your gown," she said proudly. "Now the package is in the back of the cart, but it's too much of a reach for me, so you'll have to help me take it out."

Alex strode over to the cart. "Please, allow me."

The seamstress curtsied graciously to Alex, bowing her head. "I offer you my most gracious thanks," she said politely. "Does Miss Sarah have the good fortune of your accompaniment to the ball tonight?"

"Yes," he said, quickly taking the package from the cart and looking nervously at the seamstress.

Sarah broke in, "Then am I to assume you know each other?"

"Yes," the seamstress said.

Alex abruptly handed the large package to Sarah, then caught the seamstress by the arm and led the old woman to the house, quietly whispering in her ear.

Before Sarah could ask about their strange behavior, the seamstress turned around smiling. "Come, my lady. I'll help you dress."

The woman hurried Sarah inside the house and practically pushed her up the stairs. Her enthusiasm was contagious, and Sarah couldn't get her door open quickly enough.

Once inside the room, the seamstress gingerly laid the package on the bed. "We must hurry, my lady, so we don't keep your young man waiting."

Sarah was trying to get undressed and turned around to ask her about Alex when the seamstress pulled the carefully folded gown out of its wrappings. Sarah gasped and stopped in the middle of undoing the lacing on the dress she was wearing. "That isn't the dress I requested!"

"Oh, but it is, my lady!"

Sarah was astounded. "But it's not!" She seemed unable to move, unable to look away from the gown. "I can't pay for this!"

"You already paid me, remember?"

Sarah continued to protest. All the while the seamstress nudged and prodded her until she finally had her in the gown.

Running her fingers over the skirt, Sarah admired the exquisite material. It was made of the finest blue velvet she had ever seen. Tiny white pearls were sewn along the edge of the square neckline, attractively accentuating her neck and fair skin. The sleeves were embroidered to the elbow in a crossed diamond pattern, with a pearl sewn at each intersecting point. From the elbow to the wrists a crisscrossed lacing allowed the white of the underdress to show through. The blue skirt had a raised diamond pattern sewn with silver thread, and the bottom was accented with oval blue topaz stones sewn around the hem. Sarah didn't even dare to breathe as the seamstress laced up the back of the dress.

"You won't burst the seams, my lady," the woman told her. "It's a perfect fit!"

Sarah was on the verge of tears. "It's beautiful. I can't thank you enough."

"No need, my lady. It was my own pleasure to make it for you," the seamstress said as she admired her work. "Oh! I almost forgot." She returned to the wrappings the dress had been in and pulled out a long strand of pearls and topaz stones.

"Oh, madam!" Sarah gasped.

"Here, let me put it on you." She wrapped it once around her waist and clasped it in front with one end hanging halfway down her frame. It was weighted with a silver unicorn.

"A unicorn?" Sarah started to ask, but suddenly there was a pounding on her door.

"Sarah!" Clyde's voice dripped with irritation.

"Just a moment," Sarah replied.

"Sarah, we are ready to depart, and I expect you to introduce Felicia and myself properly to your friend Alex!"

"My lady." The seamstress took Sarah's hands in hers and whispered urgently. "You deserve all the good this life has to offer; don't let the jealous ambitions of your stepfather weigh you down."

Sarah looked at her quizzically, but Clyde was getting impatient. "Sarah! You mustn't keep us waiting!"

"Coming," Sarah said toward the door.

The seamstress curtsied, bowing her head, and Sarah thought she heard her say, "my princess," but Clyde began pounding on the door and she couldn't be certain of anything at that point. She hastened to pull the latch and open the heavy door. Clyde was in midpound when he saw Sarah and froze.

He stood with his hand in the air and his mouth slightly open. It took several moments before he gathered his composure. He knew Sarah was pretty, but it had been quite a while since he had really taken time to look at her, and her overall beauty caught him off guard. She had truly blossomed into a beautiful young woman. She didn't resemble Miranda much in features except perhaps the red touches in her hair and her petite frame. Sarah was more like Miranda in her mannerisms and spirit. He lowered his hand and swallowed.

It was then that he brought his attention back to the gown she was wearing. The extravagant detailing of it was far more costly than she could have paid for, and his temper sparked again. "That dress! How did you pay for that?"

"With the money you allotted me." Sarah wasn't apologetic, knowing she had done nothing wrong.

"I'm sure we are indebted now for twice that much. How dare you spend so recklessly! How much did you throw away?"

"I paid the exact amount you had allotted me."

"Don't lie to me! I know that gown cost far more than what I gave you!"

The seamstress stepped to Sarah's side. "She paid me twenty-two silver florins! The gown is paid in full."

Clyde sputtered in disbelief and shook his head, knowing that the dress was worth at least twice that. It was a dress suited for royalty. He mumbled something about discussing it later, and then turned and marched down the hallway.

Sarah turned to look at the seamstress who just rolled her eyes and shook her head. Sarah smiled. She felt a connection to this woman.

The seamstress pulled at Sarah's skirt, pretending to straighten an imaginary wrinkle. "There now, you're a vision of beauty!" She paused and looked deeply into Sarah's face. "My, but you're the exact resemblance of your mother! It's like looking into the past and seeing her as a young lady."

Sarah's eyes grew wide with surprise. "You knew my mother?"

"Yes. Didn't I mention that before?"

"No," Sarah said softly, trying to remember her first conversation with the old woman.

"It's been a long time ago." She paused. "Now come, child. It's time to go."

Outside, Clyde marched up to Alex and stuck his hand out. "Good day, sir. My name is Clyde Berack, and this is my daughter Felicia," he said, nodding to Felicia, who had followed him.

"A pleasure to meet you," Alex said, shaking hands and then exchanging bow for curtsy.

Clyde looked at the carriage suspiciously. "And where is your driver?"

"'Tis I," Alex said with a grin.

Clyde gave him a sharp glance. "How inconvenient," he muttered as he clasped his hands behind his back and scrutinized the young man in front of him. "Sarah tells me that your name is Alex. Do you have a last name?"

Alex's eyes lit up and a broad smile surged across his face. "Excuse me." He moved around Clyde and hurried to the doorway where Sarah was now standing.

"You look . . . stunning!" He looked at her in awe. "An exquisite gown to match your beauty." He led Sarah past Clyde, whose ears were turning red as he avoided exploding at the affront of being ignored, and Felicia, who just stared at her sister dumbfounded. "Shall we be on our way then?" He opened the carriage door and helped Felicia in, then Clyde followed, cramming himself through the carriage door.

Alex then turned to Sarah. "My lady," he said as he softly laid his hand on the small of her back and gestured toward the carriage. But Sarah didn't move, and he felt like he was trying to push a small child into a dark cave, as if there were something terrible waiting in the shadows. He asked, "Is everything all right?"

Sarah shook her head. "No. I would rather not ride inside," she said calmly, but in a low, quiet voice. "Will you please allow me to ride atop next to you?"

Alex was puzzled. He had never known a lady who didn't prefer riding *in* the carriage. But in spite of her antics in the orchard, he knew Sarah was every bit as much, if not more, a lady than other women he knew. Even now, she kept herself poised, her emotions completely in check. He suspected that she had a conflict with one of the two in the carriage— most likely her stepfather. Clyde just seemed like that type of man. One who wouldn't budge, saw things only his way, and would fight anyone who went against him. He turned back and looked at the carriage. Clyde's stern face peered at them curiously through the open door.

He looked back to Sarah. If she felt uneasy about riding inside, then he wouldn't impose that on her. "As you wish, my lady." His gesture this time was now toward the driver's seat.

"Sarah will ride atop next to me," he explained to Clyde as he shut the door to the carriage. "After all, I'm her escort, and it's only fitting that she sit next to me." He turned, ignoring Clyde's sputtering about improper behavior, and helped Sarah up onto the seat before climbing up next to her.

"Does my lady also wish to drive?" he teased as he picked up the reins.

Sarah's good humor returned and the laughter danced in her eyes. "Yes," she said firmly, teasing him back. "I can, you know, although I have driven only two horses, not four."

"Well then, I shall teach you all the tricks of the trade. That is, if you're up to the challenge." Alex snapped the reins and the horses moved down the road.

"Oh!" Sarah exclaimed, now excited about prospects of her actually driving the elegant team. "I would love to try!"

"Very well. I'll show you, and when we get to the main road, I'll hand them over to you."

Alex snapped the reins again, and the four horses picked up their pace to a lope. "We shall not be late!" he called loud enough that Clyde and Felicia heard him.

Sarah held on tight but eagerly watched every move Alex made and listened as he explained the basics of controlling the four horses. It wasn't that much different from what she already knew and she anxiously awaited her turn at the reins as they approached the main road.

At last he looked at her. "Are you ready?"

"Quite."

"Shall I slow them down for you?"

Sarah reached over, ready to take the long leather straps. "No, I can manage quite well."

Alex passed the reins to her, ready to take them back if needed, but she handled them as if she had been born to it, and slowly he sat back to enjoy the ride. He breathed in deeply, sighed, stretched, then started fidgeting with his doublet. "Do you mind?" he asked. "It's a bit warm."

When Sarah looked over at him, he had the doublet unbuttoned and was in the process of taking it off, leaving him in just his white undershirt. "I don't mind, as long as you stop there," she taunted.

"Ah, you tease, but did I hear a touch of jealousy in your voice? I'm sure there are times when you wish you could do the same." He laid his doublet carefully on the seat next to him.

He was right. There were many hot days when she wished she could go around in her undergarments. "It isn't fair," she admitted. "Men have too much liberty to do as they wish."

"I admit we do what we feel." Suddenly he jumped up and threw his arms out wide.

The movement was so quick it startled Sarah. "What are you doing?"

"I'm taking the liberty to do as I feel, and right now I am feeling the wind. You should try it. I promise, I won't tell anyone."

Glancing back and forth between Alex and the four galloping horses, Sarah watched him as he balanced on the rocking carriage. She tried to concentrate on what she was doing, but she desperately wanted to turn all of her attention to him. "Someday I will, but as you can see, I'm a bit occupied at the moment." She kept the horses at a steady pace, neither giving them their heads nor letting them slow down, taking pleasure in the thought of how Felicia and Clyde must be bouncing around inside as it pitched back and forth.

Alex moved his arms along with the motion, back and forth in the breeze. The wind caught his shirt and it billowed out behind him, rippling like a loose sail in the wind. He was thoroughly enjoying himself, and Sarah started to laugh.

When Alex finally sank down on the seat next to her, the wind caught his shirt again and it billowed out, the collar slipping back down his shoulders, revealing most of his upper back. Sarah began to turn her head away, pretending she hadn't noticed. But then her head shot back and she stared intensely at his exposed skin. He instantly began to apologize and reached to pull his shirt up, but stopped just short of doing it, realizing it was too late. She had already seen.

Sarah pulled back on the reins somewhat, making the horses walk, and then gathered the long leather straps in one hand. Alex watched her out of the corner of his eye, not moving as she reached up with her free hand and with one finger brushed the skin across the top of his shoulder. He closed his eyes and breathed in deeply as her finger sent goose bumps down his back.

Sarah looked hard at the black words permanently inked into Alex's shoulder. The moment she saw them she remembered seeing similar ones on Chad a year ago. Five generations of the royal blood line. The mark of royalty. Sarah's finger ran along Alex's shoulder as she read each name out loud. "Andrew Tharon Hill, Tharon Richard Tain Hill, Richard Alexander Hill." She recognized the names of each of the past kings. "Richard Leon Hill." She stopped. "King Richard," she said, softly tracing the letters before moving to the last name. "Alexander Richard Hill." She looked at Alex. "Prince Alexander," she whispered.

He nodded in recognition of his proper title. Sarah gasped, finally comprehending, and dropped the reins.

It was more out of instinct than anything that Alex lunged forward to catch the reins before they fell to the ground. He grabbed them and yanked back. The horses, feeling the pull at their bits, stopped suddenly, sending Sarah's torso forward and then throwing her backward. Her head hit the top of the carriage with a loud crack and blackness started rolling in around her.

16. THE PRINCE

Voices swirled around in Sarah's head and gradually grew louder, then the blackness subsided and she opened her cloudy eyes, aware that Alex—no, not Alex, but the prince himself, Prince Alexander—was supporting her with one arm.

Clyde was out of the carriage and reaching up toward her. "She's hurt. Help her down."

"I'm fine," Sarah said, rubbing the sore spot on the back of her head.

"Now, Sarah, you've just had a hard blow to the head. It's not something to trifle about!"

"He's right," Prince Alexander said with concern as he looked closely at her. "Shall we have you walk around a bit? It might help." He was already nudging her to take Clyde's hand.

Sarah stepped down from the carriage and protested again. "Really, there is no need to fuss. I'm fine now." She resisted the urge to hold the point where the dull ache was shooting sharp pains through her head. She did hurt, but the soreness would eventually go away. The important thing was, she had her wits about her and there was no dizziness.

"Don't try to excuse it, Sarah. I saw what happened," Clyde said forcefully. "And with a blow like that, you shouldn't even be on your feet! Now I insist that you ride the rest of the way in the carriage!"

Now Sarah was confused. Had Clyde really seen her hit her head? But how? How much did he know? She stood up tall and forced a smile. "Really," she pleaded. "I'm quite well."

"I insist!" Clyde said forcefully.

He wasn't going to give in and Sarah didn't want to make a scene in front of the prince. Submissively, she let Clyde usher her toward the carriage. He had such a tight grip on her arm that she was sure he would leave bruises. Then she noticed Felicia's head was stuck out the carriage window and she was watching everything with wide-eyed curiosity. Sarah realized immediately what had happened. *Clyde must've been looking out the window, watching us as I hit my head,* she reasoned.

Felicia opened the door and jumped out to help Sarah in, and Prince Alexander crowded between them to offer his assistance as well. "Sarah, are you truly all right?" he asked.

"Yes," she said, peering at him from inside the carriage now. She hardly had time to think and she wished the two of them were alone to talk.

"Perhaps this will be better for you. Just rest and we'll be there soon." He disappeared from the doorway and she felt the carriage shift as he climbed up onto the driver's seat.

The prince! she thought. How stupid she must have been not to recognize him. But what of her family? Did they know? Obviously they had not recognized him before, but had Clyde heard her read the names? Did he hear her say, "Prince Alexander"?

Felicia went to climb back in the carriage, but Clyde caught her elbow and held her back. Sarah could see them both clearly from the doorway, and watched them carefully. Clyde was looking at Alex with a strange gleam in his eye.

"Your Highness?" he said.

Sarah groaned. He did know. Felicia's jaw dropped open and she gasped as the realization hit her as well. She could see the pink coming into Felicia's cheeks as she fumbled to open her fan.

"Yes?" Alex answered.

"I wish to apologize that I did not recognize you sooner."

"No apology is necessary, I assure you."

"Yes, well, if Your Highness requires company, Felicia would certainly not mind riding atop the carriage with you."

Sarah clenched her teeth together so tightly that more pain shot through her head. She moved toward the carriage door, but Clyde quickly stepped in the way, blocking her path.

"Thank you for the offer, my good sir," Alex said. "But the driver's seat seems to be a dangerous place lately. I think I shall brave it alone."

After Clyde and Felicia settled in, the carriage started rolling again and Sarah tipped her head back and closed her eyes. It was her way of showing Clyde and Felicia that she was in no mood to talk, but that didn't stop Felicia.

"I can hardly believe it!" she exclaimed. "Of all people! Prince Alexander!"

"Yes," Clyde said, sounding equally amazed. "Prince Alexander."

Felicia continued babbling on. "The prince himself, escorting us to the castle. And in the royal carriage no less. I can hardly believe it. He is so handsome! Of course I have seen him many times, but to see him up close, he is so much more comely. Such a pity we haven't been personally introduced until now. And Sarah, how silly—didn't you know he was the prince?"

Sarah made no movement, no sign that she had heard, but Felicia continued rattling on. Sarah blocked the noise out, caught up in her own thoughts. Yes, Alex must have thought she was silly. He had even asked her if she had personally met the royal family. How humiliating. Why hadn't she recognized him? She actually had seen him before on several occasions, and yet she still had no idea who he was. He must have had a good laugh.

She gritted her teeth as she tried to make sense of it all. If she would have met the king or queen themselves, would she have known who they were? Of course she would have—they would be wearing their royal . . . That was it. Now she understood. Whenever the prince was at a royal function he wore the robes of royalty and donned the royal crest. He had been surrounded by guards, and escorts, and squires, not to mention the dozens of girls that constantly swarmed around him. In fact, she had never been close to him, never talked to him, and she really never paid much attention to him. All of her interest had been in Chad.

Although Chad and Alex were cousins, they weren't exactly friends. The times when Chad mentioned Prince Alexander, his comments had been derogatory in nature. Of course Chad wouldn't have anything good to say about the man who stood between him and the crown. Few good words come from one who is jealous.

Sarah rubbed the back of her head. It wasn't her fault that she didn't recognize him. After all, who would expect royalty to be riding through the countryside unaccompanied, without even so much as a squire, and dressed . . . well, not in plain clothes, but certainly not in the extravagant dress of the royal family. Alex had hidden his secret well. Even Clyde and Felicia hadn't realized who he was at first, or surely they would've greeted him more formally. No, she was sure of it; they found out the same time she did. When she slowed the horses down, Clyde must have stuck his head out the window, and with his extraordinary hearing, overheard her call him by his proper title.

The carriage now slowed again and Sarah opened her eyes. They were inside the castle's outer walls. If she hadn't discovered his secret earlier, she would have by now, for out of the windows she could see soldiers saluting the prince, placing clenched fists over their hearts and hailing him with raised swords.

The carriage came to a stop. A small man wearing an embroidered tunic that distinguished him as someone in service to the royal family approached. "My lord, the queen awaits you in the great hall."

"Thank you, Eli," Alex said as he stepped down from the seat.

The man opened the door to the carriage and stepped aside as Alex helped Felicia out. He was wearing his doublet again, which now showed a dust mark from laying on the bench.

"Let me help you with that," Felicia said and dusted off the doublet until it was clean.

Felicia continued to fuss over him until he gently pushed her hands away and turned toward the carriage again, extending his hand toward Sarah. Abruptly Clyde stepped up, out of turn, and disembarked from the carriage, then stood blocking the door. A quiet gasp escaped Sarah's lips. It was a bold move against the prince, and she held her breath waiting to see if Clyde would further the confrontation.

Clyde tugged at his waistcoat to straighten it. "I fear Sarah is not herself yet and should rest here a while longer." He shifted his weight from one foot to another as he noticed Alexander's unwavering, firm gaze, then he continued on quickly. "I am quite sure, my lord, that many are waiting for you, so we will not trouble you any longer. I'll wait with Sarah and bring her when she's ready. But in your interest, my lord, Felicia will accompany you in."

Felicia stepped up next to Alex and slid her arm around his. "I would be honored, Your Highness," she said in a sweet voice.

Sarah sat bolt upright. She had heard quite enough, but with Clyde blocking the doorway, she couldn't do anything else but listen and wonder if Alex would choose her sister over her as Chad had done. Sarah held her breath and listened for Alex's response.

"Don't concern yourself. My obligations can wait," Alex said firmly, dropping Felicia's arm. "If Sarah is not ready then it will be *I* who will wait with her!"

The words were strong and said with conviction, and Clyde took a step back as if they had hit him in the face. He shifted his weight uncomfortably again as if he were trying to decide if there was anything else he could do. Then with a low grunt, he reluctantly stepped out of the way.

After Sarah assured Alex that she was indeed ready, he took her hand and wrapped it around his arm, then led her toward the entrance with Felicia and Clyde following. Great stones stacked one on top of the other formed the massive outer wall of the castle and towered above them. The sun was just starting to lower in the sky and the light illuminated the stones on the upper towers.

Sarah slowed her step as they drew nearer to the entrance. "My lord, I must have a word with you."

Alex must have heard the serious tone in her voice, for he turned aside and waved Clyde and Felicia on past them, watching them until they had disappeared through the massive doors.

After they were gone and Alex was sure they were alone, he focused on Sarah, who was leaning back against the stone wall with an expression he couldn't read. "Is something wrong, my lady?"

"Yes," she said firmly. "It seems you lied to me."

Alex stepped closer to her now. Close enough that if she had been standing upright and not leaning against the wall, they would have been touching. He looked down into her eyes. "I have never lied to you." His voice was low and calm. "In all the conversations I have had with you I have never lied."

Sarah looked away for a second, but then faced him again. "When we met, wasn't it lying when you told me your name was Alex without disclosing who you really were?"

Alex took a couple of steps back. "I told you how I liked to be addressed, as did you . . . Sarah. And that does not warrant my being called a liar."

Sarah knew a man's honor should mean everything to him and she was glad that he was defending his so seriously.

Alex let out a sigh and then continued on. "I try to take a couple of hours each day to escape from this insidious lifestyle, and to give me time to work on my horsemanship. Am I expected to explain to everyone I meet on those short excursions that I'm the prince just trying to get some time to myself? That would defy the purpose, would it not? And besides, as I recall the situation, I wasn't the only one withholding my full and proper name."

Sarah dropped his gaze. She hadn't given him her full name. "Sarah Antonellis Benavente, stepdaughter of Clyde Berack," she said quietly.

"Thank you," he replied politely. "Sarah Antonellis Benavente. It's a pretty name."

"And if I had known yours, I would have been saved this humiliation," she said in a whisper as she carefully laid her head back against the wall.

"There is no humiliation. I withheld my title from you on purpose." Sarah opened her mouth to protest, but he quickly put a finger across her lips to hush her and went on. "I didn't lie about who I was, I just withheld my title."

"But why continue to keep it from me?"

Alex breathed in deeply and let it out slowly. "Because it was my desire to find out who *you* were."

"My lord?" Sarah questioned him, not understanding.

"That day in the orchard . . . you attracted me," he admitted. "Not only with your beauty, but with your mannerisms and everything about you. You must understand; people act differently around me because I'm the prince. They try to impress me, and it's hard for me to know if they treat me well solely because I am royalty."

Sarah nodded understandingly.

"Don't misjudge me. I am royalty and wish to be treated as such. But there are people who treat other men with contempt, and verbally abuse others by nature, who then turn around and, putting on a mask of kindness, they flatter me. How am I to know who my true friends are? I simply wanted to see if you liked me for who I am and not for my royal station in life."

"I do understand your reasons, but when were you planning on telling me? Surely you didn't expect to hide it here tonight. I would've discovered your secret."

"Yes, I know. I was lucky that the seamstress didn't give it away. She sews for my mother, and knows me quite well, but I had other plans. I was going to tell you tonight, but I had hoped to do it in a less abrupt way. In fact, before we gained extra passengers, I had planned on stopping on the way here. There is a quiet place I like to go when I want to think and be alone in a grove of trees not very far away. I was going to take you for a short walk and tell you there. In any case, you discovered it before I had the chance to tell you."

Sarah nodded, satisfied. "I'm sorry, my lord, that I called you a liar.

But I fear now, as I was unaware of who you were, I may not have treated you as your position demands."

Alex smiled, put both hands on her arms, and pulled her toward him. "Sarah, you treated me how royalty should be treated—with sincerity and honesty." He paused for a long time and looked deep into her eyes before he continued. "And I was also sincere when I expressed my interest in you. I wish to call on you."

Sarah's heart sank. She did like Alex, but now that she knew he was the prince, the relationship had to end. "I don't believe I can allow that," she said quietly.

"You will not have me, then?"

"I can't have you. I know that it's expected of you to marry to form an alliance. I don't wish to have someone call upon me when there's no room for the relationship to grow."

Alex gently took Sarah's chin in his hand and lifted it up until their eyes met. "There is always room for a relationship to grow. Please allow me to call on you."

"I fail to see how this would be possible."

Alex pulled Sarah closer, wrapping his strong arms around her. He pressed his cheek to her head. "Let me worry about that."

17. THE MISERABLE CELEBRATION

Sarah and Alex approached the gates where two guards saluted as they passed through, and they entered into the inner courtyard of the castle. There were dozens of people mingling and visiting in the yard—a few women, but mostly men, some with drinks in their hands, others with pipes. A hush went through the crowd and in turn, they bowed to their prince. Sarah could feel the tension as some bowed reluctantly, but Alex ignored them as he escorted her toward the entrance to the great hall.

Two more guards stood at the heavy iron doors that were wide open, and music softly filtered out into the courtyard. Sarah suddenly felt self-conscious. She quickly brushed at the top of her skirt, smoothing it with her sweaty palm. She took a deep breath, lifted her head, pulled her shoulders back, and stepped through the large doors and into the great hall.

The music was slightly louder inside and the crowd instantly thickened around them. Those people closest to the entrance turned and bowed or curtsied in greeting to her and Alex. Several people eyed her curiously, obviously wondering who she was. Some acquaintances smiled genuinely, while others were surprised, with dropped jaws and soft exclamations of disbelief.

The hall, which was quite large, was completely filled with people from all over the kingdom. Several banners hung along the walls between the lighted sconces. Large windows on the west side let in scattered light from the setting sun that fell across several buffet tables loaded with all kinds of food and drink. One table boasted a whole roasted pig surrounded by roasted apples and quarters of beef. Another table had a roasted peacock with its long beautiful blue and green tail feathers on display. There were breads in all shapes and sizes, exotic fruits, cheeses, cakes and pastries, spiced beer, and spun sugar embossed with the royal crest. Many people were availing themselves of the feast, and Sarah wasn't surprised to see that the tables were a favorite place for the children to gather and play, where every now and then they snatched pieces of bread or cake.

The musicians were on the opposite side of the hall, surrounded by a more formal crowd, and the center of the room was filled with dancers. Other people stood along the walls mingling and visiting. It was there that Sarah spotted Felicia with a few other young ladies her same age, but neither Chad nor her stepfather were anywhere in sight.

Alex was nodding and greeting people as he led Sarah farther into the room. Every few steps they would have to pause as someone approached them. Sarah smiled, nodded, and then politely curtsied to each of them. She enjoyed meeting new people, and although she overheard some disapproving whispers, the people that actually approached them were friendly. She thanked the women who graciously commented on her lovely gown and curtsied to the men who commented on her beauty.

"What a lovely young lady you have with you tonight, Alexander."

Sarah turned and brought her attention to the tall woman approaching them. She appeared to be in her thirties and had an air of self-assurance.

"May I introduce Sarah Antonellis Benavente," Alex said. "Sarah, this is Lady Emelita Carlos, my mother's cousin."

"It's a pleasure to meet you, Lady Emilita," Sarah replied with a curtsy.

"Enchanted," the duchess said, and then turned to Alex. "I'm glad you're here, Alexander. I haven't seen you since breakfast, and we'll be leaving early tomorrow to return home."

"Alex!" A little boy pushed past the duchess. "I was looking for you!"

The duchess grabbed the boy by the shoulder. "Sedrick! What have I taught you?"

"Sorry, Mama."

The boy's eyes fell and he started again. "Excuse me, Prince Alexander; I have been patiently looking for you. I was wondering if you wanted to play hide and seek again tonight?"

"Sedrick!" his mother broke in. "Alexander has a lady with him tonight, and after the fireworks, you'll be going to bed. We have a long trip tomorrow."

"But Mama!" he protested, "this morning Alex promised."

"Sedrick!"

"It's quite all right." Alex knelt on one knee before the boy and winked at him. "We'll see—if it is not too late."

"Come along, Sedrick." The duchess pulled at his arm. "We must not bother Alexander any longer."

Sedrick broke away from his mother's grip. "I was not going to bother Alexander any longer. I want to talk to the lady now."

He ran up to Sarah and bowed. "Do you want to dance with me?" he asked in the most grown-up voice that he could muster.

"Sedrick!" his mother started.

"I don't mind at all," Sarah broke in. "I would love to dance with you." She took the little boy's arm and allowed him to lead her into the crowd, where he caught hold of the end of the procession of dancers snaking around the floor.

The duchess stepped over next to Alex as they both watched the odd couple. "If you do not mind my saying so, my lord, you have quite a special lady with you tonight."

"Yes, I think so too." Alex couldn't help but smile as he watched Sarah tailing his little cousin.

"I can't recall meeting her before, but then again I don't visit nearly as much as I should."

"No," Alex agreed, "you haven't met her. I myself haven't known her long, but I confess I am quite taken by her."

"Yes, I see that. She is very graceful, and yet so full of life. See how she gives all of her attention to Sedrick. That says a lot about a woman's character."

"One of her many admirable qualities."

"If my approval is worth anything, you have it; however, it's your father whom you must win over if you wish to further your relationship with this young lady."

Alex nodded. Lady Emilita's approval was certainly worth something to him. She was a wise woman with unique judgment, and his father sought advice from her on certain issues as much as he did from his own personal advisors. At that moment Alex wanted to ask her to suggest to his father what an extraordinary woman Sarah was. That alliances could be formed, not through an arranged marriage, but through convincing other countries it would be mutually beneficial, politically and financially, to form a coalition. But Alex didn't ask her to plead his case. Instead he thanked her for her sentiments and bid her goodbye in case he didn't see her before she left, and then walked into the crowd to claim Sarah back from his cousin.

Sedrick had pulled Sarah into the middle of the floor to take their turn at standing still while the other dancers moved around them. He looked up at her and tugged on her hand to pull her closer. "Excuse me, my lady," he said in his grown-up voice. "Mother says that Prince Alexander will have to get married soon. Are you going to marry him?"

Sarah blushed and opened her mouth as she quickly groped for an answer.

"Ahem," a deep voice sounded not two steps behind her.

Sarah quickly turned around to face Alex. He smiled at her mischievously and she knew he must have heard what Sedrick asked. He raised an eyebrow as if he were awaiting her answer, but she wasn't about to give him the satisfaction. "My lord," she said as she curtsied to him.

"You don't mind, do you, Sedrick, if I take a turn with this pretty lady?"

"No," he said with a shrug. "The dance is over anyway. We were the last couple."

"Thank you. You are a good man."

Sedrick smiled proudly and trotted off toward his mother.

The music died off and then began again. "May I, my lady?" Alex offered his hand to Sarah and she took it, letting him pull her close as he started to glide to the soft music, moving in a rising and falling motion and leading her in a series of steps alongside the other dancers. "You never answered the question Sedrick asked you."

"I wasn't given the chance."

"Well you have the chance now, so how would you answer?"

Her stomach was doing flips again, and she tried to evade the question. "Sedrick, the asker of the question, is gone."

"Please . . . amuse me. I'll deliver your answer to him personally."

"I think Sedrick was quite taken with me, and will probably seek me out again, so I'll be able to give him the answer myself."

"Are you saying I have to prove myself over a six-year-old to win your affections?"

"Possibly. Perhaps you need to ask Sedrick that."

He smiled and chuckled softly.

Alex was an elegant dancer and he moved her with ease across the floor as she repeated the series of steps after him. The dancing pattern moved them apart as other couples wove their way between them and then brought them back together. He stepped to her side and slid his hand around the small of her back, pulling her close to him as they moved in unison.

Each time he pulled her tighter to him he stirred a now-familiar sensation in her stomach. *I must not allow myself to feel this way,* she told herself. *Perhaps this would've been possible at a different time, but not now. The country needs allies, and the swiftest way to gain them is through marriage. I have to be sensible,* she tried to convince herself, but at that moment his strong arms wrapped around her and his breath on her cheek seemed to melt away all of her reasoning. She tried to think how she could resist his affection when she so desperately wanted it.

The music ended, but Alex didn't release her. He lingered, holding her close. People were turning toward the musicians and applauding, while others were forming into lines for yet another dance. Still he held her, and she was letting him. *What does this mean?* she thought as she pushed away from him and stepped back, breathless, and looked into his eyes, the deep blue eyes that had enchanted her and seemed to hold her captivated. It was too late to suppress her feelings—she was falling in love, and by the look in his eyes he was doing the same.

Alex stepped closer to her. "I want to introduce you to my mother."

Sarah squirmed. It was another step in a relationship that shouldn't be. "Your mother, *the queen,*" Sarah added sharply in an attempt to distance herself.

"Yes, my mother the queen, but it's my *mother* I would like you to meet."

Sarah understood. It was unfair for her to put so much emphasis on Alex being royalty. "Forgive me. I would love to meet your mother."

Alex led her across the floor to a raised balcony flanked by stairs on either side that led up to where Queen Julianna sat with two other noblewomen watching the festivities before them. She recognized Lady Mary, Chad's mother, but didn't know who the other woman was. She turned her attention back to the queen as they ascended the stairs. She was a small lady with dainty features. A few friendly wrinkles extended from the corners of her eyes, and her silky dark hair, which was showing no signs of graying, was encircled with an elegant crown.

"Mother," Alex said as he bent over and kissed her cheek. He then stepped to the side. "I would like to present my lady, Sarah Antonellis Benavente."

Sarah held her skirt out and bent into a deep curtsy. "Your Majesty."

"Ah, my dear," the queen said, reaching out and taking Sarah by her hands. "I can't tell you how pleased I am to finally meet you, for it's been you who has occupied my son's thoughts lately, but whom he still refuses to discuss in detail with me."

"Mother!" Alex protested.

She ignored him and continued, "I must thank you for coming tonight, Sarah, for if it weren't for your presence here, I believe we would also miss the attendance of my son."

"It's my pleasure to be able to accompany His Highness to such a grand event."

"Yes, and we are pleased you think so," the queen said. "I'm afraid you'll have to meet Richard at a later time; he seems to be a bit preoccupied at the moment." The queen motioned with her hand toward the back of the balcony.

There were several people standing along the wall behind them, but it was the two men in a doorway conversing whom the queen had made reference to. Sarah hadn't noticed them before, but now as she looked, it was Chad who caught her eye at first, and she realized he was talking with the king. She saw both of their mouths moving, but Chad's attention was on her rather than the king. He was staring at her, eyeing her up and down. His piercing gaze made her uncomfortable as he traced her with his eyes, and she quickly looked away.

"Sarah, this is Lady Christina Adilia Hardman," the queen said, motioning to the lady on her right. "And this is Lady Mary Elvinia Hill," she said, nodding toward Chad's mother.

"Lady Christina, it's lovely to meet you. And how do you do, Lady Mary?"

"Very well, thank you. And how have you been, Sarah?"

"Fine, thank you."

The queen looked at Mary and back to Sarah. "Oh!" she said with recognition on her face. "You must have been the young lady Chad was courting for some time."

Alex's eyes widened in shock and he cocked his head to one side, looking intently at Sarah.

"Yes," Sarah answered. "But it is my sister Felicia who has caught his attention lately. In fact, he asked her to the ball tonight."

Alex looked away from her, and shot a hard glance in Chad's direction.

"That's right," Lady Mary said. "Felicia Berack. She and your stepfather have visited me on several occasions this summer."

"Oh?" Sarah tried to mask the surprise in her voice.

"Ah, here comes Richard now," the queen interrupted and nodded toward the two men approaching them.

Chad reached them first. After he greeted the queen and her companions, he turned and bowed to Sarah, then kissed her hand. "Sarah, you look absolutely breathtaking tonight." He softly rubbed her hand before letting go. "You must save me a dance, my lady, or my evening will not be complete. Now, if you'll please excuse me, I have someone waiting for me." With that Chad turned and walked down the stairs, paying no heed to Alex who stood angrily with both hands clenched into fists.

"Richard, dear," the queen said as the king sat down next to her, "this is Sarah Benavente. She's the young lady Alexander has been spending time with lately."

"Well," he said heartily, "I'm glad to meet you. Now tell me who your father is?"

"Richard," the queen whispered as she put her hand on top of his. "They just got here. Let them go eat and dance a little before we take up the rest of their night visiting."

"Ah, very well. Sarah and Alexander, we will talk later," he said and eagerly looked around the room, not wanting to miss any of the festivities.

Alex turned away without a word and headed for the stairs, but his mother called him back. "Alexander," she said and patiently waited until he walked back to her. "The squire will fetch your sash for you." She motioned to a young man behind them. "It'll only take a moment, my son. I know you don't like to wear it, but you *are* the crown prince and by all means, you should look like it from time to time." Her voice was soft but firm.

Alex rolled his eyes but followed the squire, disappearing into another part of the castle.

Sarah walked over to the head of the stairs and watched the crowd mingling below her. She spotted Chad talking with her stepfather, then let her eyes wander around the room until she found Felicia, who was surrounded by a group of admiring young men and seemed to be enjoying herself. Sarah looked back to where Chad and Clyde were, but her stepfather was now walking away, his face looking like a thunderstorm, and Chad was looking up at her. He eyed her appraisingly, then smiled and started walking up the stairs toward her. He vainly fussed with his clothing as he walked, straightening his sleeves and brushing at his cuffs, although his focus never departed from her.

Sarah looked back behind her. The queen and king were talking pleasantly to each other, and Alex was still nowhere in sight. She didn't like how Chad was looking at her, and without Alex by her side, she felt vulnerable and trapped. This was the man that she once wanted to marry, but now she felt incredibly uncomfortable with his approach.

"Sarah," Chad said in a smooth, silky voice, "we need to talk." He paused for a moment. "Please come outside with me. I promise it won't take long."

Her stomach lurched uneasily and her heart pounded against her chest, but she forced her words out calmly. "And what, may I ask, do you want to talk about?"

"About us," he said with an icy smile.

Sarah's mouth opened. *How dare he presume. . . . After how he has acted!* "You must be mistaken, my lord. There is no *us.*"

She expected a reaction, but he held his composure, perfectly relaxed and in total control.

"Very well. We don't have to talk," he concurred. "But at the very least, may I have a dance?" He held his arm out to her.

Sarah hesitated.

"Just until Prince Alexander returns." He stood unmoving. "Surely you wouldn't refuse a short turn around the floor with an old friend," he said, his arm still extended toward her.

Reluctantly Sarah took his arm and let him lead her down the stairs and onto the floor.

"Let me see," he said casually, "it has been, what . . . six or seven years since we met?"

"Yes. Isn't Felicia waiting for you?"

"Ah, but haven't we always attended these events together, you and I?" He turned her around to face him, took her hand, and slid his free arm around her waist as he fell into step with the other couples completing a large circle.

"I suppose. But this time you asked Felicia. Is this really what you wanted to talk to me about?"

"Sarah, I want to apologize to you." His voice was low so that she was the only one who could hear him. "It was not my intention to hurt you, and I would like to resolve these injured feelings between us.

"I did bring Felicia tonight, but only as my friend. In truth, I believed my bringing her would make you happy." He saw her confused look and continued, "Your family is so important to you, and I wasn't much help through your mother's illness or your mourning. I decided to become better friends with your sister so you could see I truly care for not only you but all of your family. Even your stepfather. Clyde and I have been doing a lot of business together lately."

Sarah raised her eyebrows in surprise. She had known that Clyde had taken some business advice from Chad, and she knew that they discussed politics on a regular basis, but she had no idea that they were actually doing business together. And had it all been because Chad was trying to show her that he cared about her family?

"Please accept my apology," Chad continued as he gently pulled her closer to him. "I know our relationship has been strained, and that's why I drew myself closer to your sister and your stepfather. It was my subtle way of trying to be near to you—to begin to close the gap between us."

Sarah thought the explanation was far-fetched, yet his expression seemed sincere and she could see he was attempting to smooth things over between them. She considered the apology as they danced along. They had been friends a long time, and she didn't want to make an enemy of him.

She forced a smiled and inclined her head. "Although we have grown apart this last year, I do value our . . . friendship—"

"And I too, my lady. Your kindness knows no bounds. And now my happiness knows no bounds." Chad added a few extra dance steps here and twirled her with a flourish, causing the surrounding dancers to laugh.

The two continued to dance, and just as he complimented her on completing a particularly complicated step, Chad pulled her closer to him and put his lips to her ear. "I can offer you everything the prince has to offer," he whispered, and then quickly slid his lips across her cheek to kiss her.

Taken by surprise, Sarah was unable to avoid the kiss, but quickly turned her head to avoid further contact. It was then that she saw Alex standing near the bottom of the stairs, watching them. He now wore a sash embroidered with the royal crest along with a gold pendant that draped across his shoulders. His hands were pulled into fists, and his face was hard and drained of all color. Alex shook his head, then spun on his heel and headed for the door.

Sarah tried to pull away from Chad, but he held her tight and pulled her close again. "Everything he has to offer. . . . In time, even the throne."

"Let me go!" she cried. "Why are you being like this?" Sarah flung her arms out, breaking loose from his grip, and ran toward the door. She wanted to reach Alex, but he had already disappeared, swallowed in the crowd.

* * *

Distraught and angry, Alex pushed through the people, ignoring those who tried to greet him, until he stepped through the heavy doors and into the courtyard. He took a deep breath. The air was cool. The sun had gone down behind the massive walls and darkness was beginning to cover the castle. This end of the courtyard was still crawling with people, all standing under the bright lanterns posted near the stone walls. He looked around and then quickly headed to the far end of the square, where he disappeared into the dark shadows near the large wall.

He leaned against the cold stones and quietly cursed, and then walked to the corner where he opened a small gate that led into the garden. The garden was quiet, away from everybody, and the thick shrubbery that surrounded it muted the noise from the courtyard and the castle beyond. A soft glow lingered on the horizon, leaving just enough light to make out the brick pathway.

As far as he knew, everyone needed some form of escape from the pressures of the world. His escape was to ride horses. His father's was hunting. His mother's was this garden. It was large, with winding paths that meandered around flowering shrubs and bushes, all of which his mother could recite by name. He walked slowly along the path until he came to the first stone bench, and then sat down. Only then did he notice the figure walking down the path toward him. He held his breath as he watched the woman's figure emerge from the shadows, and then frowned with disappointment.

"Madam, I wish to be left alone."

"Forgive me, Your Highness." Felicia walked closer until he could see the tears in her eyes. "I didn't know what else to do, but I won't trouble you any longer." She slowly turned away, but lingered, looking pleadingly back at him.

"All right, what can I do for you?" he asked, trying to keep the exasperation from his voice.

"I don't wish to bother you."

"And I don't wish to drag out this conversation. It's not in my nature to turn away a lady who is in need of something. So I beg you, tell me what it is that you need."

Felicia walked over to him. "I only wish to leave. I know why you are out here and wish to be left alone, and it is the same reason why I can't ask my escort to take me home."

"Lord Chad?"

"Yes, Your Highness. I only ask you because . . ."

Alex shook his head and dropped his face into his hands as he rubbed his temples.

Felicia stepped closer to him and then gingerly sat on the bench next to him. "Are you all right, my lord?"

There was no answer.

"I don't know what has come over Sarah," Felicia said softly to him. "And I don't know what her intentions are with Lord Chad, only that their actions make me tend to think . . ." She paused for a moment and then gently placed her hand on his back, attempting to comfort him. "I'm sure that you were as shocked as I, and that is why I ask for your services. Not only did you provide my ride here, but I presume that you also wish to leave."

Again the faint sound of footsteps echoed on the pathway.

"My lord?" Sarah called quietly. "Are you here?" She came closer. "Your Highness, is that you?" She stopped short. Through the shadows she could see Felicia sitting next to Alex with her hand resting on his back. She stood motionless, waiting. Finally Alex raised his head. He stared blankly at her and said nothing. She waited for some kind of response—anything.

"My lord?" she pleaded.

Alex slightly shook his head. "I have nothing to say to you."

"Please!"

"No," he said, not looking at her. "I am sure Lord Chad is waiting for you."

Sarah took another step toward him. "Alex, please."

He quickly put a hand up, halting her approach. He shook his head at her and then looked away, hiding the pain in his eyes.

Sarah looked at Felicia, who glared back at her and then began to gently rub Alex across the back of his shoulders.

Sarah turned quickly to hide her own pain and disappointment and then ran from the garden and out into the courtyard. She dropped her head down, avoiding eye contact with the droves of people as she passed them, and hurried out through the gates.

18. THE RETURN HOME

Sarah walked past people, horses, and the line of carriages until she found the one that had brought them to the castle. Fresh horses had been hooked up to it and, like the other carriages, it was surrounded by footmen, drivers, squires, and stable hands.

She said nothing to the men who were gathered together in small groups laughing and conversing, but walked to the back corner of the carriage, next to a wall, and stood, unsure of what to do next. The fireworks hadn't started yet and there would be more eating and dancing afterward. She guessed that it would be several hours before the others were ready to leave. She wasn't going back in, so she decided to wait. But wait for what? A long uncomfortable ride home? How awkward would she feel when the others finally came? No, she wasn't going to wait for them. She was going to leave, and she was going to leave now.

It was safe enough to walk from the castle to the manor in the light of day, but at night. . . . At night the village and the roads beyond it were not safe. There were people who lurked about the streets at night, mostly drunkards that would kill in order to obtain a few pieces of silver and others who would do unspeakable things if they happened upon a woman. She looked at the group of men closest to her. *No,* she thought, *if I request a ride home from them, they might need to get permission to leave, and that would get word back to the prince.* Sarah shook her head. Clearly Prince Alexander didn't want anything to do with her right now, so ducking her head again to avoid any attention, she walked away.

Sarah stood in front of the stables and looked around. She had told Alex that she wanted to see his family's establishment, and that is how she would explain it if she were caught and questioned about wandering around.

There were three buildings. The smallest was most likely used to store equipment or perhaps was the place where stable hands bunked. The largest structure, she guessed, was the stable that housed the horses for the cavalry soldiers. There were two guards standing outside and three other mounted soldiers slowly riding toward them. She couldn't see anyone by the third building, and that is the one she went to, slipping in through the open door.

It wasn't quite as large as the other stable, but it could still house forty horses or more. Two aisles ran lengthwise through the building, with stalls along either side of each. Two large lanterns hung above the doorways at each end and several hung from the middle rafters, giving ample light to the whole room. The mixed smell of hay and horses fell over her as she took another step, and youthful laughter rang through the building. She strained her eyes enough to see two stable boys at the far side of the building on the opposite aisle. She could just make them out, crouched down, playing some sort of game. They laughed and she heard the faint sound of dice rolling on the stone floor.

She looked around again, making sure there was no one else that she had missed, and noticed that fewer than half of the stalls were filled. There were three or four white horses like the ones hooked to Alex's carriage, a beautiful dappled-gray horse, and two bay horses looking out at her from their stalls. Just then a black horse raised his head, snorting and pawing at the ground. It was Alex's Friesian stallion, and he was only a couple of stalls down from where she stood.

She quietly walked over to him and carefully, silently, lifted the latch and squeezed through the gate and into his stall.

"Shh, big fellow," she whispered as she stroked his mane. She kept glancing around nervously, startled by every sound. *This is ridiculous*, she thought. *But what other choice do I have?*

"You know me. Remember? You've given me a ride before," she whispered in the stallion's ear.

Tack hung outside every stall, so she reached through the stall gate and gently took the bridle off its hook. The horse whinnied and Sarah stroked his neck again. "Shh. Don't worry. I only need a ride home and I promise I'll have you returned tomorrow."

She rubbed the bridge of his face and slipped the bridle up over his head. The metal bit clanked as he took it in his teeth, and she darted a look toward the two boys squatting in the far aisle. Neither one looked at her, but surely they would notice the horse coming out of his stall.

She hesitated for a moment and then, with a deep determined breath, she finished fastening the bridle. With the reins in hand, she lifted the latch and quietly pushed the gate open. The horse stepped out onto the floor with a clip clop. The boys still kept their attention on the dice between them, and Sarah judged the distance between her and the door. In just a few seconds she would be safely outside. She tugged on the reins. The horse's shoes clacked with every step on the stone floor, but she kept moving, holding her breath.

"Aaayyy!" one of the boys laughed. "You left a stall open and a horse is getting out!"

Sarah froze as she heard the second boy start laughing.

"Well I can't stand up and go get it, now can I?" They both started to laugh.

"Nor I!"

Sarah peeked over the horse's shoulder and saw the boys rolling onto their backs, a bottle between them. "They're drunk!" she said in a sharp whisper. *They can't be older than eleven or twelve,* she thought. She shook her head as she looked at them one more time and then led the horse outside.

It was now fully dark, and she stood for a minute to let her eyes adjust to the darkness. Without warning, the sky lit up with a streak of light that exploded into hundreds of small sparkling lights, like a flower blooming in the night sky. The sight was beautiful to her but terrifying to the young stallion, who whinnied and pulled back, rearing and kicking out with his massive front feet. One rein pulled from her hand, but she held tight to the other.

"Easy, boy," she soothed as she pulled on the rein. She spotted several rags that were used to wipe down the horses after a hard run, and she grabbed one and rubbed it on the horse's nose, moving it up toward his eyes. Another streak of light shot through the air. Quickly she moved the rag over the stallion's eyes. The firework exploded with a crack. The horse, blinded from the sight, now had to deal with only the sound. He stomped uneasily while she tied the rag on, all the while talking softly to him. At last he calmed down, and she took up the reins and led him away.

Trying to avoid attention, she led the horse away from the stable, using him to shield her from the people she passed. She quickened her pace as she approached the guards, who stood at the castle gates, but they only glanced at her momentarily before turning their attention to the lighted sky, allowing her to pass by unchallenged. Finally, she was through the gates.

She waited until she was farther down the street before she stopped and pulled the blindfold from the stallion's eyes. The fireworks still exploded every now and then, but with the stallion facing away from the commotion and with trees and buildings to block out most of the exploding light, she was able to keep him from rearing and bolting off. She waited until the fireworks stopped, but even then the stallion still pranced nervously, bobbing his head up and down and pawing at the ground. She did her best to calm him, then using a short rock wall to stand on, she managed to slide her leg over his back and pull herself up onto the nervous horse.

It had been a long time since she had ridden bareback, and it felt strange to her. Her heavy gown wasn't making her any more comfortable. The horse pranced along uneasily. She wondered if he had ever been ridden bareback before—or perhaps he wasn't used to being ridden at night. Things looked different in the dark. They headed through the village, and the street that had been alive with people just that morning was now quiet and deserted, except for a light here and there and the shadow of a person or two ducking into corners or darting across the street. The clop of the horse's hooves echoed across the cobblestones beneath him, the sound intensified by the silence around them. She nudged the stallion steadily on, slowly passing shops, taverns, and cramped apartments that people called home.

She saw movement from the corner of her eye, and she watched as a dark figure emerged from the shadows and made his way to the middle of the street.

"Good evening, my lady."

The voice was harsh and husky, and instinctively Sarah tightened her grip on the reins, her senses heightened. As she drew closer to the figure, the moonlight fell upon his face. He was unkempt, with filthy gray hair hanging down around his shoulders. A foul odor drifted up to her, and she glared at him, willing him to stay away from her. She wanted to urge the stallion into a gallop, but wasn't confident she could remain astride the horse at that pace, especially bareback.

The man smiled menacingly, revealing several black and rotting teeth. "Ah, my pretty, you must be lost; the castle is the other way."

"I am not going to the castle," Sarah replied firmly as she eased the stallion on.

"What's the hurry then?" he said, stepping in front of the horse and blocking the road.

"I ask you to move." Sarah tapped the horse's ribs with her heels, moving him forward.

"No need to be rude." He reached up with a dirty hand and grabbed a rein, pulling the horse to a halt.

An anxious feeling rose from the pit of her stomach. "I insist that you release the horse at once!" she shot back loudly.

"All in good time, my lady." He held tight to the rein. "Perhaps we can reach an agreement that will benefit us both." He smiled again at her. "The roads are dangerous at night. 'Twould be a shame if somethin' happened to you. So I propose you give me somethin', and in return I'll make sure no one else bothers you."

Sarah struggled to control her shaky voice. "I have no money, and so I ask again, let go!"

"Now, no need to be rash; as I said before, it's unsafe, dangerous for a maiden like yourself, and I'm not askin' for money, just your company for a short while."

A sickening feeling swept over Sarah, followed by anger. "You speak of my virtue, sir. Now step aside!"

"I warn you, if you won't give it, then I'll take it." He reached his hand behind his back and pulled a long knife from under his shirt.

Panic flooded over Sarah and she dug her hills deep into the stallion's flanks. "Hyaw!" she yelled, sending the horse bolting forward right into the startled man, ramming him in the shoulder and knocking the breath from out of him. He gave half a cry, but it was cut short as he was sent sprawling backward onto the street so fast that the knife flew from his hand and landed with a clank. Concentrating on staying upright, Sarah let the horse bolt down the street unrestrained.

Outside the village, the horse slowed to a walk on the dark road, which was lit only by the moon and filled with eerie shadows and unearthly sounds from the trees. Sarah gathered the reins with shaking hands and began to cry as she thought about what almost happened. Wanting only to reach the safety of home, she directed the horse to pick up the pace.

In her own small stables, Sarah thanked the large black horse and closed the gate to the stall. She looked at her hands. They still shook, and she couldn't help but start crying again. She ran to the security of her house and up to her room, shutting her door tightly behind her, and sat on the bench beneath her open window. The moon and stars lit up the sky, and as she pondered how there could be such beauty on such a terrible night, she laid her head on the windowsill and watched the road until she drifted off to sleep.

Sarah stirred halfway between sleep and consciousness, not fully realizing where she was or what was going on around her. There was a noise—some kind of sound growing ever so slightly louder, something she wasn't quite fully aware of as she drifted in and out of sleep until the sound drew nearer, bringing her to her senses.

She raised her head from the windowsill. The moon softly illuminated the dark landscape below. A carriage creaked as it rolled along, approaching the manor. The lantern swinging from it cast its light over the four white horses pulling it. As she stared at it, the memories of the night came flooding back to her.

She peered through the night and could make out two persons sitting atop the driver's seat, with two more men on horseback following behind. She squinted, trying to make out who they were.

"Alex," she breathed out quietly when they were close enough that she could see the royal sash across the chest of one of the men sitting atop the carriage. *Is he only returning Clyde and Felicia, or am I partly the reason for his presence?*

She looked at the two men following on horseback.

Or perhaps they have discovered the missing stallion and have come to . . . She stopped herself from finishing the thought, knowing that what she had done might be considered as stealing from the royal family.

The carriage rolled to a stop below her window. Alex looked up at the manor; the light from the carriage lantern illuminated his somber face. Sarah quickly ducked to the side of the window, hiding herself from his view. She watched from the corner as he climbed down and opened the carriage door, then assisted Felicia and Clyde as they stepped out. Felicia babbled on about the spectacular display of fireworks, and graciously thanked His Highness for his services. The words of their idle conversation drifted up through her window, and Sarah leaned against the wall until she heard Alex's voice, then peeked out again. He simply bid them a good night and climbed back up on the carriage.

"Please, Alex," Sarah whispered. "Please don't leave."

He didn't hear her, but she silently continued to beg him. *I need to talk. Please, I need to explain. Even if you never call on me again—give me a chance to explain.*

She stepped in front of the window, letting the moonlight land on her, almost crying out to him, but she held her breath. She waited. Alex nodded to the driver, who cracked the reins, and the carriage started moving.

"Please Alex," she whispered. "Look up." Nothing. Tears sprang to her eyes, blurring her view as the carriage rolled back down the road.

She turned and threw herself on her bed, burying her face in the covers. The door shut downstairs, and the footsteps and muffled voices of Clyde and Felicia ascended the stairs. Felicia's door shut and the sound of Clyde's footsteps came down the hall, stopping momentarily outside her door, and then continued on again until she heard the door to his bedroom close.

"I'm glad you didn't knock, for I wouldn't have answered," she muttered. "Although, if it were Felicia, I'm quite certain you wouldn't have gone to bed until you knew that she was home safe. But then again, I'm not Felicia." Tears began to dampen the bed where her face lay, but she was careful not to make any sounds that would be heard beyond her room.

Eventually Sarah slipped out of her extravagant gown and into her nightdress, but sleep didn't come easily. The night seemed endless for her as she drifted in and out of awareness, and visions of Alex and Felicia sitting on a garden bench, Chad's evil stare, and a filthy man coming at her with a knife infiltrated her mind. But for the most part she had lain there, feeling only a dull ache, tossing and turning as she watched the moon move across the sky and eventually out of view from her window. At last the darkness faded and a soft glow edged the horizon.

"The stallion!" Sarah bounded out of bed. "I could still return it and no one would be the wiser," she said as she pulled an old gown from her wardrobe.

She certainly didn't want Clyde to find out about the stallion, and she needed to hurry if she was going to get him out of the stable by the time Joshua made his rounds doing chores. "If I leave now, with God's speed, I'll be home before Clyde awakens. Hopefully after the late night, he'll fancy sleeping in," she told herself as she pulled on her dress and tightened her lacings.

She gripped the wooden handle of her brush and started pulling it through her hair while she eyed herself in the mirror. "I should at least be presentable . . . Oh, what have I gotten myself into? And what will I say when I come sauntering up with the prince's stallion?" she mumbled. "Perhaps they will send for the prince himself. Yes, it would only make sense—after all, it's his horse. And that would at least give me the chance to explain to him."

She felt a spark of hope. She laid the brush on her dressing table and took one last look in the mirror, then snuck out on tiptoe, hurried down the stairs, and fled through the house.

The sun was just casting its first rays across the gardens, sending shimmers of light glistening across the blanket of dew that covered everything, and she kicked the little droplets of water from the grass with the toes of her shoes as she walked.

It was quiet inside the stables except for the sound of the stallion shifting his weight in the stall. He looked at her when she came in, and she saw the recognition in his dark eyes. He swung his head up and down as if he were giving her permission to approach him.

So magnificent, she thought. *Truly a horse fit for a king. It's good that Joshua turned our horses out to pasture. It would be a shame to have them stalled next to such a grand specimen.*

"Look at you, almost too big for the stall, yet so gentle. You saved my life last night, you know." She sighed. "What I would give to own such a horse!"

She began to open the stall, but as she did so her gaze strayed down the length of the building, and then she gasped. Her hand flew up to stifle a scream, her heart now pounding rapidly against her chest. She stared at the two feet extending from the last stall. At first she feared that the filthy man from the village had somehow followed her, but the boots were too well made to belong to the thug she had encountered last night, nor did they look like the boots she'd seen Joshua wear.

Who was this? She dared not move or make a sound. Yet there was no movement from the unidentified boots. *Dead? Sleeping? Perhaps drunk or unconscious? And who?*

19. THE STRANGER IN THE STALL

Sarah waited, but the body that protruded from the stall remained still. She listened closely and could almost make out the deep rhythmic sound of the man's breath. *Good—not dead. At least I suppose that's good.* Quietly she inched over to the stall and peeked over the wall.

Stunned, she gripped the edge of the wooden plank and pulled herself closer to get a better look.

"Prince Alexander . . . sleeping in our stables?" she uttered with bewilderment.

His eyes flickered open and the instant he saw her he sprang to his feet. "Sarah! I . . . I didn't expect to see you here . . . in the stable," he stammered, running his fingers through his hair to dislodge some loose strands of hay.

"And I didn't expect to see *you* here, Your Highness." She looked away as he finished brushing off his shirt and breeches, straightening himself. "Have you been here all night?"

Alex ignored the question and walked past her to the stable door, looking around to make sure they were completely alone.

"Before I explain," he said, "I need to ask you something, my lady. I need to know . . ." He broke off without finishing.

"You may ask me anything, Your Highness, and I will answer you truthfully."

He turned from the doorway and faced her. He seemed uneasy, his blue eyes deep in thought, his expression solemn. He beckoned with his hand, then walked outside behind the stables, out of sight of anyone who might come out from the manor.

Sarah followed him to a small clump of trees. She felt a few drops of water on her arm and looked to the sky. The sun had now fully appeared over the horizon, and no clouds were overhead, but more tiny drops of water landed on her cheeks. "A sun rain," she said softly. That's what her mother used to call it. Sarah loved the rain, but even more so, she loved rain that fell from a nearly cloudless sky through bright rays of sun. Apparently Alex didn't mind it either. He did nothing to shield himself from the light drizzle, but tipped his face up to it and ran his fingers through his hair.

She walked over to where he stood and watched the rain glisten on his hair and face. She could tell he had something to say to her, but it seemed as if he didn't know where to start.

Sarah dropped her gaze. "How long have you been here, my lord?"

"All night," he admitted.

Surprised, she brought her head up to look at him again, "But I saw you leave . . . You came back? But why?"

"I needed to talk to you," he said simply.

Sarah looked around again. "I see no horse or carriage. How did you come?"

"I walked."

"You walked?" The words came out sounding more alarmed than she had intended them to. "And at night?"

"You were nowhere to be found last night," he explained, "and upon returning from taking your family home, I found my stallion missing from the stables and knew."

Sarah blushed.

"It was better that I walked," he said, "to make sure you weren't along the roadside somewhere, to go slow enough and quiet enough not to miss anything in case . . ." He stopped again and looked at her. "That horse could have thrown you, or someone could have attacked you . . ." The words caught in his throat.

"It's a dangerous thing you did, Your Highness."

"And you, my lady. That's why I came afoot."

Sarah couldn't believe what she was hearing. Prince Alexander, with no concern for his own safety, had taken care to make sure that she hadn't fallen in harm's way. Again she thought of the filthy man she'd run into in the village. The thought still terrified her. "Did you encounter any danger, my lord?" she asked carefully.

"I am yet in one piece, as you can see," he said with a wry smile.

She suspected his humor covered a darker truth. Attacks on the roads at night were more common than not. She eyed him carefully. He wore the same clothes as he did last night, except the sash bearing the royal crest had been exchanged for a sword and dagger that now hung from a leather belt buckled around his waist, and she wondered if they had recently been used.

"Sarah, before I say any more I need to know . . ." He paused, focusing his attention on her. "Tell me, what is your relationship with Lord Chad?"

"I have no relationship with his lordship. Not now."

"And last night?" Alex held his breath.

"Last night was his doing, not mine. Believe me, I don't wish to be associated with Lord Chad. He has revealed a side to me that I'm fearful of, and as of last night I have severed any connection with him."

Alex took in a deep relieving breath and sank to his knees as if he no longer had the strength to stand. "I thank God," he said quietly.

Startled, Sarah took a step back, looking down at him. "I don't understand, Your Highness."

After a long moment, Alex slowly pulled himself back up on his feet. "I have spent most of my life trying to keep what is rightfully mine from Lord Chad's coveting hands. He's my cousin, and for that I love him, but he is hungry for power." Alex clenched his hands into fists and looked away for a moment. "In some cases, I've allowed him to manipulate situations and take from me without consequence." He looked back at Sarah. "But last night was too much. I can't tell you how I felt when I found out he'd been courting you. And then to see him with you. . . . I knew he would try to win you over again once he knew that I was your escort. Your affection is most precious to me, and to see him try to take that away. . . . My heart was ripped from me last night when I saw you together."

Alex slowly dropped his gaze. "But then I did no better. I caused pain to someone I hold dear." He reached out and took Sarah by her hands and then looked into her eyes. Light rain fell on her cheeks and clung to her eyelashes, and tiny droplets of water formed in her curls, then ran to the ends and dripped off, only to have other drops form in their place.

He took a deep breath and then knelt down again on one knee. Still holding her hands, he looked up at her. "Sarah," he said softly, "I have come to apologize and ask your forgiveness. You sought me out, and I turned you away. You are a remarkable lady and have been nothing but honest and kind to me . . . and I mistreated you. I'm truly sorry. I prayed all night that God would spare me the pain of losing you. I ask your forgiveness, and if you would . . ." He paused, taking in a deep breath. "I renew my petition to court you. Please say yes."

Sarah fought to control her emotions. "You can't be sure of this."

"I can. As God answers prayers, I am sure."

"Prayers?" Sarah asked as she tugged at his hands to get him to stand up. "And I pray that you won't lose your crown over this."

Alex stood back on his feet. "Are you still worried about that? You think I would lose my crown if I were to marry you?"

Sarah nodded.

Alex pulled her close to him. "I won't lose the crown over my choice of whom to marry. I'm not betrothed to anyone. It's my choice, and I won't have that right taken from me."

Sarah took a deep breath, trying to sort out her thoughts. Alex continued to hold her hands and watched her patiently.

Finally she spoke. "Only yesterday I learned you were the crown prince of Calibre. It's a great responsibility for anyone who walks by your side, my lord."

"A responsibility I know you'll handle well or I would never have asked."

"I thank you for your confidence."

"So . . . do you offer me at least a chance?"

Sarah nodded. "Yes."

Alex's eyes lit up and he took her in his arms and pulled her to him. "That's all I ask—a chance to prove myself to you." Slowly and with some hesitation he lowered his head, and when she didn't pull away, he softly pressed his lips to hers.

20. MEN OF DARKNESS

Market Street was empty this morning, even more so than Chad had expected, and it did nothing to improve his foul mood. Last night hadn't gone anything like he had planned. He rubbed his burning eyes. It was all starting to wear on him. He had come to Market Street in hopes of finding something to raise his spirits. A woman who would dote on him and flatter him—or at the very least, something to buy—something new and exotic that would bring him some sort of pleasure, even if it was short-lived. But all his hopes had faded. The streets were empty. The vendors weren't out yet and the shops were still closed. The dancing and other entertainment had gone on late into the night, and he didn't expect to see a lot of people out this early. Perhaps a few shops would remain closed today, but this? His mood worsened and he regretted coming altogether.

Chad climbed off his horse and handed the reins to his escort. "Wait here," he told him.

The light rain that had fallen earlier left puddles in the middle of the street and Chad cursed when he stepped in a muddy pool, splashing his clean boots. "Blasted rain. No doubt it'll keep everyone in their pitiful houses today," he muttered as he moved to the edge of the road, trying to walk in the dry areas next to the shops.

He looked up and down the street again, looking for a pretty face. In his opinion there was nothing like the soft touch of a woman to bring a man out of a foul mood. But there was no one. Only a hunchbacked old hag who sat in front of a small shop across the street.

Chad cursed again. He considered the act of charming women an art, one that he thought himself very good at. After all, he never had to stoop to visiting a brothel, or paying a woman for her company. And why should he? Given time, he could make even the most austere women fall for him. He didn't steal their innocence from them, but found it more to his liking to charm them into wanting him, and then keep them dangling, which gave him the advantage.

He clenched his hands into fists. He had certainly not had the advantage last night. Felicia had been his next target for entertainment, but everything had been ruined. When Sarah had shown up wearing that stunning gown, he had second-guessed his choice between the sisters. But more than anything, he had been driven almost to madness by the fact that she was being escorted by his cousin Alexander. What could she see in him, anyway? The man would never fulfill his royal potential . . . He'd see to that himself.

His eyes narrowed as he looked down the street. His fists clenched tighter, digging his nails into the flesh of his palms. Hate welling up inside of him, he turned his face and spat onto the ground, then quickly walked farther down the road.

"Out of my way, you buffoon!" Chad growled at the man laying in his way. Without waiting for a response he swiftly booted the man, who let out a low groan but still made no attempt to move. "You disgusting, stinking animal!" He kicked the man again before stepping over him and continuing down the street. He walked toward an obscured doorway but paused before he entered as he noticed a rider in the distance. His face went white with recognition and he narrowed his gaze spitefully, then quickly ducked through the door and into the establishment.

The tavern was dark and he stood for a moment, letting his eyes adjust to the dim lighting. The room was saturated with the ripe smell of whiskey mixed with the stench of unbathed men. Looking around he counted five men, not including the one slumped over a table at the far end of the room. These were men who had no morals, men who had no families, or they wouldn't be found in such a place so early in the morning. He had come here for a quick drink, just something to ease his mood, but since he had seen the rider, he now had another idea. . . . He stepped farther in and raised his voice. "I seek to employ a couple of men." Heads turned in his direction. "It's not much in the way of work, but I pay well." One man waved him off and went back to his drink, but three others approached him.

Two came together, obviously friends. One was tall and bulky, a stupid-looking man, and his partner was short, thin, and wiry. Another man came from the shadows of the far corner, and his smell reached Chad before he did. He had long, greasy gray hair that hung tangled to his shoulders, and he looked as if he hadn't washed in years.

Putting the edge of his sleeve to his nose to filter the air, Chad said, "I have a problem." He lowered his voice and continued. "I wish to be rid of it."

"A problem, eh?" the wiry man said with a chuckle. "Who is it you want killed?"

Chad inhaled sharply at the man's forwardness and quickly glanced at the others to see their reaction. They stood quietly, still listening as if nothing out of the ordinary had been spoken.

Chad nodded to them. "I see we understand each other." He moved to the door. "If you will, please step outside with me for just a moment."

He ushered the men outside. They blinked and shielded themselves against the sun as if the very light would kill them. These men were truly creatures of the night.

"Now remember, I'll make it worth your while," he said and then raised his arm, pointing up the road at the man who had passed by on horseback moments ago.

The men looked at the rider and then recognition dawned on them. "Blimey, the prince?" the big brute said in a hoarse whisper. "Are you mad?"

"We aren't that daft," said the other. "I would sooner kill me own mother than take a try at the crown prince."

"I said I would make it worth your while," Chad broke in.

"Yes," said the big brute, "and at the cost of our own lives if anything goes wrong." He shook his head and turned to walk back into the tavern.

"You can do it yourself," said the other man, who then followed his friend back into the darkness.

Chad looked at the third man, who was rubbing his shoulder. He stared after the prince and then smiled at Chad, revealing his rotting teeth. "I remember that big black horse," he said as he rubbed at his shoulder more intently now. "We had a run-in, last night."

Chad looked at him, expecting an explanation and wondering if the man was sane.

"There's a place near the river that grows poison hemlock. The slightest bit put in his food or drink will kill him quickly. I will only need to—"

"No," Chad interrupted and the man scowled indignantly at him. "No. I wish him to have at least a fighting chance."

The man grinned. "That will cost more."

"Very well." Chad reached to his side and pulled his dagger from its sheath. "This was a gift from His Majesty the king"—he turned the blade back and forth showing the fine craftsmanship—"forged from the finest Damascus steel. The handle is carved from wood imported from Africa." He tipped it, showing the large ruby embedded in the end of the handle. "I'll give this to you now, and you'll have three times its value when the job is done. I don't want to know the details of how or when you'll do it, I just want him dead by the next full moon . . ." Chad's words trailed off, echoing in his ears, and he noticed his voice sounded strange and unrecognizable even to himself. He pushed aside the strange feeling, consoling himself with the thought that within four weeks, his cousin would be out of the picture. Slowly but deliberately, he handed over the dagger to seal the deal.

21. THE CROWNLESS PRINCE

Alex glanced bitterly at his father and then, fuming, he stood up and headed for the door. He couldn't believe what was happening. He thundered through the door, swinging it into the unsuspecting guard on the other side and sending the man almost tumbling to the floor. Without even an apologetic look, Alex stalked down the dimly lit hall of the castle, trying to put more distance between him, his father, and the rest of the men that made up the king's council.

"Alexander."

Alex cringed at the sound of Chad's voice coming from the room behind him. Ignoring his cousin, he walked on. Lord Chad was the last person he wanted to deal with now—and was no doubt the cause of all of this. The sound of footsteps running up behind him made him even more agitated. His muscles tightened and he gritted his teeth like a wild dog about to attack.

"Alexander," his cousin called again.

Chad's voice was sweet and calm, like he was talking to his best friend, but Alex knew better. Chad reminded him of the story his mother used to tell him of the wolf dressed in the sheep skin that would come right into the flock, undetected, free to kill as it pleased.

"Alexander," Chad said again, now right behind him. "Where are you going in such a hurry?"

Alex, not able to stand it any longer, spun furiously around to face Chad. "Why ask me where I go, what I do, or whom I am with, when you can ask your spies? And tell me, why does it concern you to know of my whereabouts?"

Chad's stunned look only lasted momentarily before he regained his usual calm composure. "My lord," he said easily, "whatever you do affects the whole kingdom." Chad began to fluff up the sleeves of his doublet. "You rushed out of the room so quickly, and I merely wanted to ask a simple question. One that all of us would like to know." Chad motioned with his hand back to the room where the king and the rest of his council still waited. "Which country do you plan to marry us to?"

Alex sprang forward, putting his face next to Chad's. "I will not marry into another country!" he said, sharply growling each word into his cousin's ear.

Chad took a step back. "You would go against the king's order?" he asked calmly.

"The king's order? Oh how you twist the truth!" Alex shot back. "It wasn't the king who proposed the insane idea of arranging an alliance— within a month!—through a forced marriage. Do you forget? Or perhaps you take me for a fool. It wasn't the king who initiated it, but his advisor— whose new son-in-law, I'm told, has recently been employed as head steward over your entire household."

Chad's lips tightened and his hand slowly moved to rest on the hilt of his sword. "Surely you're not suggesting that I have influence over His Majesty's advisor because I employed his son-in-law."

"What man wouldn't feel obligated to return favors to the one who bestowed such a grand position on his only daughter's husband?"

Chad's calm disposition was now gone. His brow furrowed and his eyes narrowed as he waved a hand toward the room behind them. "I'm not responsible for this," he said angrily. "Our lands on the northern border are at war. Sacrifices must be made. I, myself, have agreed to lead your men back to Midway—a suicide mission that could've been avoided if you had stayed your ground! Why your father ever trusted this matter to you escapes me! Which country you choose to marry into will affect us all. It will determine how long I am to be in those God-forsaken, lawless border lands pursuing an impossible victory!"

"You selfish dog. I pity you that you must leave the comfort of your pampered surroundings and sacrifice a little to serve our country for a time."

"And I pity you, that you too must sacrifice for the country," Chad echoed sarcastically.

"I will not be forced to marry!"

"No. You're right," Chad said calmly, regaining control of his voice. "I am selfish, but not you. You won't forsake your own country, your own obligations for selfish desires. No, you won't let your people down. You will do what the council has demanded and will marry to form an alliance, or . . ." Chad stopped himself.

"Or what?" Alex asked, demanding an answer. "Renounce the crown?"

"No, you'll choose to marry. My only regret is that I'll be at Midway and won't be able to see you wed. However, I will do one small thing to ease your burdens. Although she may be unsuitable for you, I know you have feelings for Miss Sarah Benavente, so I will personally take care of her for you, and you may be at ease knowing she'll be well loved by me."

Alex gritted his teeth and sharply turned away. Willing himself to move, he strode down the hall in great, heavy strides, trying to put some distance between himself and Chad before he lost control and did something that he would later regret.

"Alexander," Chad called after him. "I advise you to be cautious. These are dangerous times, and one can't be too careful. It would be a shame if something were to happen to you."

* * *

Sarah pushed open the kitchen door and slipped through but still wasn't quick enough. "Ned," she called after the cat that had darted into the room between her legs. "Come back! You need to stay outside."

"I'll get him, mistress," Catherine said. "The master has been asking for you. Bade me to tell you as soon as you came in. You'd better hurry. He is in the study."

Clyde was hunched over his writing desk frantically scrawling on some paper and paused for only a moment when Sarah walked in. "A letter came for you earlier," he said, pointing to a parchment envelope sitting on the edge of his desk.

Sarah picked up the letter and ran her finger across the royal crest impressed into the red circle of wax. "This seal has been broken," she said examining it more carefully.

"I never noticed," Clyde grunted without looking up. "The carrier must have been careless."

"Perhaps," Sarah said, not believing his excuse.

Clyde dipped his quill sharply in his ink bottle, sending small splatters of black ink onto his desk. "I'm very busy, so take your letter and go."

Sarah crossed the hall into the parlor, and sat in front of the window before pulling the letter out of the envelope.

Dear Sarah,
I have a matter that I greatly desire to discuss with you.
Please make yourself available this afternoon. I will come as
soon as my duties allow and expect to arrive at your house at
half past two.

Sincerely yours,
Alexander

Sarah read the letter two more times, but couldn't make anything more of it. What could he possibly want to discuss?

"Oh! Pardon me, miss," Amanda said when she came bustling into the room, carrying a dingy cloth. "I thought no one was in here. I'll return later to do the cleaning."

Sarah looked at her, puzzled. "Wasn't this room cleaned yesterday?"

"Yes, my lady," Amanda said with a smile, glad that her work didn't go unnoticed. "But the master requested that it be done again. Says an important visitor is expected today."

Sarah raised her eyebrows. "Did he tell you who?"

"No, my lady. Would you like me to go inquire of him for you?"

"No." Sarah ran her thumb across the broken seal of her letter. "I think I know who he's expecting to come." Sarah tried to guess at the motives behind her stepfather's unsolicited screening of her private letters. Although she didn't feel like it was beyond Clyde to pry into her relationship with Alexander, she still felt like it was somehow connected to the only other man who would care about her involvement with the prince—Lord Chad. Just then she thought back to the ball and remembered that Chad had mentioned that he had been doing business with Clyde lately. Perhaps it was time for her to do a little snooping of her own. Abruptly she stood up. "Amanda, do you know what time it is?"

"Yes, miss. Just past one."

"Good. Have Joshua saddle our horses, and fetch me from my room in half an hour."

"Very well, my lady."

Sarah was ready when she heard the knock on her door. "Come."

"It's half past the hour, miss," Amanda said. "Joshua is waiting outside with the horses."

"Thank you." Sarah grabbed her cloak and pulled it on. "I suspect that around half past two, Clyde will be asking where I am. At that time—but not sooner—please let him know that Joshua and I have gone to collect this month's rent from the tenants."

"Very good, my lady."

Sarah rushed down the stairs and stood outside of Clyde's study, reviewing her plan in her mind. If her stepfather was expecting her to meet the prince in an hour, he wasn't going to let her take his financial ledger and go running off to collect rent. She needed to get the book without him knowing. She had recorded the rents and other miscellaneous items in his ledger before, and it had never been of much interest to her, but today she wanted to take a closer look at his finances. If Clyde had been doing any business with Chad, she wanted to know exactly what it entailed. Sarah drew in a deep breath and calmly walked into the room. The scratching of Clyde's quill immediately stopped and he looked up, his eyebrows deeply furrowed.

"Yes?" he demanded. "What do you want?"

"Oh, nothing," she said easily. "I was just wondering if you minded if we dine early this evening. Perhaps about four?"

Clyde's eyebrows raised slightly with interest. "Is there a reason to be eating so early?"

Sarah moved closer to the writing desk. "No reason," she said slyly as she glanced down at his desk, eyeing the stack of sealed letters. The top one had been addressed to Lord Chad Hill.

Clyde sat back in his chair and tapped his finger on his chin.

Sarah suppressed a smile, knowing that he was coming to the conclusion that she hoped he would—that perhaps her expected guest might like to dine with them. And at this very moment, Clyde was probably thinking that it would give him the perfect opportunity to eavesdrop, and perhaps to glean any useful information, or influence some political matter.

A broad smile spread across Clyde's face. "I suppose it would be fine. What is Cook making?"

Sarah frowned. "A stew, I think. I was hoping she'd fix that venison dish that you told us about when you went to Darthing last month. I remember you saying it was fit for a king."

"Yes, it was a grand meal. Not much else I remember about that night," he said with a laugh. "The wine was good as well."

"I think Cook would do the meal justice if you would give her the details of it as you remember."

"Very well," he said, pulling himself up to his feet.

As soon as Clyde had passed her, she quickly leaned over his desk and snatched his ledger from under the pile of papers. At the same time, she tried to make out Clyde's writing on the unfinished letter. She could only make out a word here and there—something about the war, Midway, and loyalties to a certain unnamed leader. Holding the ledger behind her back, she followed Clyde out of the study, and when he was engrossed in describing the venison meal to Cook, she slipped out the back door to where Joshua was waiting.

What was Clyde up to? Who was the leader that was mentioned in the letter, the one to whom they should remain loyal? Clyde must not have mentioned names for fear the letter might be read by someone other than the intended recipient. The secrecy piqued her interest, and Sarah thought about going back inside to see if she could get a better look at the unfinished letter, or at the very least, find out to whom he had addressed it. But then she thought better of it. If she went back in now, it could ruin her plans.

She quickly thumbed through the ledger, not knowing what she was looking for. Everything looked normal as she scanned the recent entries on one page and then another, working her way back through the month. But then her heart seemed to jump up into her throat as she flipped to a new page. A rather large amount of money was marked down as being paid to Andrew Smyth, one of the king's advisors. What business would Clyde have with Andrew Smyth? Sarah flipped the pages back to the previous month. There she found another entry for the same amount of money, but this entry showed that it was money paid to Clyde from Lord Chad Hill. She quickly scanned back farther, and again found the same pattern of entries. One paid out to Andrew Smyth, and one paid to Clyde for the same amount from Chad. She flipped back through more pages, finding similar entries for the past four months.

"You ready, miss?" Joshua asked impatiently.

Sarah looked up abruptly. "Oh, uhh, yes. Yes, we had better get started," she said, tucking the ledger under her arm as she moved over to the horse and allowed Joshua to help her mount.

Sarah decided to take the back way, which would take them past the the northern fields collecting rent from the tenants and ending at the Scotts' cottage, then following the road up in front of the manor. They went quickly, accepting the payments, marking it in her stepfather's ledger, then moving on to the next cottage. Finally, Sarah thanked Mrs. Scott at the last cottage and trotted her horse all the way up to the crossroads. She kept her eye on the manor as it came into view and strained to see if there was a carriage or any horses in front, hoping that she had been quick enough. "It must be close to half past two," she said out loud.

"Yes, my lady. We wasted no time in collecting today," Joshua called from behind.

She pulled on the reins and stopped in the middle of the crossroads looking both ways. She had a clear view of the manor now and could see as far in the other direction as the bend in the road. "He isn't here yet," she said, letting out a long sigh of relief.

"What was that, my lady?" Joshua asked as he caught up to her.

"Nothing. Just thinking out loud." She looked down the road again. There was no sign of him. She was sure that Clyde was awaiting the prince's arrival, but Sarah wasn't about to receive Alex in the sitting room where Clyde's sensitive ears would be able to pick up every word spoken. But now she would have to depend on Alex's promptness if her plan was going to work. Clyde would be looking for her any moment now and she would be easy enough to find. It was well known that the prince had a reputation of arriving late to certain affairs, but she had a feeling that it was a matter of choice and not just a bad habit. On issues of importance, she suspected that he would have no problem with being prompt.

"Is something wrong, miss?" Joshua asked her.

"Yes," Sarah said stalling. "I think my horse is favoring his left foreleg. Will you check it for me?"

"Yes, my lady." Joshua swung down and squatted next to Sarah's horse and ran both hands expertly up and down the leg. "Nothing unusual, my lady. No heat, no bumps." He picked the hoof up and examined it for rocks and checked the shoe for fit. "Not even so much as a pebble. Step him out and let me see him walk."

She turned the horse down the road and let him walk.

"He looks fine to me," Joshua said. "If it pleases you, I'll take a closer look at him when I get him back to his stall."

Sarah wasn't listening to Joshua. She was straining to hear something else.

Joshua now heard it too. "Someone's comin'," he said just as three horses rounded the corner. Alex was in the lead astride his familiar black mount, and two guards were following.

"My lady," Alex said, riding up to them. "Tell me you're not leaving."

"No, I'm here to meet you," she told him, then turned to the surprised Joshua.

"Take this home," she said, handing him the ledger. "I'll be along shortly."

Alex waved to his two escorts. "You may go, too. I wish to speak alone with Miss Benavente. I'll meet you back at the castle. Please tell Sir Tyson I'll be there shortly."

Alex waited a moment longer as he watched the two guards reluctantly head back down the road, and when they were finally out of sight, he swung down from his horse and helped Sarah down from hers. He took her hand and held it. "It's good to see you," he said warmly. "And I'm glad you had the forethought to meet me out here."

Sarah nodded. "I thought it would be best."

"Indeed it is." Alex paused, gathering his thoughts, and then he began, "Sarah, I'm faced with a most difficult decision and I've spent many hours pondering what to do. I'm not here for your advice or opinion, but to ask for your support and respect for my decision."

Sarah braced herself. This didn't sound good. She gave his hand a squeeze to encourage him. "If I'm to support something, then I must first know what it is."

"Yes," said Alex solemnly. "But first you must know that our relationship did not influence my choice."

"Please, tell me. What have you chosen to do?"

Alex glanced around. "I tell you this in the utmost confidence that this conversation will stay between us and none other," he said, lowering his voice.

Sarah nodded.

"I share this with you because I want someone in whom I can confide, and there is no one I would rather confide in than you."

Sarah silently nodded again.

"I have chosen," Alex said even more quietly, "to relinquish my right to the crown."

Sarah gasped and pulled her hand away from his. It couldn't be. She loved Alex, but she wouldn't want him to give up the crown, even if it meant that they could be together. It was his birthright. She knew that some people didn't want him to rule, but he was capable of it and given the chance, he could be great. "But why?" she said, shaking her head in disbelief. "I don't understand. Why would you do this?"

Alex's eyes narrowed. "Let me explain," he said quietly, but with a more forceful tone. "This isn't something I've been rash about. I've been thinking about it for several months now, and I believe it's the best thing to do for the country. I was considering this option even before I met you. I've only been waiting for the right time to do it. A situation has recently come up, and now the time is right. I had hoped that the situation would change, that I wouldn't have to give up the crown, but unfortunately, due to the circumstances . . ." Alex shook his head. "This morning my father held a council and it's been required of me to marry, within a month, to form an alliance. Although this is not why I chose to cede the crown, it does give me the opportunity to do it without suspicion."

Sarah looked horrified. "So why would you do it?"

"Surely you must see, it is better this way. There are numerous people in the kingdom who already expect it will happen."

"But you shouldn't act so rashly because of the opinion of a few!"

"No," Alex broke in, "let me finish. Our country needs strength and unity now, and I can bring neither. You know my reputation. I was unpopular with some of our people before I made the decision to retreat from Midway, leaving it to the Austrians. And now many of our people have no faith in me." Alex quickly looked away, the frustration apparent on his face. "The time is growing near for us to take back Midway, and when the word gets out that I'm sending our soldiers back, there will be dissension. I risk a rebellion among my own people."

Sarah stood silent for a moment as she stared at Alex. "Then it is true? You are sending soldiers to take Midway back?" she asked, feeling a little out of place, as if she were intruding on something she shouldn't.

"Yes, I am sending them back." Alex tightened his fists and flung them in the air, scaring both horses. "I'd lead them back myself, but I can't lead our people when they have no desire to follow me! There has been an uprising and two attempts on my father's life since the fighting broke out. If he were to die and leave the crown to me, our country would be divided. There are so many people who oppose me that war would break out within our own country if I were crowned king. That would be an enormous advantage for the Austrians."

Sarah took a step back. "But think to whom the crown will fall. This is exactly what Lord Chad wants. He said something to me at the ball, I must tell you—"

"Nothing you can tell me about Lord Chad will surprise me."

There was a long silence between them. "But Lord Chad intends to take—"

"Lord Chad," Alex broke in, "is a great leader. The people love him. His men are loyal to him."

Sarah shook her head, thinking of what Lord Chad had told her at the dance. "His intentions aren't honorable."

"Perhaps, but our people will be united behind him."

"No! You can't do this!" Sarah cried.

"I have no other option! I won't have our people divided! Lord Chad may not have the purest intentions, but our country will be greater with him as the future king."

Now Sarah was beginning to understand the intent of the letter Clyde had been writing. Lord Chad was the leader that was obtaining the loyalty of Clyde and other merchants and businessmen. Could this be related to the transactions in Clyde's ledger? Why would Chad give money to Clyde, who would then give it to the king's advisor? She grew sick as the answer dawned on her. Chad had been bribing the king's advisor and covering it up by funneling the money through Clyde. "Your Highness," Sarah said, "Lord Chad is conspiring to steal the throne."

Alex turned and angrily kicked a rock, sending it bouncing down the road. He turned back to Sarah, hurt filling his eyes. "He has done nothing that I can prove against him."

Sarah clenched her teeth together. If only she had kept the ledger, she could've shown Alex proof of Chad's treason. Perhaps she could return to the house and get it. She could somehow take the letters from Clyde's desk as well. "Come with me now. I may have something of interest."

"No!" Alex said sharply. "I'll hear no more about Lord Chad's devious-ness today." He turned away from her, dropping his head. "I can't even get my own soldiers to return to Midway under my command," he said, exas-perated. "They refuse to serve under me. I'm sending Lord Chad because it's he whom they trust and will follow."

"Perhaps he'll perish in the battle," Sarah said hopefully, then covered her mouth with her hand. "I'm sorry, that was wicked."

Alex shook his head. "No need to apologize, but also no chance of that wicked little thought coming true," he said calmly. "They will succeed. I have planned every detail so carefully, there's no chance of failure."

Sarah walked over to him and took his hand in hers. "If you say our soldiers will succeed, I believe you. Therefore you must wait until after Midway has been recaptured and then the people will see your leadership has been wise and trustworthy. Once they see the outcome there will be no division."

"Perhaps, but if I'm to give up my right to the throne, I must do it by the time the council has set for my marriage. Under the cover of avoiding a forced marriage, there will be few objections brought up. It's the only way for a smooth transition with as little dissension as possible. Our country will be strong and united behind a new leader in whom they trust. He'll then come back from Midway triumphant, and with such a grand win, the people will be heartened and strengthened along with our troops. We'll secure our borders and return our nation to peace."

"I beg of you," Sarah pleaded. "Don't do it. There must be another way."

"I see no other option."

"I do," Sarah said softly. "You can marry as the council has requested."

Alex's eyes flashed with anger. "I will not! All I ask is that you respect the choice I have already made."

Sarah saw the pain in his face. It wasn't easy for him to admit that his own people would rather have his deceiving cousin crowned over him. She wanted to tell him about Clyde's ledger, about the letters, and what Chad had told her, but she could see that such small details wouldn't change anything. He wanted his people united, and it was more likely to happen with Chad as ruler instead of him. "Please forgive me. I do respect a man who makes his choices based on the good of others, and I see that your intention is for the welfare of your people. It's your choice, and I respect that, but please consider withholding your action until the month's end."

"Yes, I will do that. And I am pleased to have your support," he said, pulling her close. "Now I must go. I have people waiting for me at the castle. I'll send word to you when I can come again."

"Soon?" she asked.

"Soon," he said. He pulled her to him and held her tight for a moment, then brought her hand up to his lips and softly kissed it. Then he mounted his horse and rode away.

Sarah mounted her horse, turned toward the manor, and saw Clyde, red-faced and panting, as he ran down the road toward her, his big body wobbling back and forth with every stubby stride. He walked the last few steps, clutching his side and gasping for air.

"What . . . were . . . you doing?" he demanded as he took in big gulps of air.

"I'm sorry, didn't Amanda tell you? Joshua and I went to collect the rents."

"I see, and had a secret rendezvous with the crown prince while you were at it!"

"It would've been a rendezvous had the prince known he was to meet me here, but since he was unaware of my plan, I would call it more of an ambush!" Sarah kicked the horse and let him run all the way back to the manor, leaving Clyde sputtering and cursing.

Once inside, she went to her room and waited for Clyde. Surprisingly, it wasn't a long wait. She had been there for only a few minutes when he appeared in her doorway, still red-faced and breathing hard, with drops of sweat streaming down his brow.

"I have one question for you," he growled. "What did you and the prince discuss?"

"It's of no concern," Sarah said calmly.

"Anything that involves you concerns me. I will ask one more time. I demand that you tell me—what was said between the two of you?" This time his voice rose dangerously.

"I will not speak of it," Sarah said firmly. "It's a private matter."

Clyde was turning more purple than red now, and his veins were standing out on his neck and forehead. "That's your answer?"

"It is."

"Very well," he said. "You've made your choice, and so must I." Clyde silently turned and walked out of the room.

Something was wrong. Clyde never retreated until he got what he wanted. Surely she hadn't heard the end of it. And what should she do now? Was she supposed to wait for him to return? Or was she free to go about the rest of the day as normal? Or perhaps she should leave. Her instincts told her that something was building, and it would be best if she weren't around to see what it was. She heard a horse galloping away and hurried to her window. It was Clyde, but where was he going so quickly? Again Sarah had the thought that she should leave, but then she thought better of it. What could he do to her now, anyway? Surely he couldn't make her talk if she refused. At last she decided it was best if she just stayed in her room.

She lay back on her bed and rehearsed in her mind everything that Alex had told her.

* * *

Clyde pulled his horse up sharply near the turn in the road and dismounted. Prince Alexander wasn't anywhere to be seen, but that wasn't who he was looking for. He followed the path through the trees until he reached the large protruding oak stump marked by the plucked weed that lay across it, indicating that his counterpart was already there. He looked around, scanning the thick foliage

A moment later, Lord Chad silently emerged from behind a large tree. Although they were completely alone, he darted nervous glances in every direction. "You're late," he whispered, walking up to Clyde. "I've been here for more than half an hour."

"The prince himself decided to take a visit out my way," he explained. Chad's eyes lit up, so Clyde hurried on to curb his excitement. "I didn't discover anything. He met with Sarah out on the road and he was gone by the time I got to them. Sarah refuses to tell me what they discussed."

Chad's face fell momentarily but then he shrugged. "It doesn't matter. I have an idea of what he might have been telling her. But that's another matter. Now, how about we get on to our business?

Clyde nodded, trying not to appear too anxious. He had been curious about the secret meeting and hoped that it would prove as lucrative as others had in the past.

Chad stepped closer. "I have a proposal," he said, lowering his voice. "It's about the judge's position. I know that you are aware that there are several likely candidates besides yourself vying for the position." He paused and then drew in a deep breath. "But what if I were able to guarantee you the judgeship?"

Clyde smiled. This was even better than he had hoped, but still, he felt the need to proceed cautiously. "What will I have to do for it?"

"Not much." Chad said with a shrug. "I'll even pay you for it."

Clyde stroked his chin thoughtfully. "Go on."

"I only want Sarah's hand in marriage."

Clyde took a step back in shock. "Sarah?" he said, not able to withhold the venom in his voice. "I thought your intentions were toward Felicia!"

"The situation has changed, my friend."

Clyde waited for further explanation, but he knew a man of Lord Chad's stature didn't need to explain himself. Still the offer was contemptible.

"I remember you mentioning that your sister could take Sarah in for a time. I think that might be best while we work out the details. Anyway, think about it, my friend." Chad patted him on the shoulder then turned to leave. "I will come by later with the contract written up and the money."

22. MURDERER IN THE SHADOWS

Alex was deep in thought as he rode his horse slowly back to the castle. He was perplexed by Sarah's reaction to his decision to renounce the crown. He had expected her to respond more positively than she had. He thought that she would've been happy at his refusal of a forced marriage, and he had been caught off guard by her concerns over Chad's fitness to rule. He hated to relinquish the crown to his cousin. He knew how ambitious and devious Chad could be, but he felt that deep down Chad was really a good leader and would ultimately do what was best for the country. So why did he feel so awful now? He wasn't as certain about his decision now as he had been a few hours ago.

He leaned forward and patted the horse's strong neck. "I wish you could advise me."

Suddenly Alex felt exploding pain as a heavy branch slammed into his back, knocking the breath out of him and sending him flying from his horse. The stallion whinnied and jumped forward in fright. Just as Alex felt himself hit the ground, a man jumped on top of him. Alex gagged as he breathed in the man's stench, then he rolled, throwing the person off. Quickly he jumped to his feet and spun around to face his assailant.

The grubby man growled through yellow gritted teeth as he looked at Prince Alexander. The stench of his unwashed body hung in the air and Alex took a step backward to avoid the smell as much as to avoid the attacker. The man shifted his weight from one foot to another as he waved a dagger back and forth in front of him. Suddenly, he lunged, dagger outstretched.

Alex jumped to the side dodging the blow, but a sharp stinging sensation ripped through his arm as the man swung around wildly and sliced the blade through the his sleeve. Ignoring the pain, Alex sprang forward, grabbing his attacker's arm just as the dagger came around again for another strike. Using the man's momentum, Alex pulled him forward and sent him sprawling hands first down on the road.

Alex turned, facing the assailant again. He could feel the blood oozing from his arm and the coolness of his sleeve as it stuck to the fresh wound. Quickly he assessed his injuries without looking at them. He guessed that the cut wasn't too deep.

Slowly the man stood up and his lips parted into a caustic grin. Alex crouched, his arms open, poising himself for another attack. He narrowed his gaze on his opponent and noticed that the man's eyes kept flickering to the side. He refused the urge to turn and look at what had caught the man's attention, but in an instant, he took stock of his surroundings and a low branch on the edge of his vision told him that he was dangerously close to a tree.

The man sprang forward again, swinging the dagger. Alex could have easily jumped back, but not wanting to risk backing himself against the tree, he jumped forward, narrowing the distance between them. The man's eyes widened in surprise at the unexpected move and Alex took advantage of the flicker of hesitation to grab the man's arms and pull him forward, propelling him into the tree behind them.

A loud crack sounded as the man's head collided with the trunk, but Alex didn't let go. Instead he jerked the man back, swinging him around and sending him sprawling again onto the road. The dagger fell between them, and Alex grabbed it quickly, picking it up long before the other man had recovered.

He could see the man wasn't going to come up with another attack, so he held the dagger in his hand and examined it. It was made of Damascus steel, and the handle bore a large red jewel. Alex had seen this dagger before. Could his cousin really be this foolish? He glared fiercely at the man, who was sitting on the ground, nursing his skinned and bleeding palms.

"I beg you, please have mercy on me!" the man cried as he cowered below Alex. "I was coerced. I was forced to do this. I knew it was a bad idea. Please, please have mercy on a poor man," he begged pitifully.

Alex tried to think quickly. Should he confront his cousin with this man? Or should he send the man away and deal with the problem another way?

* * *

Sarah drew her attention to her window as Clyde rode back up to the manor. She had never learned what errand he'd hurried off on, but nothing seemed unusual until a couple of hours later when a carriage pulled up and stopped in front of the manor. No one got out. The carriage was empty, and Sarah had a foreboding feeling about it. Within minutes, she heard voices coming up the stairs.

"No, Father! Please, please don't do this," Felicia cried.

"I will deal with my family as I see fit," he boomed.

Just then her door flung open. Clyde stood between Amanda and a distraught Felicia, the smell of apple brandy hot on his breath. "Sarah, pack your trunk. You're leaving!"

Sarah stared dumbfounded at him.

"My sister has sent word that she'll take you, and given your disregard for my authority and recent unladylike behavior, I think it best!"

Felicia, now sobbing, turned toward Sarah. "This is all my fault. If I hadn't started seeing Chad. . . . Why didn't I confide in you, Sarah? I don't want you to go—I want us to be friends again, like before Mother . . ." A sob caught in her throat, then she turned to her father, reached out, and grabbed his arm. "Please don't send her away, Father," she begged.

Clyde shook off Felicia, ignoring her pleas. "You'd better hurry," he said to Sarah. "The carriage is waiting for you."

Felicia, unable to control her sobs, turned and ran down the hall to her own room. Amanda came in wringing her hands and began to gather things from around the room. Clyde watched for a moment and then left, closing the door behind him. Sarah still stood, staring blankly out the window at the carriage, not sure of what had just happened.

"Oh, Miss Sarah," Amanda choked. "What are we to do?"

"I must go," she said numbly as she began handing things to Amanda, who carefully packed them into her trunk. She went through her possessions, gathering and packing them mechanically, and sooner than she had expected, she was done.

There was a knock at her door. "Enter."

Joshua poked his head in. "Come to carry your trunk down, miss," he said quietly.

"I'm ready." Sarah pulled her cloak on and looked around the empty room. It didn't look that much different. Her bed and dressing table were still the same. Her bench and dressing screen were still there, but they all seemed so lonely somehow, as if they too didn't want her to go.

"I'm ready," she said again and walked out into the hall. Felicia came out of her room with tears still streaming down her face, and Sarah realized they had never been apart for any extended time. She reached out and took Felicia's hand. "Please don't cry. I'll be back soon."

Felicia shook her head. "Mother never came back . . . and now I'm losing you. I'll be all alone. Please don't go. I'm sorry. I'm sorry I've been so jealous of you. Please try to come back soon. I'll try to persuade Father as well. I know we can be the sisters Mother wanted us to be."

Sarah looked at Felicia. They had grown apart, and she too knew their mother would be disappointed if she could see what had happened between them. They would have to put aside their differences if they were going to revive their friendship. She said a quick, silent prayer for strength, then reached out and took her sister in her arms in an attempt to heal the wounded feelings between them. "I'm sorry too, Felicia. Things will be all right. You'll see. And I promise I'll come back."

Felicia wiped her face and nodded. They walked down the stairs together and out to the carriage where Clyde stood waiting.

Catherine came rushing out of the house and handed Sarah a wrapped bundle. "Sliced meat and bread for your trip," she croaked. "We'll watch after Pooka and Ned for you, my lady," she said, wiping her eyes. "Please come back to us soon."

Sarah gave Catherine a hug, then turned to Amanda and hugged her. At last she embraced Felicia, struggling to hold back her own tears. Then she straightened herself up and with all the dignity and grace she could muster, silently walked past Clyde, and climbed into the carriage. With one last wave out the window, she was gone.

Inside the carriage, she choked down her emotions. Everything had happened so fast. She looked out the window one more time. Clyde had already turned and was walking into the house; the others stood there waving to her through their tears.

Sarah sat back and numbly wiped her face as the carriage gently rocked back and forth on the road. After several minutes the carriage slowed down and moved off the edge of the road. Sarah's heart jumped. Had Felicia convinced Clyde to call them back? She slid over to the window and peered out.

The carriage had moved over to make way for the small party of riders coming their way: Lord Chad and five men following in his shadow. Chad was smiling and playing with a large purse that hung from his belt, and as he passed, he turned his head and looked into the carriage. Sarah ducked back, but it was too late. He'd already seen her. And the image of his face was burned into her mind. He wasn't surprised to see her leaving in a hired carriage; the look on his face was one of understanding and satisfaction. Sarah sat back and tried to make sense of what was going on as the carriage picked up speed again and rolled down the road.

* * *

Clyde sat in his room, his glass of brandy nearly empty in his hand. His stomach knotted with frustration. Sending Sarah away would only temporarily relieve his discomfort. He still had to make his decision about her. Swallowing the last of his drink, he set his glass down and looked around the room. There was no evidence that anything feminine had ever been there, but the room still brought back memories of Miranda. Lovely, vivacious Miranda, the only woman he had ever dared love. The woman who couldn't love him back. The woman who was so devoted to Sarah, the daughter of another man! Why couldn't she have loved him as much as her previous husband?

He let out a groan and flung his arm in frustration, purposefully knocking two books from the nearby table and sending them flying across the room. They hit the floor with a heavy thud, accompanied by a lighter tap of metal. Slowly he stood then walked over and pushed the books aside and bent to pick up Miranda's heart-shaped pendant.

Clyde stared at the necklace for a moment. Miranda didn't think that he knew what it was, but he knew. He knew by the way she would finger it when she was pensive or after quiet moments when he tried to express his love for her. He ran his fingers over the heart, still staring at it. Miranda had taken it off when she got sick and was never able to put it back on; it had lain there on the table, forgotten. Forgotten, overlooked, and neglected—just like him.

His breath steadily grew more rapid as the anger built inside him. He closed his hand tightly around the pendant as if to squeeze Miranda's attachment from it. They could've been happy together, he knew—if it hadn't been for her previous life and the attachments that came with it.

All at once he flung the door open and raced down the stairs and out the back door to the stable. Inside the dim building he stumbled to the anvil and leaned heavily upon it, his body quaking with rage. Then with quick deliberation he placed the necklace on the anvil and with one fluid motion grabbed the hammer and, letting out a cry of grief, he swung the heavy tool over his head and brought it down, shattering the pendant with a sickening clang. He stared at the pieces for a moment, then dropped the hammer into the dirt, swept the remains of gold onto the ground, and walked outside.

With his anger only slightly abated, Clyde trudged around the manor and saw Lord Chad riding into the yard.

23. THE MIDNIGHT ENCOUNTER

Alex paced one more time around his bedchamber and paused by his open window to look out at the cloudless night. He had waited long enough. Walking quickly to the door, he pushed it open just wide enough to stick his head out and look around. The lamp outside his door had gone out and he blinked, trying to focus his eyes in the darkness, as he searched the blackened hallway for the guard. Since the attack on him a couple of days ago, his father had ordered guards outside the sleeping areas of the castle until the matter was investigated, but Alex didn't need an investigation to know what was going on. His eyes adjusted to the darkness and he spotted the guard, who was passed out, lying against the wall. The large pitcher of ale Alex had given him earlier lay empty next to him.

He slipped out the door and silently crept down the long dark corridor. It made him feel foolish, sneaking down the halls of his own castle like a thief. Suddenly he stopped and cocked his head to one side. He could hear the soft sound of padding feet moving toward him from an adjacent hall. They were soft and light, most likely those of a woman. Alex quickly backtracked and ducked around the corner, then pressed his body back against the cold stone wall as he listened more carefully. The footsteps were moving away. He peered around the corner and from the faint flicker of her candle, he recognized his mother's chambermaid.

Again, he cautiously crept down the long corridor, now with heightened senses, determined to go unnoticed. Along the way he had to duck into two more passageways to avoid being seen, and once he even slipped into a small room where he found a maid sleeping. He was surprised that there were still people walking around at this hour of the night. Finally he peered around the last corner at the guard who lay motionless only ten steps in front of him. He smiled grimly at how this simple technique had worked with both guards. The large empty pitcher was turned completely upside down next to the now unguarded door, and Alex moved forward, stepping over the large man who was sprawled across the hallway.

Putting his ear to the door, he listened, then budged it open a crack. Warm air flowed out, hitting him in the face. He waited, listened, and pushed the door farther, then farther still until he was able to slip through. Then he closed the door as slowly as he had opened it.

His eyes were already used to the darkness and he could easily make out the dim outline of the room. A hint of red embers lay dying in the fireplace, and the air was thick and stifling. A huge tapestry hung on one wall, not merely a decoration, but keeping the heat in as well, and the window next to it was completely hidden by a heavy curtain. A large four-poster bed took up most of the room, and the curtains that hung around it were pulled back, allowing full view of its sleeping occupant.

Alex stepped onto the thick rug and moved closer until he was hovering over the dark figure in the bed. Slowly, he pulled the dagger from his belt and turned it over and over in his hand, rubbing his thumb over the large embedded ruby as he eyed his sleeping cousin. Chad was a deep sleeper. Alex had spent many nights with him when they were boys and he'd always found it hard to wake his cousin. Now it seemed unreal that he was standing over him with a dagger. What had brought matters to this? The past years ran through in his mind, ending with the image of the failed murder attempt by his cousin's hired killer.

Alex gripped the dagger, realizing that he could never kill Chad. He was, however, going to leave a lasting impression on his cousin. He looked around the room again and saw where Chad's clothes had been neatly laid out on the overstuffed chair by the fireplace. Quietly, he walked over to them and picked up Chad's long belt. With one sweeping motion, he cut it in two with the sharp dagger and then placed both pieces back down next to the clothes.

He turned and looked at Chad, who was still sleeping soundly, then quietly walked to the far side of the room. He pulled the chair away from the small writing table and put it next to the bed, halfway hidden behind the heavy bed curtain, and then sat down and waited. Normally Chad liked to sleep in late, but Alex guessed that it wouldn't be long before he would start stirring. Chad was a guest in the castle that night because in a matter of hours he would be assembling the one thousand men that would accompany him to Midway. The anxiety of it all was sure to have him up early.

Alex was right. As soon as the first soft light began to glow around the curtain that hung over the window, Chad began to stir. Alex leaned back in his chair and adjusted the bed curtain to conceal where he sat. Chad rolled over once, then twice, and then slowly sat up and groaned. He tossed the covers aside and dragged himself to his feet, and then shuffled over to the fireplace, cursing at the coolness of the room, and poked at the ashes with a long fire rod. Without finding a single hot coal, he hung the rod back in its place and grabbed his clothes. Groggily, he stepped into his breeches, almost stumbling in the process, and then pulled his shirt on followed by his doublet. Finally he reached for his belt. He grabbed one end and pulled it up toward him. As it came off the chair, the other half fell on the floor with a thud.

From his hiding place, Alex restrained a chuckle.

Chad stood there dumbfounded, staring at the piece of belt on the floor. Then he slowly leaned over and picked up the broken belt, looking carefully at the cut edges. If he hadn't been fully awake before, he was now. He spun around wildly, scanning the room.

Alex stood up and stepped out into the open, and when Chad saw him, he choked on his breath, stepped backward, and visibly went rigid as he recognized the dagger Alex gripped tightly in his fist. Instinctively his hand slipped down to where his sword would've normally hung, but there was no sword and no belt to hold it. There was nowhere to go, and even if he had time to turn and grab his sword where it lay against the chair, it most likely wouldn't do him any good. Alex was quick and very skilled in the art of fighting. Chad opened his mouth to speak, but his mouth was dry and no words came out.

Alex approached until he stood just outside striking distance. "Cousin," he said, trying to control the anger in his voice. "These are dangerous times. One can't be too careful. It would be a shame if something were to happen to you."

Chad's jaw dropped open as he recognized his own words being thrown back at him, and sweat instantly beaded on his forehead.

Slowly Alex pointed the dagger toward Chad. "You seem to have misplaced your dagger. It would be awful to find yourself without it when you need it most."

Chad felt his face flush. "Y-yes, my lord," he stammered. "I have been careless."

"I trust that you'll be more careful from now on." Alex turned to leave the room, setting the dagger on a table as he passed.

Chad followed his cousin to the doorway, his heart pounding. He looked dumbfounded at his unconscious guard sprawled across the hall.

* * *

Several hours later, Alex walked to the corner of the small council room where a desk and several bookshelves stood. Removing a false panel at the back of the desk, he pulled out a large piece of rolled-up parchment and placed it on the table in the center of the room. He clasped his hands behind his back and walked around the room again, then back to the window to watch the crowd growing beneath him in the courtyard. Downstairs, the great hall was full of men and women of the court awaiting his father's official order for the soldiers to depart for Midway. Throngs of people were gathering outside to bid farewell to the soldiers. Alex couldn't help but wonder whether there would have been such support if he were the one leading the army. Somehow he doubted it.

He watched as a group of men from the sword maker's guild came into the courtyard, proud to see their own craftsmanship playing a part in the soldiers' attire. He eyed a group of nobles. It was hard to recognize people in the crowd when looking down on them, but he recognized a few, one of which was Clyde Berack, who kept tipping his round face up when he laughed. He was now deep in conversation with Lord Bening. He guessed that the dark-haired young lady with them was Felicia. It was Sarah whom he wanted to see, but he couldn't find her in the crowd.

A heavy knock on the door brought his attention back to the more pressing issues at hand.

"Lord Chad to see you, Your Highness," the guard said as he stepped aside to make way for Chad. He closed the door behind them, leaving them alone.

Chad bowed politely to his prince and then stood quietly, almost humbly. For once Chad had nothing to say, no sarcastic comments to offer. Alex relished the moment and turned to look out the window to hide his smile. He wanted to savor the moment, but this small triumph over his cousin was not quite what he thought it would be. There was a sense of bitterness and remorse that accompanied it. After a long moment, Alex moved to the large carved wooden table and sat down, then motioned for Chad to take the seat across from him. He did so quietly, avoiding eye contact with Alex. Neither one mentioned their encounter earlier that morning, but it was obviously still on Chad's mind. It wasn't something that he would likely forget—or forgive—anytime soon, but there were more pressing matters at hand now.

"You've been called here because I need to inform you of our plan of attack before you depart," Alex told him.

Chad smiled, the look of humility dissolving instantly on his face as he tipped his head back and chuckled. "Plan of attack? You have one? I must admit I'm quite surprised. Why did you wait until now to disclose these plans?"

Alex calmly eyed Chad. "It's best, at times of war, to guard your points of strategy and only reveal them when necessary, as I'm sure you know."

Chad shook his head dismissively. "It's easy enough to sit here in your castle planning your so-called strategies, but it's quite another to implement them in the thick of the battle."

Alex forced a pleasant smile and said calmly, "Why do you try to undermine everything I say? Have you come to listen and do as I command, or shall I dismiss you now, and turn control of the army over to my commander at Midway?"

"Ah yes, your trusty commander, Don Jordan. You can't trust that fool. Every time I try to correspond with him, all I get are reports on the weather at Midway. You know there's no one better to lead the army than me, and if you don't mind, I do have my *own* plan of action."

The smile fell from Alex's face. "No!" he said forcefully as he thumped both fists on the table. "I will not allow you to do some fool thing, risking lives when you know nothing of the situation! You will execute my plans exactly, or I'll remove you from command!"

Chad waved a hand in disgust. "Didn't you receive the report regarding your leadership? Your decision to go back to Midway has been met by outward objections from people all over the kingdom. It also stated that *I* was the acceptable choice to lead the troops back so that *I* can take care of the problem that you created—to clean up your mess!"

Alex's eyes narrowed as he leaned over the table and spoke in a low voice. "You think that because you command these men, you command the crown. But let me remind you, Cousin, that I'm still the crown prince of Calibre, and therefore have the power to remove you from this position. Do you wish to be relieved of your post?"

Chad glared at him. "No," he finally admitted.

"Then I suggest that you pay very close attention to what I tell you."

Defiance flashed in Chad's eyes but he simply nodded.

Alex sat back in his chair, keeping his eyes on his cousin. "My plan was laid out completely before I left Midway a month ago and has worked perfectly thus far. If you execute it as I tell you, you'll not lose a single man in battle." Alex stood up and grabbed the rolled parchment that he had taken from the secret compartment in the desk and spread it out, revealing a detailed diagram of Midway.

"I have studied Midway and know every inch inside its walls," Alex explained as he flattened the map. "In addition to the front gate, there are four other weak areas where one can enter, assuming that they're not guarded. The first two are the guard tower windows, one here and the other one here." Alex pointed to two spots on the map. "Both towers are on the north wall bordering the river." He traced his finger along the line depicting the river. "The windows can only be accessed by crossing the swift waterway."

"I have heard of this. Precisely how high are the windows?" Chad asked, eyeing the map.

"It varies with the rise of the river. The river is elevated now, but the windows are still so high that a ladder or rope would be required to gain access to them. The walls are actually built into the river's edge. Therefore, building a bridge or platform below the windows is not possible."

Alex continued, ignoring the shaking of Chad's head. "The third vulnerable area is a small tunnel thfat runs under the north wall and dumps into the river here." He pointed again to a small mark on the map. "The tunnel is long and narrow and can only be traversed on hands and knees. This end of the tunnel is blocked off with bars, and with the heavy rain storms this season, the river has swollen and flooded the tunnel. It's been under water for the last six weeks."

Alex continued, "The last weak area is this section of the wall here." He pointed again to the diagram. "It's the shortest and most vulnerable section of the wall, but is still high enough that a ladder or rope is required to make it over, and it's on the south side, which borders the gorge. The cliff on which the wall is built is solid stone. However, as it tapers off and drops into the ravine, it turns to shale. The shale spreads the length and depth of the gorge. See how the walls are extended here? The only way to gain access to this south wall is by coming up from the bottom of the gorge."

Chad shook his head. "This is your plan? You can't expect me to take an army into Midway using any one of these ways. You're mad if you think those *weak spots*, as you call them, are accessible! It can't be done, I tell you!"

Alex sat back in his chair and grinned for what seemed to be a long time, pleased with himself. "Exactly, Cousin. How right you are. No army can get into the city through any one of those ways. Nor can any army get out of Midway using any one of those ways."

Chad looked up, bewildered. "What are you saying?"

Alex stood up, still grinning, and leaned over the table toward Chad. "I'm saying that what appeared like a retreat was actually a trap. And one that worked quite well."

"A trap?" Chad questioned. "I've heard nothing of a trap."

"Of course not. Do you think the Austrians would've come into Midway if there were any rumors of a trap?"

"But as a member of the king's council, I should've known."

"No one knew but me, Commander Jordan, and the king."

"But why such secrecy?"

Alex walked over to the window and gazed out. "The Austrians outnumber our men three to one. Our victory couldn't have been left to chance on the battlefield or we would've failed. The only way we could outmatch them was in strategy." He turned and walked back to the table, looking sternly at Chad. "You know all about spies . . . well, the Austrians have many. If a single word got out, our method would have been unsuccessful. Even our own soldiers had to be convinced that we were truly retreating. With our own troops believing in the farce, there were no suspicions on the Austrians' part. We had already withdrawn from the border, abandoning our fields and cottages. The Austrians knew that they outnumbered our army and that we had just gotten word that they were planning an attack on us while we were encamped in the fortress. It was a guaranteed victory for them, and we knew it. If they were to gain control over the bridge into the city, we would have had no escape, so they weren't surprised when we abandoned the fortress right before their attack."

Chad stared at the map in front of him again. "Yes, but they still outnumber us three to one, and now they have the advantage of occupying the stronghold."

"No. The advantage is ours. Every detail has been planned." Alex sat down in his chair. "You see, they took their entire army into Midway to celebrate our retreat, save eight guards posted on the bridge, and they failed to notice that I had left behind my commander and a large group of soldiers hiding in the forest not far away. Remember that last shipment of supplies that I had sent to me at Midway, the one full of wine?"

Chad stared blankly at him.

"You remember. It was the shipment that made you so enraged that you wrote letters to everyone on the king's council depicting me as a drunkard who thought I was on holiday instead of tending to matters of war."

Chad's face hardened, but he didn't speak.

"Well, contrary to what you might think, I didn't drink a drop of that wine. But it was well used on the night the Austrians came into Midway. I believe it was two days before they were sober enough to notice that their guards on the bridge had been replaced by our own men. By that time, it was too late. We had control of the only reasonable way out of the city, and those men who attempted to come out were killed. You yourself said that the weakest areas of Midway were not adequate to take an army through, and after several failed attempts, they came to the same conclusion."

"How long do you intend to keep them there?" Chad asked.

"By the time you and your men arrive, you may very well walk through the gate and declare victory. What few men that are left will be more than willing to surrender to you."

"How can you be sure of this?"

"One cannot live long without food and water."

"But when you retreated, you left all of your supplies there. The Austrians could live for months if they rationed it."

"I told you," Alex said calmly, "every detail has already been planned. Didn't you wonder why, with every order of supplies, I had several empty barrels shipped? It looked like we were getting large shipments of food and supplies, when in truth, we were just getting enough to survive. By the time we left, we had exhausted all of our supplies and those in the city. Even the granaries were emptied. All of the food barrels we left were filled with sand, save a top layer of apples, or flour, or salted fish, giving the appearance that they were full of food. They had drunk the shipment of wine within two days, and when they opened our barrels of beer and ale, they quickly discovered that they were poisoned. At first they lowered buckets through the guard tower windows to bring water up from the river, but the river water made them sick. The only source of drinkable water was through a well here." Alex pointed to a mark on the map. "I had it covered and then filled in. Then we built a stable over the top of it. The report I received last week stated that they had been digging, trying to find the well, but their attempts have been unsuccessful. Three shipments of supplies have been sent to their army, but Commander Jordan was able to intercept all of them. They're getting desperate, and the report I got earlier this week informed me that they've made several attempts to send men across the bridge or out the tower windows by night. But all have been in vain, as we have bowmen all across the river and at the bottom of the ravine. The report I received today stated that there has been hardly any movement reported inside the walls for the last three days. What soldiers are left will be weak and unable to fight. Your victory, Cousin, has already been secured."

* * *

The wind blew across Alex's neck and he shivered, pulling his cape tighter around him. It was an unusually cold morning and seemed to be getting worse. He directed his stallion up the village street, then turned and watched the hills behind him disappear in the approaching storm. He felt bad about spurring his horse on and leaving Philip, who was now undoubtedly caught in the raging storm. But Alex had been so upset when he left Sarah's house that he had grabbed the reins from Philip and bolted away before the servant could even climb on his own mount.

The wind whipped up behind him, the cobblestone street growing darker from the storm clouds and the dust that was being picked up with it. Ahead he could see the castle, but he wasn't going to make it there before the storm caught him. He tightened his eyes into narrow slits as the darkness settled around him and windblown dirt began to sting his face. His cape caught in the wind, whipping to the side and up under the horse's neck. The horse reared and Alex balanced himself, leaning forward in the stirrups. "Easy boy," he coaxed, but the horse came down hopping. He pulled tight on the reins, but the large stallion was still dancing, so Alex swung down quickly and gathered the reins. "Easy. Easy, boy."

The wind came up again and flashes of lightning slashed through the ever-darkening clouds. The horse pulled back, jumping to one side and then the other, as Alex did his best to stay out from under his hooves. Just as the horse was showing signs of settling, a large piece of loose brush tumbled up the street and caught between the stallion's hind legs. The horse leaped forward, knocking Alex to the side and pulling the reins from his hands as it bolted up the street toward the castle, leaving its rider with long, red burning streaks across his palms.

Alex grimaced, not from the painful leather burns on his hands, but from the thought of how the guards would laugh at him for arriving home after his horse.

He started walking toward the castle. He was nearing the end of the street when he heard a whooshing sound behind him. He turned and stared at a wall of rain rushing up the street. The few people that were still outside were now finding shelter in the nearest shops and he did the same, stepping through the door of a little shop just as the rain hit.

He watched the downpour for a minute before closing the door and turning to examine the little room. It was dark, but just enough light filtered through the window for him to see that the shelves were piled high with bundles of cloth and sewing supplies. Dresses hung along the walls, and a large man's cape hung by a doorway leading into a back room, which seemed even darker than where he was now. He stepped farther in and found a large piece of neatly folded black fabric. He ran his fingers over it and discovered a picture of a skull embroidered in black thread, almost unnoticeable on the black cloth. *A death shroud,* he thought.

He looked around the vacant shop again and noticed several red tunics carefully folded on a shelf. He stepped closer and saw that each one was embroidered with the unmistakable emblem of Lord Chad's house. *The shopkeeper must have connections with Chad,* he thought.

"Hello," he called. "Shopkeeper . . . is anyone here?"

"Just a moment, Your Highness," a scratchy voice called from the back room.

Alex squinted through the darkened doorway, astounded that the shopkeeper could see him let alone know who he was. "I'm only seeking shelter," he called back. "And then I will take my leave."

"I see," said the voice. "Do you seek shelter from the storm or from your troubles?"

Alex didn't answer.

"It doesn't really matter," the voice continued. "I'll provide both. But how peculiar that you come to me. I thought that I would have to seek you out, but here you are. You make it so easy for me."

"What's this you speak of?" Alex demanded, his hair now on end. He remembered how Chad had hired someone to kill him and thought that someone else might have been hired to finish the job.

"Your troubles. I'm going to get rid of all your troubles."

"And what do you know of my troubles?" Alex called as he drew his sword and cautiously stepped closer to the doorway that led to the back of the shop.

"Come! Come into the back room and I'll show you."

Slowly Alex stepped through the door, sword at the ready. Around a dressing screen the light from a small lantern illuminated the face of his mother's seamstress.

24. THE CONTRACT

Sarah sat on her bed, picking out all of the needlework she had done yesterday. Finally, she flung the piece of material toward the foot of the bed and flopped back against the feather pillows with an exasperated groan. "It will never be good enough to satisfy her!" she muttered to the empty room. Even though the room was tastefully decorated and comfortable enough, Lady Pendleton preferred dark, somber colors, and Sarah missed the familiarity of her own home.

Suddenly there was a heavy pounding at the main entrance of her aunt's house, and she wondered who it would be, though she assumed it would not be a visitor for her. She had been quite lonely since she had arrived, which seemed nearly a lifetime ago. Sarah counted back the days trying to remember exactly how long it'd been since she was forcibly shipped off to her aunt's for "proper tutelage," as Clyde called it. She pulled a pillow over her face to muffle the moan. "Nearly four weeks!" Four weeks and she hadn't heard of Alex relinquishing the crown or of any plans for a marriage. She ached for any news from him, and ached to leave this miserable place and be home again.

"How long am I supposed to stay here in this prison?" she asked out loud. Four weeks without being able to ride any of the horses, even though several in the stables were broke for the saddle. Four weeks without anyone her age to speak with. Lady Pendleton restricted her conversations with the hired help to only necessities. "Idle conversation encourages friendship. Hired help is just that—hired," her aunt had told her. The widow liked everything stuffy and formal. Not once had she heard any laughter, and the only music she'd heard was so depressing she'd have been better off chopping an onion. Thank heavens for her daily walks. At the very least they afforded her some time away from the rigidness of the household.

She sighed. She missed Felecia. She missed Alex. She missed her cat, Ned, and Pooka. She wondered if someone was taking care of the pony or if Clyde had gotten rid of him.

She lay back and contemplated the path she might take on today's walk when there was a heavy knock at her door. "Enter," she said forcefully, just as Lady Pendleton had taught her. She picked up the discarded piece of cloth just as the door opened and one of the servants came in.

The young girl curtsied. "Lady Pendleton requests your presence in the drawing room."

Sarah got up and hurried out of the room, knowing that her aunt would be cross if she thought she had dallied along the way. Outside the drawing room she paused to straighten her skirts and gather her composure. She opened the door and slowly walked in. "Good afternoon, Lady Pendleton." She walked over and gave the woman the compulsory kiss on the cheek.

"Ah, Sarah. I've the most wonderful news from my brother Clyde." She motioned for Sarah to sit across from her.

Sarah's heart skipped a beat, and she tried to read her aunt's face, hoping that the letter bore no news of Alex passing his stewardship to Chad. Perhaps Clyde was just writing that all was forgiven and that she could return home.

"Here—let me read you what he writes," her aunt said, then cleared her throat.

"Oh, here it is. This part says, 'I write to inform you that I have signed a marriage contract with Lord Chad Hill. He and Sarah shall marry when he returns from the borders. I would that you prepare Sarah with the most proper of manners and impress upon her the expectations and status of a lord's wife. We are most happy about this fortuitous reunion of theirs.'"

Her aunt folded the letter back up. "Then he goes on about other details you needn't concern yourself about," she said, not noticing Sarah's blanched face and vacant stare.

"When?" Sarah asked, her voice faltering.

"When? When Lord Chad returns. I suspect it will be in a matter of weeks, seeing that he has been gone for nigh four weeks now. Since the wonderful news that his plans were successful in retaking Midway, I suspect it won't take him long to secure the border. He'll be home before you know it." The woman spoke hurriedly. "There is much to do. We need to shop for your trousseau. Of course your mother left you some things, but if you're to be a proper lady, there will be special things that you require. And of course an appropriate wedding dress."

"A matter of weeks?" Sarah nearly choked. "But . . . Chad has been gone all this time, so how could Lord Clyde have signed a marriage contract with him?"

Lady Pendleton stiffened. "Your stepfather signed the contract the day you left. He didn't want to inform you prematurely. He wanted you to have time to learn how to be a true lady without your head in the clouds."

"Inform me prematurely? He determines my entire future and doesn't wish to inform me? How long have you known?" She trembled as she spoke, trying to control her anger.

"How long I have known is of no importance to you." Her voice was cold. "However, if you must know, this letter is the first I have received on the subject. I don't always approve of my brother's motives. Be that as it may, I do agree with his decision in withholding this information until now. You have improved greatly since you've been here, and I think you wouldn't have done so had you known beforehand of the match."

Sarah stood, quivering as she tried to suppress the anger and hurt building up inside her, yet she remembered what had been drilled into her over the past few weeks. "With your permission, I would like to withdraw."

Lady Pendleton nodded. "Before you go, I have a letter for you." She held out a sealed envelope. "It's from Felicia."

Sarah took the letter and quietly thanked her aunt before walking out of the room. As soon as the door was closed behind her she ran upstairs as quickly as she could. She entered her room and tossed the letter on her bed, then walked to the window and looked out. She couldn't stay here any longer; she had to be outside.

She flew down the stairs as fast as she could, her skirts hiked up to her knees. She didn't care who saw her and she didn't care if she did receive a vicious scolding from the old woman.

She ran out to the stables and called to one of the stable boys, "Which is your fastest horse?" The boy pointed to a lanky white Spanish mare, and grabbing a saddle, Sarah headed for the stall amid the protests of the young boy. Sarah ignored him and adeptly saddled the horse, then lowered the stall bar, quickly stepped up on the horse, and spurred him on through the open doors. The horse bolted and Sarah finally let the tears flow.

An hour later she returned and was amazed to find that her brief escape was still unknown to her aunt. The breeze wafting into her room through the open window soothed her as she lay on her bed and rubbed her fingers over a corner of the letter she held in her hand.

Dearest Sarah,

I hope that this letter finds you in the best of health. The house is empty and lonely without you and I miss you immensely. I must beg your forgiveness for my behavior. I have not been as a sister should be. It wasn't until you left that I truly realized the full extent of my actions. I have grieved deeply knowing that I have injured you and I pray that you can someday forgive me.

By now, I'm certain you know of the marriage contract that Father and Chad have signed. This also adds to my grief, for now I see the true, wicked nature of Lord Chad and it weighs heavily upon my heart that you would have to wed such a dishonest man. I have tried time and again to speak to Father about the matter. All he says to me is that it is settled. Do not despair. I have not lost hope and I will again try to persuade Father to see reason.

Of other news and good tidings, Ruth and John, the lower land tenants, are expecting their third child. They asked me to convey their best wishes to you. Amanda still takes Pooka to market every week. Father tried to sell him, but we convinced him of the pony's usefulness, and so he stays. Lord Chad is still at the border. It is not known when he will return, but it is confirmed that they were indeed successful at retaking Midway. Prince Alexander called shortly after your departure. He and Father spoke at length, but of what I don't know. It is rumored that he has now left the country. Some say he is searching for a bride so that our country may be bound with another. Others say he has fled his responsibilities and will relinquish the crown. I don't know what to believe.

Please forgive me for such a short letter. I have much to prepare as Joseph Savell is to visit again today. Do you recall Joseph? He's the son of Andrew Barnett Savell, one of the court's high judges. He requested a dance at the celebration, and he asked if he could call. Since then he has called twice every week. He is so very kind and gentle with my feelings. He is not as handsome as Chad or Prince Alexander, but that doesn't matter. He treats people with great respect, which, I daresay, is a lot more than Lord Chad has ever done.

As I close this letter I plead with you for your swift return. I know that Lady Pendleton doesn't always espouse the ideals our dear mother taught. However I pray that if you will comply with her, it will speed your return home to us. I ache to see my dear friend and sister again. It is so very lonely without you.

Love from your devoted sister,
Felicia

Sarah read the letter several times, each time hoping that it would somehow reveal more information, but to no avail. She was happy to know that Felicia had a suitor who would be kind to her, and it helped to know that her sister also understood her anxiety about the marriage contract. And she had forgiven Felicia. Her sister had probably been just as much a victim of Clyde's scheme as she was.

The man had changed since the death of his beloved wife. He had been so completely devoted to Miranda and didn't want to see her dreams die, and so Sarah understood why he had inserted Felicia into her failing relationship with Chad. Besides, it was more advantageous for him to put his own daughter into that relationship than his stepdaughter. Clyde obviously resented her, and the more she thought about it, the more she understood. What she didn't understand was why he had changed his mind and again wanted her to marry Chad.

She remembered the look on Chad's face as she was leaving the manor and had to believe he was responsible for persuading Clyde to change his mind. Could Chad have made a deal with Clyde for her hand in marriage, just so he could take her away from Alex? She recalled what Chad had said at the ball, and what Alex had told her about his cousin coveting all he had, and it seemed to fit. Chad would have her as his wife, and somehow he would find a way to have the crown too.

25. THE HATED RETURN

Sarah poked her head out the carriage window again to look around at the familiar surroundings. She had been scolded twice already for doing so, but now that her aunt had fallen asleep, she couldn't resist looking out at the world she had so deeply missed. She had such mixed feelings about returning home. She longed to be back with Felicia and to learn more about Alex, but returning also meant that her wedding was now only three days away.

The last two weeks had been miserable. After discovering her betrothal to Chad, Lady Pendleton had forced her to prepare for the unwanted union. As soon as they had gotten word of his return from Midway, she was told to pack and make ready to return home. Now here she was on her way back for the wedding. Her wedding. Sarah had tried to push for a later date, but Chad had written and insisted that it be done promptly. She tried to reason with her aunt by saying that their names hadn't been called out at church for the proper amount of time, but Lady Pendleton explained that their names had been called out every week since she had left, at Clyde's request. Sarah's efforts had been useless, and she would be forced to marry in a matter of days.

"They're here! They're here!"

Sarah stuck her head out the window again and saw Felicia waving her arms and jumping up and down in the courtyard. Catherine and Amanda came running out from the house and Joshua came running around from the back. Sarah put a hand on Lady Pendleton. "We've arrived," she said, gently nudging her aunt awake.

Clyde had come out by the time the carriage rolled to a stop, and he helped his sister from the carriage, leaving Joshua to assist Sarah.

Felicia ran over to Sarah and threw her arms around her, kissing her on the cheek. "You're finally home. I have missed you so much! Come, I'll help you freshen up," she said, taking Sarah by the arm. In a whisper she added, "I have so much to tell you."

Up in her old room, Sarah threw her traveling cloak over the dressing screen and then sat on the bed next to Felicia. "You said you had much to tell me. What news do you have?"

Felicia took Sarah's hand. "I'm afraid it's about Prince Alexander."

"Go on," Sarah said cautiously.

"I found out what father told him when he came to call on you right after you left. Amanda overheard their conversation and I pried it out of her." She paused, taking a deep breath. "Father told him that it was *you* who agreed to the marriage contract with Chad."

"What?" Sarah exclaimed with a gasp.

"That's not the worst of it," Felicia said solemnly. "Father then said that you had confided in him that the king had commanded Alex to marry within a month to form an alliance and that you didn't want to hinder the prince's duties, and that's why you agreed to marry Lord Chad and moved away until Chad returned from Midway."

Sarah shook her head. "I never told him such a thing! I can't believe it. What must Alex think of me?" Tears now brimmed in the corners of her eyes at the notion that Alex now thought that that she had betrayed the confidence he had given her. "Did Amanda tell you how Alex responded?"

"Just that he seemed hurt and angry. He stormed out of the house, jumped on his horse, and rode away on a dead run."

Sarah brushed at a single tear trickling down her cheek. "Has he returned? Has there been any word about him?"

Felicia frowned mournfully. "He hasn't returned, but there have been rumors. . . ."

"Tell me," Sarah said quietly.

"I heard that he left Calibre shortly after and made arrangements to meet a princess from another country, although I don't know which country. There've been so many different rumors as to which one. Lord Chad came over a few days ago to work out the wedding details with Father and I know it was wrong, but I stood outside the room listening. He said that the king and queen have received word from Prince Alexander. He has met a bride and he is bringing her back this very week." She let her words trail off. "Wedding arrangements for them are already in process."

Sarah brushed at another tear and nodded her head as she forced a smile. "At least he didn't relinquish the crown."

"Relinquish the crown?" Felicia asked, stunned. "Why on earth would he ever do such a thing? After the great success at taking Midway back, the entire war plot was made public and the credit is all going to Prince Alexander. Everyone was talking about it in town yesterday—what a great strategist he is and such a dedicated leader. You should see it, Sarah, even the shops have flags hanging with the royal crest on them and Prince Alexander's name. I must say that Lord Chad hasn't been pleased at all."

Sarah smiled slightly. "I am glad to hear that."

"Father wasn't, nor were several others. They've been protesting, saying that the credit is due to Lord Chad. There have been many reports that have slandered the prince, but it was discovered that someone has been paying to alter the reports so that they didn't favor the prince. The corruption has been going on for quite some time, and an investigation is being done. Nothing has come of it yet, but father will be the one looking into the matter."

Sarah raised her eyes in surprise, so Felicia continued. "Lord Chad announced that Father was awarded the new judge's position and will start right after the wedding. He's already been paid an advance. Chad gave him a large sum the day you left, and I saw him give Father some more money when he was here the other day."

Sarah gritted her teeth. *So, Chad killed two birds with one stone. He handed the judge's position to Clyde and with a token payment, secured his innocence in the investigation and bought my hand in marriage.* "And I'll be forced to marry this evil man," she said quietly.

"What?" Felicia asked curiously.

Sarah shook her head. "Nothing. The investigation may be impeded, but at least Alex will retain his right to the throne." She paused for a minute. "And what have you heard about my wedding?"

"Oh Sarah, I wish there was something I could do to stop this marriage."

"So do I," Sarah said, looking at her sister who now had tears in her eyes as well. "Oh, don't fret, Felicia. After all, it was mother's wish that I marry Lord Chad."

"Mother had no idea how devious Lord Chad really is," Felicia said sternly. "You know that if she were here right now she wouldn't allow this to happen."

Sarah nodded. "I know. If there's a way out of this, then I'll find it. Now tell me what you know."

"I'm afraid I don't know much more than you. However, I did hear that you're to be presented to the king's council the day after tomorrow. Chad mentioned that it's a tradition for council members to present their bride to the rest of the council. Perhaps you could take that opportunity to make a plea."

"Perhaps," Sarah said thoughtfully.

"You're also to stay in the castle that night and on the next day, you'll be prepared there for the ceremony. Then Father and I will come and escort you to the church."

"I don't think I can go through all that," Sarah admitted. "Maybe I could run away and—"

"Sarah! No!" Felicia exclaimed.

"I know," she said patting Felicia's hand. "I won't run away, but I will make a plea to the king's council."

* * *

With hopes of somehow thwarting Lord Chad's plans, Sarah spent hours searching the manor for her stepfather's ledger, and for any letters that might hint at Chad's involvement in his conspiracy against Alex, but nothing could be found. She knew she couldn't make a case against him without proof. No one would believe her. And once they found out that she really didn't want to marry him, they would simply think that she was accusing him to stop the wedding. With no evidence in hand, she arrived at the castle with only her determination to somehow get out of the marriage contract.

"My lady, it's not customary for guests to arrive near the stables. It would be far better to take you to the entrance," the steward said after Sarah insisted on stopping the carriage.

"No!" she said, her reply sharper than she had really intended. "No, thank you. I need the walk to clear my head. I'm not feeling quite myself. But thank you for your concern." The man nodded, gave a slight bow, and then waved the carriage on, leaving her to walk the rest of the way.

Sarah hadn't seen Chad yet, but she knew that he would be there to present her to the council, and she only had an hour left to gather her thoughts of what she wanted to say to them. She pulled her skirts up around her ankles so that she could step without soiling her gown as she walked past the stables. If she hadn't been so intent on her thoughts, she would've paid more attention to the conversation between the two men who were just around the corner of the building.

"Do you think she'll be pleased?"

"Pleased? I think she'll be overjoyed. At the least I hope she will."

Sarah should have recognized the voice of the second speaker, but she was preoccupied with her situation and her desire to convince the council that they should allow her to withdraw from the marriage contract.

As she hurried around the corner, she ran right into one of the men. "I beg your pardon! How very clumsy of me." Strong hands reached out and steadied her as she rocked on her heels. She looked up at the man that she had unintentionally assaulted. He was about her height, perhaps just a bit taller. He had shoulder-length golden hair, and the sunlight brought out the slightest kiss of red in it as he took a step backward. His eyes were an intense blue and they lit up as a smile spread across his face.

"Are you all right?" he asked her.

He had a thick accent that seemed familiar to her, but in the moment she couldn't place it. "Yes, thank you," she said, staring at the young man in front of her. "I beg your pardon, but you seem very familiar to me. Perchance, have we met?"

He grinned broadly, turning to someone that was just out of Sarah's sight, and asked, "Alex, should she know me?"

Her heart leapt at his name, and then she noticed Prince Alexander standing not far behind the well-dressed stranger. He was staring at her, his face completely expressionless.

She curtsied deeply, "I beg your pardon for my clumsiness, Your Majesty. Forgive me for interrupting." She didn't wait for a reply, but picked up her skirts and practically ran to the gated entrance of the inner court. She had hoped the walk would clear her mind, but seeing Alex had only served to unsettle her even more. She hurried inside the gates and paused to catch her breath and gather her composure. Alex was the last person she had expected to see.

Half an hour later, Sarah stood in a parlor adjacent to the council room and waited, her thoughts still on Alex. The members of the council were now coming in and she watched them as they all filed past her into the large meeting room. No one spoke, but they nodded, acknowledging her presence, and then moved on. She hadn't realized there were so many people involved in the council, and as time passed, she was thankful that she had chosen to wear her dark red gown, which didn't show the water marks left from her perspiring hands. The king entered and paused, looking into her face, and then offered her a kind nod of his head. She curtsied deeply and gave him a pleading look, but it went unnoticed and he turned to join the others in the council room.

A couple of other men filed past her, deep in conversation, and following behind was Chad. Sarah's stomach tightened with a sickening feeling as he approached her with a calculating look on his face. He walked around her, looking her up and down with his dark, brooding eyes, as though he were appraising an item he wanted to purchase. Standing behind her he leaned in, pressing his body up against hers as he grabbed her arms and restrained her from moving away.

"Why aren't you wearing that exquisite blue velvet dress?"

She didn't answer.

"No matter. You're just as beautiful as I recall. You'll make a pretty prize for me yet," he said, not bothering to whisper.

Sarah's heart sickened and she began to tremble.

"Lord Chad. The king wishes a word with you. It's best not to keep him waiting."

Sarah's head shot around to where Alex stood stone-faced in the doorway.

"Soon, Sarah, you'll be mine." Chad pressed in tightly to her, emphasizing the ownership of his last words before releasing her. Then walking past Alex, he glared hatefully at the prince and strode confidently into the crowd of people in the other room.

Sarah stood before Alex, visibly upset and trembling with fear. She wished he would take her in his arms, or at the very least say something that might soothe and quiet the panic welling up inside. He did neither.

After Chad had disappeared into the other room and they were alone, Alex spoke. "It might be a while before you are called in. Is there anything that you wish me to convey to the council?"

Sarah lost her composure and dropped to her knees, trying to choke back her tears of frustration. She didn't want to be there, knowing that Alex would be marrying another, and she was betrothed to his enemy. Her whole life would be filled with misery if she married Lord Chad. She couldn't help but imagine that life and the countless awkward moments when she would be in the presence of Alex, and how she would be forced to watch as Chad tried to come between Alex and the crown.

"My lord," she begged. "Please don't let this happen. Please tell the council that I don't love Lord Chad. Please tell them this is a mistake. I don't want this, with all of my heart and soul I don't want this."

Alex reached his hand down to pull her up, then spoke quietly. "It pains me to see you so distraught, my lady. If it is not your wish to marry Lord Chad, please tell me, what *do* you want?"

Sarah looked at him with beseeching eyes. "What I want is not possible."

Alex's voice became softer still. "Sarah, tell me."

She looked into his face. "It would not be proper—I understand that you are engaged."

He studied her face for a moment as if he wasn't sure what to say. "More or less," he finally replied tentatively. "But I need to hear something from you . . . I was told that it was *your* choice to marry Lord Chad."

"It's not true. Nor did I break your confidence by telling Clyde any of what you told me. That must've been Chad's doing."

"Thank you for that," he said in a whisper. "I assure you, Sarah, I will do everything within my power to ensure your future happiness." The prince looked as if he were considering saying more when a man walked into the room and Sarah recognized him as the handsome blond-haired gentleman she had bumped into near the stables.

"Am I late?" he asked hesitantly.

"No," Alex replied, motioning him to come over.

"Sarah, may I introduce Prince Michael Don Delacor of Kyrnidan. Michael, this is Miss Sarah Antonellis Benavente."

A small jolt ran through Sarah at the introduction of Prince Michael. It wasn't common for royalty from different countries to get together unless they were attending to certain matters, and she fearfully wondered if Prince Michael was Alex's future brother-in-law.

The young man smiled sweetly at her, then excused himself and walked into the room where the others were.

"Sarah, it will be a few minutes before you're presented. Please don't worry—all will be for the best." He bowed respectfully and walked into the other room, leaving her utterly alone.

Sarah looked around the empty room, then eventually sat down in one of the overstuffed chairs and tried to force herself to relax. It wasn't long before she heard whispers coming from the hallway and then someone appeared in the doorway. It took her a moment before she recognized the woman as the seamstress that had made her ball gown. Behind her was a tall gentleman Sarah didn't recognize.

The old woman wore a large, dark shawl, and it dangled to the floor as she leaned over and kissed Sarah on both cheeks. "Sarah, my dear, it's been such a very long time. How are you?"

Sarah was confused at the woman's presence there, and stumbled over her words. "Uhh . . . fine . . . very well, I thank you."

"I fancy that you were not expecting to see me here," the seamstress said. "Although I am here quite frequently, sewing and altering items for Her Majesty. But never mind that. I'm here, and that's all that matters." She turned back to the gentleman that had followed her into the room. "This is one of my old friends, Mr. Moylan."

Sarah turned her attention to the man, seeing him for the first time. He was tall and thin but had broad shoulders. His dark hair was intermingled with silver, and although he smiled approvingly at her, she could see that his brow was creased with worry.

He bowed to her. "Sarah, it's a great pleasure to meet you," he said with an accent.

She smiled up at him and nodded.

"Sarah and I met a couple of months ago," the seamstress said. "I made a gown for her to wear to the centennial celebration."

Sarah confirmed the statement with a nod and the seamstress continued.

"Oh, and what a gown it was, and it fit perfectly if I do say so myself. Do you remember when I was measuring you in my shop? I measured your shoulders and I saw the birthmark on your shoulder. It certainly was distinctive."

Sarah nodded again with a touch of embarrassment and saw the man's eyes widen in interest.

"Birthmarks are certainly important," he said. "They qualify a person as unique. Would you mind if I took a look at yours?"

Sarah raised a hand to her chest, her mouth open in shock.

"I apologize, my lady. I mean you no harm," said the gentleman. "Carlina here"—he motioned to the seamstress—"said it was on your shoulder. Ladies in my country often have gowns that expose their shoulder, so to me it didn't seem an offensive request. I certainly don't wish to cause you distress. Perhaps it would help if I explained that I've taken a special interest in birthmarks lately and have looked at hundreds. Forgive my asking again, but I would very much like to see yours, and I assure you, I will be quite discreet."

Sarah didn't say anything but glanced between the tall gentleman and the seamstress. "I don't know whether I can be comfortable with this," she finally said.

The gentleman nodded and sat quietly for a minute as if he were contemplating something significant. "I see," he said gently. "Perhaps if you could think of me as a friend, the request would not seem so odious. I would like to offer you something as a token of friendship."

"What are you saying?" she asked.

"Well, I see you are here waiting to address the council for something. Perhaps I could assist you in that. I spent many years of my life as a royal advisor and am proficient in matters of debating law."

Sarah studied him thoughtfully. "I wish to be released from a marriage contract."

The man nodded. "I believe I can help you with that. My opinion does have some influence on several of the members in there. I'll do what I can for you." He paused, then added, "Would this be considered a sufficient favor to ask a small one in return?"

Sarah let out a long sigh, but seeing this as her only chance, she nodded in agreement and turned around, allowing the seamstress to move the edge of her gown down just enough for the gentleman to look at the birthmark.

He reached up as if to touch it but refrained from running his fingers across the thick red scar. "That is a special mark indeed." He began to blink rapidly, as if something had gotten in his eyes. "Please excuse me," he said with a bow, and then hurried from the room.

Sarah pulled up the shoulder of her gown and sat quietly, wondering at the man's eccentric behavior. She looked at the seamstress, who just sat down next to her and patted her hand. After a few minutes the man returned, completely calm and collected. He sat down next to Carlina and they fell into a light conversation. Sarah was just realizing that the two shared a similar accent when she noticed the man was addressing her.

"Sarah, would you tell me about Miranda, please?" he said.

"Miranda?" she asked in surprise. "My mother? I don't understand."

He was slow to respond. "Because I knew her very well a long time ago in Kyrnidan."

She stared at him, not quite certain how to respond. She hadn't even known that her mother had ever been to Kyrnidan. She had never talked about that country or any friends she might have had there. Sarah was just about to question him when the door to the council chamber swung open and a steward entered the room. "Sarah Antonellis Benavente," he called out.

Sarah stood, her nervousness returning, and she desperately looked toward the seamstress and the gentleman and wondered if he had really meant what he said about offering to help her get out of the marriage contract. But how could he? He didn't even know any of the details. She began to consider bolting, but then the gentleman stood up and with a smile of encouragement, took her by the arm and led her toward the council room, the seamstress following behind.

26. THE LOST SECRET REVEALED

Sarah was relieved that she didn't have to enter the room alone, and to her surprise, the council didn't question her two escorts. She put her hand on her stomach to settle her nerves and took a quick look around the room. Three large oak tables formed a half circle with the members of the council sitting along the back side, giving each one a perfect view of the three occupants who stood in the middle of the floor. Seated at the center of the head table were King Richard and Queen Julianna. They were flanked with Alex on their right side and Lord Chad on their left. Prince Michael also sat at the head table along with two other foreign men who were dressed with a royal crest on their shoulders. The king's advisors and the other councilmen filled up the rest of the seats.

The steward stepped in front of them and tapped his staff on the stone floor. "Sarah Antonellis Benavente, along with Mrs. Carlina Sarter Fales and Apollo Kaplan Moylan."

Sarah curtsied deeply and marveled at how the steward had known the seamstress's name along with Mr. Moylan's, and she was still taken aback at how they all seemed to accept these two accompanying her. She looked at Chad, and her stomach turned and her head spun for a moment, but Mr. Moylan stepped closer to her and discreetly reached out and steadied her.

Three chairs were brought to the center of the room, and once seated, the old seamstress patted Sarah's hand and smiled broadly at her. Sarah couldn't return the smile. Her hands were wet with perspiration and her cheeks felt clammy. She took a deep breath and tried to calm herself, but when she looked around at all the solemn faces in the room, the knot in her stomach tightened at the thought of addressing so many people.

"Now, let us finish today with this marriage business," the king boomed so that the whispers instantly quieted. "I believe Prince Michael wanted to address us first."

Sarah cringed inwardly as she realized that Alex's marriage contract was going to be addressed first, and she couldn't help but think how cruel he was for making her sit through it.

The steward tapped his staff on the floor again. "Michael Don Delacor, crown prince of Kyrnidan."

Michael stood. "I'm here representing my country in regards to the marriage contract between Prince Alexander and my sister. We have evidence to present to this court concerning the identification of my sister. I ask that Apollo Moylan speak on behalf of my family." He waved to the tall gentleman seated next to Sarah.

Mr. Moylan stood and took a step forward. "I am Apollo Kaplan Moylan."

Sarah stared at him in shock as she realized why the council hadn't questioned his presence in the room. He was there as a representative for the marriage contract between Alex and the princess of Kyrnidan.

The king acknowledged Apollo and he continued. "Eighteen years ago Queen Natalia Rankin Delacor gave birth to a child. At the time I was King Michael Delacor's chief advisor. Samuel Leegen, the king's second advisor"—he motioned to the man seated next to Prince Michael—"and I were in attendance at the birth. As soon as the babe was born, we took her and placed upon the back of her left shoulder the permanent mark of heritage and royalty of the firstborn. It was only then that we found out that there was a second child, a boy. Only myself, Samuel, and the attending physician knew there had been two children born. We believed the boy could fulfill a long-foretold prophecy—a prophecy that, in the end, we had put too much belief in—despite our best efforts."

Apollo paused and Prince Michael looked up, meeting the tall counselor's gaze. Sarah was just wondering about the sadness that she detected in the prince's eyes when he glanced at her momentarily before averting his gaze.

Apollo cleared his throat and continued. "So we took the boy and also put on his shoulder the mark of royalty, the sign of the firstborn, and then returned him to the queen. Because of political situations, it wasn't wise for the girl to be raised in the castle and that very morning I delivered the baby girl to a woman of impeccable reputation. For the safety of the child, she took the baby and left Kyrnidan. At my own request, no one knew where she went. Eventually the queen learned of her daughter and we searched for the princess. But it wasn't until Prince Alexander requested a marriage contract with King Michael for her hand in marriage that we discovered her whereabouts."

Sarah found the story of the missing princess intriguing, but she was becoming increasingly anxious about her own petition. She was fidgeting with her skirts when she saw Apollo turn and gesture to Alex.

Alex stood. "I have a signed marriage contract for Princess Sarah, daughter of King Michael Delacor and Queen Natalia Rankin Delacor. If she will have me," he added and then turned, looking right at Sarah.

Sarah's breath caught in her throat at the sudden mention of her name and she quickly looked around with anxious surprise. Had she missed something? Suddenly she felt Carlina nudging her to her feet.

"He's talking about *you*, Princess," the seamstress whispered.

What? This made no sense! Surely they weren't talking about her. She wasn't a princess that had been spirited away at birth. She was Sarah Antonellis Benavente, and she had been born in Spain. Her mother was Miranda, and her father Antonio had passed away before she was born. She was certain who she was, yet her heart began to pound in her ears and she could almost hear Miranda's voice calling to her as she had every night, *I love you, my sweet princess.* Sarah opened her mouth to say something, but her mouth went dry and no words came.

"Sarah." Alex spoke again, directly to her. "I'm asking for your hand in marriage."

She was speechless. She shook her head as if she could shake off the confusion mounting inside her. Her mind was reeling as she tried to piece everything together. Frustration welled up inside her as she tried to grasp at the enormity of what they were suggesting. She didn't know what to say or how to react, but Chad seemed to know exactly what to do.

He jumped to his feet and bellowed, "I have signed a marriage contract with this woman's father and I demand that it be upheld!" He trembled in his anger as he stood, glaring at the other council members.

Prince Michael stood up. "Need I remind you that Clyde Berack is not her father?" His voice matched Chad's in volume but had much more control. Sarah's head spun. *This must be a mistake!*

"This is all a lie!" Chad swiftly moved toward King Richard and leaned over the table. "It's a lie that he concocted just to spite me!" he yelled, pointing to Alex. "I had my contract first. I demand *my* contract be upheld!" He pounded his fists on the table. Apollo grabbed the staff that the steward held and shoved the end of it into Chad's chest.

"You have no claim to her." Apollo's voice was cold and threatening. "It is not a lie." Apollo stepped forward, pushing Chad with the staff until he flumped back heavily into his chair. "I know! From the beginning, I set these events in place. I was the one who held the babe while she was marked. The identical mark is now on her brother as well." He nodded towards Prince Michael, who stood. He held Sarah's gaze for a moment and then slowly turned around.

A hush fell over the group as the prince of Kyrnidan reached up and began to pull his collar to the side. Sarah's eyes were riveted to where his skin was slowly being revealed. Her breath caught in her throat as the edges of a scar began to emerge from beneath his shirt. A shock jolted through her when at last the whole image was revealed—a scar . . . like hers.

"And I have seen that same mark now eighteen years later on the back of the left shoulder of this woman." Apollo pointed toward Sarah.

The seamstress rose and pulled Sarah to her feet. "From two witnesses, this truth will be established," Carlina said, her voice firm with conviction. "I found her out when I was measuring her for a gown. She indeed carries the mark of the crown of Kyrnidan, burned into the back of her left shoulder."

The room seemed to spin and Sarah shook her head to clear her thoughts. She was only vaguely aware that the seamstress's steady hands were turning her around so that her back was facing the council members. She put a hand on her chest to steady her breath as she felt the neck of her dress being pulled to the side. A collective gasp filled the room followed by hushed whispers. Then Sarah felt Carlina's soft fingertips brush across her own scar. She closed her eyes but in the darkness she could still see that same identical scar on Prince Michael.

Abruptly Sarah turned around, her mind reeling. "If Your Majesties and honored councilmen will excuse me," she said in a shaky voice. "I need a moment alone." She curtsied to the head table and quickly made her escape out the door. When she was halfway down the large hallway she pulled up her skirts and began to run. She needed some time to understand all of this. *Princess?* she thought. Her mother had always called her princess. *But I can't be. No, Miranda was my mother. She had to be! They've made a huge mistake.* The thoughts flooded her mind and tears began to blur her vision. This wasn't what she had expected. Princess of another country? A different family? How could Alex have withheld this truth from her? Her feet flew down the stairs and she headed for the only place she knew she could truly escape: the stables.

With her skirts up nearly to her knees, she darted down the corridors, not caring who saw her or what they might think. She burst outside and continued to bolt across the grounds. She heard Alex calling to her but she ignored him. As she came around the corner of the stables, she lost her footing on the cobblestones. She bruised her knees as they hit the ground and scraped the palms of her hands, but it only momentarily detained her. She stood and staggered a couple of steps as she gathered her skirt again. Alex called her name again but still she didn't stop. Suddenly his strong hand grabbed her elbow.

"Sarah."

She pulled away, violently wrenching herself free.

"Sarah!"

This time he grabbed with both hands and spun her around to face him. She tried to shake him off and put her arms up to push him away, but he held her until she stopped struggling. Then cautiously, he reached up to brush at her tear-smudged cheek.

She dropped her head and blinked to clear the mist from her eyes. "How could you have not told me?" she said without even trying to hide the bitterness in her voice.

"I couldn't tell you. It needed to be verified." Slowly he released her and watched her guardedly. "I know you must be confused at all this, and you'll need some time to comprehend it, but please give me the chance to explain things." When he was sure that she wasn't going to run off again, he walked into the stable and grabbed a saddle, then headed toward one of the stalls.

Sarah watched him with a touch of resentment. "What am I supposed to do? My whole life has been a lie, and it seems everyone knew it but me!"

Alex let himself into the stall of a tall brown horse and proceeded to saddle it. "Would you like the marriage contract with Lord Chad to be upheld?"

Sarah shook her head. "No, of course not!" she said scornfully. "I thought you understood that."

"I understand that now. But I was led to believe that you welcomed the union. And I believed it because I knew you would rather have me go through with a forced marriage than relinquish my crown as I had planned."

Alex was right, but when he looked at her for a response, she just folded her arms defiantly.

"But none of that matters now," Alex continued. "All that matters to me is that you oppose the marriage with Lord Chad. I would have hated to arrest your new husband for treason after we finish the review of his financial accounts."

Sarah's defiant look was replaced by a hopeful one. "You know, then, that he's the one that has been bribing people and falsifying the reports against you?"

"Yes. He's been doing it for years now. And we are in the process of acquiring the proof as we speak." He finished saddling the horse and then led it out of the stall and handed Sarah the reins.

"What's going to stop me from riding away to someplace where you would never find me? Like my mother, Miranda did," she added.

He entered the next stall over and began to saddle another brown horse. "Hmmm. Amada is a fine and fast horse. However, she's not quite as fast as her mate here. You probably would just be reaching the gates before Amador and I caught up with you."

Even though she couldn't see his face as he strapped on the saddle, Sarah knew that he was smiling, and it maddened her.

Then his tone became serious. "But more importantly, I don't think you would avoid your responsibilities."

"I didn't ask to be the princess. Especially not of a strange country!"

Alex put his hand on her arm. "Sarah, no one in your position, or mine, ever asks for these responsibilities. We are born into them." He helped her up on the horse and then mounted his own.

She thought about spurring her horse on and making an attempt to outrun Alex, but at the very least, he owed her some explanations, so she allowed him to follow. She led him back to the orchard where they first met, and along the way, Alex began to explain things to her.

He told her how he had found himself in Carlina's sewing shop and how she divulged her suspicions to him. "The old seamstress is more involved than you think," Alex informed her. "She was Queen Natalia's— your mother's—seamstress years ago in Kyrnidan. It was that referral that helped her here in Calibre to obtain clients such as my own mother, and it was her connection with both royal families that gave her the credibility we needed when she and I returned to Kyrnidan with word of their lost princess."

"And you, knowing that I was the princess of Kyrnidan, went there to ask for my hand in marriage, which conveniently fulfilled your obligation that the king's council put on you."

Alex frowned. "No. I didn't go to fulfill any obligation. I went for you." He turned and looked at her. "You should've known that I wasn't going to give you up to Chad, even if you had agreed to a marriage contract with him."

At the orchard, Alex helped her down from her horse and they slowly walked through the trees together. Sarah shook her head in frustration as she tried to process all the new information swirling through her mind. "How can King Michael sign a contract for a daughter he never even knew he had?" she questioned.

"He did know of you," Alex said. "The physician who assisted at the birth gave up the secret on his deathbed. At first your parents didn't believe the story, but when questioned, Apollo and Samuel did admit to it, and despite the fact that they saved your life, they were imprisoned for the act. Although Kyrnidan has gone through continuous bouts of unrest, they felt it was safe enough for you to return at that time, but unfortunately, Apollo didn't know where Miranda had taken you. That was eight years ago, and they've been searching for you since. So you see, your father did know of you. He just didn't know where you were. Apollo and Samuel were released and sent back with me to verify that you truly are the princess, and now that it's confirmed, they'll be pardoned for the crime."

Alex reached out and took Sarah's hand, then turned her around to face him. "Your mother and father may not know the details of their daughter's life, but they do love her." Alex paused as Sarah considered his statement, then continued, "Your father agreed—insisted, in fact—that our marriage contract is to be void if it's not what you want. And that is why Prince Michael is here: to find out what it is you really want. If you don't want to marry me, they hope you'll return and reside in Kyrnidan. They wish to know you, and would like you to know them as well."

Sarah paused thoughtfully for a moment. "If I marry you then the two countries will become allies. It will not only be what our country needs, but will undoubtedly strengthen and help bring peace to Kyrnidan as well."

Alex nodded his head somberly. "Something that will fulfill a long-time prophecy in that country, I am told."

Sarah drew in a deep breath and reached her hand up to her shoulder, where she could feel the raised bump of her scar through the cloth of her dress. She could already feel the weight of her birthright's responsibility being placed upon her. Alex reached out and gently pulled her hand away from her shoulder. "Sarah, your father wants only your happiness, as do I. I do not want you to marry me out of obligation. But tell me, at one time, your deepest desire was to be with me. Now that it's possible, have your feelings changed?" He looked into her eyes as though he was searching her soul.

"I didn't expect such a dramatic change of events," she admitted grimly. "And my feelings are in turmoil. So much has changed in such a short while. . . ." She saw the hope in his eyes begin to fade and her heart swelled with compassion. Though much *had* changed, her feelings for him had not and she could not torture him by letting him think otherwise. "Alex, I do wish to be with you—with all my heart."

His face broke into an infectious smile, and in his excitement, he picked her up, pressing his lips to hers and twirling her around.

"I thought I was going to die when Clyde told me that you had agreed to marry Chad," he said, setting her down again. "I thought there was no hope. And then the seamstress told me who you were, and I could see a ray of light. I just prayed that things would work out."

Sarah returned his smile. "Well, I suspect that things *are* working out," she responded, inwardly resolving to come to grips with the new changes in her life, to be the princess that Miranda had always thought her to be. They strolled through the orchard and Alex told her everything he knew about her mother, father, and her brother, Michael. They continued to talk until the sun started setting, then they climbed back on their horses and rode back to the castle.

27. ROYALTY RESTORED

"Hello there," called Prince Michael as Sarah and Alex rode up to the stables in the dimming light. "I'm glad you're back. You both ran off so quickly, you missed the grand finale to the meeting."

"What was that?" Alex asked as he jumped down from his horse and handed the reins to a stable boy.

"Lord Chad. They recovered some of his records showing that he bribed one of the king's advisors and falsified reports about you. The records also showed that he had quite a following of men, enough to start a rebellion. He was rewarding them for their support by putting them into high-paying positions. It appears that he's been scheming to snatch the throne away from you for years. They took him into custody for treason while they finish the investigation."

"They arrested him?" Sarah said, her mind reeling from the implications.

Michael nodded. "I'm so glad you didn't want to marry *that* man, Sister." He reached up and helped her down from her horse. "Do you mind if I call you *Sister*?"

"No, not if I may call you *Brother*," she replied shyly. She liked Prince Michael very much, and after listening to Alex talk about her brother, she wanted to get to know him better.

"I'd be honored to be called your brother," he said as he pulled her to him and gave her a warm embrace. "You should've seen it. Lord Chad put up a fight and Apollo used the steward's staff to knock Chad's feet out from under him. He landed flat on his back in the middle of the room and suddenly began pleading for mercy." Michael looked carefully at Sarah. "He gave up the names of all of the businessmen who supported him in his treachery." He paused and looked at his newfound sister with concern in his eyes. "Clyde Berack was mentioned," he said softly.

Sarah closed her eyes briefly. "I knew that he was involved. What will happen to him?"

"They'll take him into custody and there will be a trial. At best he'll probably be cobbling the streets or doing other public services for quite a while."

Sarah shook her head. "He used to be a decent man, you know, but after my mother died . . ." Sarah gasped and her hand flew to her mouth. "Poor Felicia! She'll be all alone."

Her brother's face lit up again. "Actually, we discussed Felicia, after Lord Chad was removed from the room."

Sarah looked up, concern clouding her face. "But why would the council talk about Felicia?"

"Yes," Alex jumped in, "why discuss Felicia? Surely she did nothing wrong in all this."

Michael shook his head. "No, she isn't accused of anything. We discussed her because she was raised as a sister to the princess." He looked at Sarah. "The council wishes her to be well looked after. She'll have the choice of living with her aunt, or she'll be allowed to stay with you in the castle."

"I fear she won't want to leave the manor, but I can't leave her alone."

Michael smiled slightly. "From what I understand, she won't be alone for very much longer."

"What do you mean?"

"The high judge. I forget his name . . ."

"Andrew Barnett Savell," Alex put in.

"Yes. Well, he mentioned that his son is very taken with Felicia and will be making an offer of marriage soon."

"Joseph?" Alex asked surprised. "It's about time he married."

Sarah let out a long sigh. "Oh, I am so glad to hear it! Felicia told me of his interest—and that she returned his affection. And Brother, thank you for coming out here to tell us."

Michael blushed. "Actually, I came out here because I wanted to see the much-talked-of new addition to the stables."

"You mean she's arrived?" Alex asked.

Michael nodded. "Just before you got back," he said with a grin. "She is a beauty, just as you described her."

Michael took Sarah's arm and carefully wrapped it around his own. "Come," he said as he led her toward the stables. "I believe Alex has a surprise for you."

Alex took her other arm, and the three walked into the stables where in the first stall stood a tall, sleek, snow white mare.

"Oh, she is beautiful!" Sarah exclaimed. "What's her name?" she asked, stroking the mare's broad forehead.

Alex beamed at her. "She's yours to name."

Sarah stopped stroking the horse and gave Alex a questioning look.

He took her hands in his and pulled her closer. "Sarah, my love, she's my wedding gift to you."

Sarah gasped and then squealed as she jumped into his arms. "Oh Alex! Thank you! Thank you so much!" she said and then kissed him firmly on the lips.

"I assume the marriage contract my father signed is now indeed official," Michael said with a laugh.

Sarah was famished by the time they walked into the castle. Michael excused himself, and Alex ordered a plate of food to be brought to Sarah's private quarters, then led her up the stairs to the rooms she had been given. At the entrance he pulled a key from his pocket.

"Do you plan to lock me in so that I can't run away?" Sarah teased him.

"I thought about it, but actually your belongings were brought this afternoon and this key belongs to one of the trunks. Felicia said that it was your dowry chest from Miranda." He opened the heavy door and let her enter.

The first room was a reception area with beautiful padded benches, carved tables, and a few paintings hanging on the walls. The candles placed around the room illuminated several large trunks. She could see into the next room where her sleeping chamber was, and beyond that was yet another room.

A servant appeared at the doorway with a platter of food and drink. Alex thanked her for it and took it inside, setting it on one of the small tables.

"Can I get you anything else, my lady?" the servant said.

"No, thank you."

"Very well. I shall be back later to assist you, my lady."

"Assist me?"

"Before retiring, my lady. To change into sleeping clothes?"

Sarah shook her head. "Thank you, but I won't be needing you. I've always been accustomed to doing things for myself."

"As you wish. I shall, at any rate, come and turn your bed down for you."

Sarah thanked the servant again and dismissed her, then went and sat next to Alex, who tried to hide a mischievous smile. "What?" she demanded.

"Oh it's nothing, really," he said, and picked at the food on the tray. "And they thought *I* was nonconforming," he said under his breath.

Sarah swatted playfully at him, then knelt down next to the large chest that contained her dowry and placed the key in the lock.

Alex stood up quickly. "Would you like me to leave so you can sort through your belongings?"

"No. Please stay. I've been alone so much lately, and I want to share this with you."

Alex knelt down next to her and helped her lift the heavy lid.

On top was a large quilt that she knew Miranda had spent countless hours stitching. It was a beautiful blue, and intricately made. Sarah pulled it out and laid her cheek to it, and Alex fingered the delicate stitching with admiration.

"I remember watching her make it."

Alex breathed in deeply. "It smells of lavender."

"Mother loved lavender. She must have packed lavender sachets in the chest with it." She closed her eyes and allowed the scent to bring memories of her mother to the surface.

Next she pulled out a bundle of papers tied with purple ribbon and sealed with red wax. She was eager to read them, but even more eager to see the next item, so she set them aside for now. She reached in and pulled a gown from the cherished items. It was exquisite, long and white, and elegantly beaded.

"Her wedding gown?" Alex questioned.

Sarah nodded and stood up, holding the dress up to her. "From her marriage to Antonio. She must have meant for me to wear this on my wedding day."

Alex moved over to her and gently placed a hand on her cheek and looked into her eyes. "You'll look so beautiful in it."

Sarah smiled and looked down at the dress as she tried to swallow the lump growing in her throat. "What a lovely treasure," she whispered. Then the packet of papers sitting on top of the blanket caught her eye again. Gently she laid the dress aside and picked up the packet.

She ran her finger across the wax seal that had been stamped with a tiny figure of a unicorn. Carefully she pulled it from the papers, leaving it in one piece. Inside she found two official documents. One had her name written on it: Sarah Antonellis Benavente. It was a certificate of name. She held the document so both she and Alex could read it. She knew by the olive branch in the corner of the page that the naming had been certified by a cleric. "I've never seen this document before," she said quietly. She set aside the piece of parchment and reviewed the one behind it. This one had a different name. Sarah Elizabeth Rankin Delacor. Sarah recognized the royal name of her birth family.

"Look," Alex said, pointing to the bottom. "Here's Miranda's signature. The other certificate didn't have it."

Sarah looked back at the first document and found only the signature of the cleric. She unfolded the remaining papers and discovered that it was a letter written in Miranda's hand. She was eager to read the letter but paused, afraid that she might get too emotional.

Alex sensed her hesitation and put his arm around her. "It's all right," he encouraged quietly. "Go ahead."

Slowly she began to read the letter out loud:

> *My dearest Sarah,*
>
> *As I sit to write you this letter my heart is full. There is so very much that I wish to tell you, and I hope and pray that you will somehow understand. Dearest Sarah, you have been all that a mother could hope for in a daughter. You are a delight, with a sharp mind and a tender heart. I know that this will likely be a terrible shock when you learn the truth. I hope and pray that I will be able to tell you myself, but I feel in my heart that I will join my parents and beloved Antonio in the life to come before it is time to tell you the truth. So I write you this letter in the event that I am unable to disclose my secret.*

Sarah stopped and looked up momentarily. "She must have written this when she was sick." She blinked her eyes several times and then turned back to the letter.

> *My darling Sarah, there is no easy way to tell you, so I will be straightforward. As much as I love you, and for all the years I have cared for you, I am not your mother by blood.*

You were born to another woman—Queen Natalia Rankin Delacor. She is the queen of Kyrnidan, our homeland. At birth, you were given the royal mark of the firstborn—the sign of the crown placed upon your shoulder. At the time, prophecies predicted the firstborn to be a male child. Situations were volatile in our country. Minutes after you were marked, the queen gave birth to your twin. The baby was a son. They marked him as the firstborn as well, and then the king's advisor, Apollo Kaplan Moylan—fearing for your life due to previous threats—brought you to me within hours of your birth.

I had known Apollo for many years. He was a great man of honor, and I knew him to be trustworthy. Know this: if it had not been a matter of grave concern, he never would have removed you from your birthright. Do not harbor anger or resentment for him. It must have been a terrible burden on him. But he has always been completely dedicated in his service to his king and country.

Taking you as my own and hiding who you really are meant leaving what life I had and making a new one in a country far away. After a hasty departure, we traveled and eventually made our way to Spain. There, I found a cleric who, as part of his devotion to the Lord, had decided to take a vow of silence for the last few years of his life. I waited, and the day before he was to take his vow, I went to him with you in my arms and I poured out my soul. I believe that ours is not the only secret he kept. He held you in his arms and saw the mark of royalty. He listened with patience and understanding. Then he blessed you with your name, Sarah Elizabeth Rankin Delacor. As was the law we both signed the naming certificate. Then he signed another with the name you have always known, Sarah Antonellis Benavente, although that document was never legalized by my signature. I kept it only as a precaution, in case your identity was questioned. Soon after, we continued our travels on into France and eventually to Calibre, where I married Clyde.

I know that Clyde has had difficulty understanding my total devotion to you. And I know that Felicia has noticed it also. I hope and pray with all my heart that they will one day understand and forgive me. I have always loved you as my own and felt also an extra responsibility to compensate for the loss of family you unknowingly suffered. Please understand that you and Felicia have been my life's delight.

The day may come when you meet your blood parents, your twin brother, and perhaps other siblings. My dearest Sarah, I have loved you as deeply as I have loved Felicia. You have always been and will always be my precious daughter. May the good Lord continue to bless you.

With all of my eternal love,
Your mother,
Miranda

Sarah set down the papers and, picking up the dress, she buried her face in it and cried softly. "You'll always be my mother. I promise to make your sacrifice worth it."

Alex wrapped his arms around her and pulled her to him. "She would be proud of you."

Sarah nodded. "I understand now—why she did what she did. She protected me for all those years, not allowing anyone to know who I truly was, but doing all she could to give me the same opportunities I would have had in the home of my birth. If she could only see that all her hopes have been fulfilled."

"I think she knows," Alex said as he leaned down and brushed his lips against hers. "And I also love you, Sarah. My sweet princess."

ABOUT THE AUTHORS

Jennifer K. Clark and Stephonie K. Williams are sisters by chance but became friends by choice when a year of rooming together at college taught them how to get along. Now stay-at-home moms, separated and living in different parts of the county, they still manage to work together on various projects that Jennifer willing admits to as harebrained ideas, some of which have included: producing a music video, inventing and hosting community fantasy day camps, and coauthoring this book. Stephonie has a love for writing and is a technical buff (computer nerd) who loves dragons and felines and spends her time scheming up new harebrained ideas. Jennifer lives on a hobby farm with a variety of unique animals and has a special love for horses. She spends a lot of time with the characters in her head, putting their stories down on paper, and in her spare time she tries to comply with her sister's crazy ideas.